Baking

for

Dave

Melissa Palmer

Baking for Dave

All marketing and publishing rights guaranteed to and reserved by:

Sensory World
A proud imprint of Future Horizons

Phone: 800•489•0727

Online: www.sensoryworld.com

Email: info@sensoryworld.com

ISBN: 978-1935567677

Contents

Contents

Chapter 1

Eric

The nervousness came like a thousand little bugs, rushing over her with tiny legs that prodded and itched until they found what they wanted and crept in through her pores. She could feel them moving under her skin, scuttling just beneath the surface.

Don't pick.

It was easy to pick at her head, to scratch it all away like a big mistake. All she had to do was settle her hands up under her cap. She could lose her fingers in the long strands of brown hair tucked just beneath her wooly, just a few scratches, so she wouldn't flap. Flapping made people stare.

She fought the urge with everything she had. The man behind her, the one who smelled like an old can, made it quite hard.

"You wanna move it along, honey?" His voice was hard, and he pressed the last word in a way that school nurses and grandmas never would. He was telling her he was annoyed. She didn't look, but she could tell he had hardening of the arteries and liked beer from the way his voice scratched and because of the acidic smell that burst out with his question. It didn't mix well with the bitter punch of coffee and the hot sugar scent that fought to hold off the yeast smell and the faint aroma of the bleach stuff they always use in these places to keep the counters clean. The register clicked and dinged. The lights flickered above and buzzed above like a giant insect ready to eat Iris alive. Heat pushed off from the annoyed man and it bristled against the back of her legs from ten inches away. He didn't take care of himself, this man with the heavy voice. His eyes were no doubt narrowing as he shifted his weight from one foot to the other. He would open them wide if she started flapping, like she wanted.

"Sometime today?" He prodded.

Iris didn't answer. Instead, she reached her hands up into the front of her cap, settling them between the soft wool and the twists of her hair. The little bumps on her scalp where hair met skin felt good. They made crunching noises like old fall leaves under her fingertips.

"Mind your business or you can get outta here." Eric shouted while leaning over the counter and waving at can man as if he were shooing a fly.

The poppy-seed bagels were set out next to the onion bagels, not the ones with sesame seeds. The chocolate chips were on the bottom shelf with the egg bagels. Nothing was as it should have been, which made her itchy inside. It was a sticky, worried feeling that made her sense that something was about to go terribly wrong.

"Take a breath, kid." Eric was a lion of a man, but he was gentle with Iris. His mane of long brown hair was pulled back in a ponytail when he worked at the store. Through his big beard she couldn't see his lips, but she knew he was talking to her. He was the kind of man who harkened back to an era of pool-stick barroom brawls and poker games turned shootouts, with big square shoulders and hands that could pass for stones. Even so, he was always gentle with Iris. His voice was rough, but it smoothed the edges like sandpaper.

"In through the nose and out through the mouth, like this." She followed his instructions out of habit and necessity, though the air was thick and pungent with morning meats. She tried to blot them out and focus on the dark blue veins that snaked up his hands. They ran like two rivers up to his forearms, twisting around the tattoo that rested there, a breezy scene with palm trees on a beach.

"That's right Iris, focus."

He slid the phone from his pocket and laid it down in front of her where the blinking buttons caught her eye, and she couldn't help but follow the patterns. "Good things," he eased. Sure she was settling, he nodded as he was speaking softly, like what he was about to do was for them only. He hummed a tune so lightly it could have passed for a sigh. Her shoulders slackened like a weight had been lifted.

"A bagel, please?"

He sang a phrase to a tune she knew, and not for the people in line but just for her. "Now, what'll you have?"

Her face had changed in a matter of seconds, melting from the tense mask it had been. The voice was loud and her words came out in a bark, one note repeated like a demand, but Eric knew she wasn't shouting. "A blueberry bagel, with strawberry cream cheese, please." She let out the deep breath with a puff of her cheeks, and Eric held up his fist for a knuckle bump before looking at the man behind her with a scowl.

"Can I get another blueberry bagel with strawberry cream cheese and wrapped in waxed paper?" She ticked off the order methodically as if she were calculating a problem only she could see, robotically, as she made sure not to look at the goods on the shelves. She gazed at the palm fronds, and the bright sun that hung on Eric's arm like a tiny orange.

"I would like three of the big cookies. A biscotti. Two biscotti, and a sweet bun with raisins? Is that a new phone, Eric?"

Gadgets made her forget.

Her bag of treats hit the counter with a thump.

"Hungry?" He asked.

Iris' eyes went donut wide, she was sure he was making fun of her until she remembered about sarcasm. It was quite the opposite. Her stomach had felt like it was about to turn upside down and sideways, but Eric was making a joke.

"I'm not eating it all now," she added, like labored punctuation. "Silly." She unpacked and repacked her extra food in the little bag, folding over the top so the edges didn't touch. "Some of it is for later."

He winked. "Just in case."

She handed Eric a crinkled ten dollar bill from her pocket, which he promptly put back in her hand.

"Ah, yeah. Having a big day at school, right? I thought it was tomorrow?"

"No, it's definitely today." Her voice jumped in volume, but he didn't seem to notice. Sometimes it did that.

"It's not every day you get a chance to be on *Dance Magic*."

She shrugged lopsidedly with the best sideways grin she could come up with. She'd wanted to raise one eyebrow like in the cartoons. It was a trick she loved to pull out at times like this, when someone said something preposterously ridiculous, but it would've blown her cover. Instead, she did the unthinkable, something she hated to do to Eric, who'd been nothing short of a hero and always more than a true friend. She lied.

The door clanged behind her with Christmas bells. She heard Eric's voice calling with the usual plaintive urgency, "Say hi to Maisy for me."

He said that to her every time. Silly, considering he'd see her this afternoon.

Nonetheless, the deed was done and she was grateful Eric was who he was, especially this morning. Anyone else and her plan would've been dashed into a thousand pieces.

The sun was very hot today, and it was searing her skin like the untrue words had burned on her tongue. She wasn't a good liar, but in all his years knowing her, Eric had known Iris to speak nothing but the truth. When she nodded vaguely at his questions, he had no reason to question her response. *Dance Magic* was a popular show and all the girls in her school watched it—all the cheerleaders and ballet girls, all the track team and drama kids. It was a shared thread that seemingly held her school together.

Today, *Dance Magic* had picked Woodrow High to hold a local audition. It had presented Iris with the opportunity of a lifetime, but it necessitated employing a manner of speak with which she was not familiar. However, Eric had made it easy. She had lowered her head when he asked if she was excited. She had lifted her eyes when he asked if she'd planned a routine. Technically, that wasn't a lie. It was only when he asked her directly that the words caught in her mouth like molten peanut butter.

Her mouth stung with the thought of it.

"What are you going to dance to?" Good old Eric was so direct. It was one of the things she'd come to admire about him, but she'd planned this for so long, she couldn't think of it as a lie. She had to think of it as a script.

"Do you really have to ask?" She averted.

He smiled easily with a big sigh, as if the answer had been as plain to see as a butterfly perched on his nose.

"Dave" There was no question in the way he said it to her. It was only sweet recognition, for which she was so thankful.

Iris cut through two yards and an alley while holding tight to her precious package. She could hear the little ones chirping, singing like birds about the teacher's dirty looks, as she slipped into the little thicket between Myrtle Lane and East Harlow, clean through the woods behind the elementary school. She avoided all corners, hated right angles, and ended up reducing the distance. When she arrived at the boulevard, she realized she had made great time by deciding not to cross the street and heading toward her school helped her time even more. She doubled back the opposite way straight to her house.

Chapter 2

Grace Is Gone

I t wasn't a question anymore, no longer a daydream or conversation Iris lingered on over breakfast that stretched into dinner. This was as real as it got, no fantasy or pretense.

Murph had said she needed to focus on real life more, hadn't she? Session upon session with the puppets and squishy clay, she and her therapist worked on drawing pictures together about what was happening *right now*.

This was happening right now and, if she didn't let it, she might not ever get the chance again.

She imagined she was mist slipping in the storm door, silently pushing through the entryway with the palm of her hand, steady and quiet. When she was little, she walked on her toes. For years, she tottered room to room on the balls of her feet, never letting her heels touch the ground. Kids in school would try to push her off balance, the mean ones at least, and they made fun and pointed, because that's the kind of thing some people did. What they didn't know was that the laugh was on them.

Iris had perfected the tiptoe at an early age, and it was working for her now. One sound could throw off the whole plan. One creaking floorboard or loss of balance could mean waking Maisy, and then, the jig would be up. That was a saying people used when their plans went awry. It originated in the Elizabethan era when "jig" meant trick. This wasn't a joke, so if she made a sound, it would all be over. She was stealthy and light as she tiptoed through the back hallway to her room where she settled herself in an excruciating display of muscle control, lowering herself by the millimeter onto the bed. She reached below thinking of her arms as plastic putty, gently bending beneath the springs without a sound.

Her room was a marble tomb. She was inside the great pyramid awaiting the ancient mummy's arrival. If she stirred, the beast would be there in moments, but Iris wouldn't let that happen. She breathed deep, fearful that her heartbeats would shake the walls. The booming would rattle her lamp and sway the two stacks of boxes next to her closet. The magazines would spill all over her floor, but the two towers didn't bobble. The pictures weren't moving on the walls. They didn't shift with what felt like the earthquake rumbling inside her, nor did her special rocks quake and tumble to the floor, as she thought they would.

This was her imagining things. This was the stress she needed to control.

She closed her eyes and thought of blue. She made herself the color that meant calm and oceans, clear skies and berries. The rumbling, hulk feeling slid away from her, like old skin. She had to learn to be a chameleon and let things go, Murph had said, and it worked.

Her backpack was almost full, but there was just enough room in the front pocket for the parcel from the bagel store. She rolled the bag into a thin little sausage, tucking it inside. Then she touched everything she'd packed to make sure she hadn't forgotten a thing. She moved from pocket to clasp to the tiny hidden pouch with the zipper, lingering on the smooth surface of her new license. It felt warm to her even now, like the laminate would peel up and adhere to her fingers forever like extra skin.

The box towers stood taller than she did and leaned together in a large V next to her closet. They made for the perfect hiding place for the last thing she needed. She grabbed the stick hidden there and stuck the end of it into her backpack, so it shot up into the air like a knight's sigil flag. She piled her most important items into an oversized bandana and folded it into a neat bundle she attached to the end. It was a hobo stick, just like she had seen in the old movies, and it was perfect. Satisfied, she turned around in a circle for one final inspection. Her black-and-gold dragon with the orange fire in pastels hung perfectly on the wall hanging evenly and smoothly. The ice-cream stick bridge that connected her pony collectibles to the world of fighting amphibians she'd made out of plastic bricks was intact, free of obstacles and threats. She lined up the two factions in parallel columns on either side of the bridge, straightening each one three times before the smooth feeling replaced that rough feeling inside her. It was like sand in a bathing suit, the worried dread feeling that filled her stomach up like a hot water balloon when the lines weren't right. No one would move her things while she was gone. Maisy knew not to touch them, even if they disagreed on the matter. She assured herself of that.

There was only one more thing to do before she could set out on her journey. She touched each of the smooth rocks that framed the one-gallon fish tank on her dresser.

"I have to go on this adventure, Sophie." She said to the magenta betta fish that swam up to the tank's edge, as if responding.

"You're going to be okay, all right?" She plunked the pellet she pulled from her pocket into the tank and the little fish turned a flip, flaring her fins like a tiny flamenco dancer.

"Eat this." She touched the cool plastic of the tank and gazed without blinking at the silky fin that waved behind the little fish like a flowing gown. "I will be thinking of you."

Before tiptoeing out, she took one last look at Sophie, her best friend in the world. It was hard to leave her behind. The extra key was in the third slot of the secretary desk by the front door. It was a musty fossil of dark wood that creaked every time it was touched. A hundred years ago, it might have been used for letters and inkwells. Now it was a resting place for dust bunnies, scraps of paper, broken key chains, discarded shoelaces; all sorts of things lived there that the world had forgotten, and of course, Maisy's spare key. Iris hovered before the heavy lid, closed in an ominous seam across the top, trying to will the old wood not to whine or moan when she pulled it open. To make things worse, old Oscar had appeared as if summoned. The chubby cat was as vocal as he was nosy and as grumpy as any old-timer she'd ever seen in a movie when he didn't get his way. He rubbed his head against her knee begging to be petted, so she instinctively slipped a foot from her shoe, providing belly rubs before he could protest. His soft purr was like a warm little motor against the bottom of her toe. It heated her from the outside in and made her feel—not ticklish—like she could do what she had to do.

She was stealthy now and light like a cat burglar with Oscar as her sidekick. It was her strategy to be feline. She pulled the lid open in one motion, and though it let out a dull thump as the latch settled, the wood didn't squeak at all. There was a grassy museum smell inside, which Iris tried to ignore, extracting the key like a surgeon on a mission to save a fading patient. Oscar had flipped to the other foot, and meowed softly in gratitude for the whole operation. She crunched her toes in his squishy fur and held her breath as she pushed the lid back as quickly and silently as she could.

If all went well, Maisy would sleep until school was long over. An hour or so after the final bell rang, she would roll out of bed and have her breakfast at 4 p.m., as always. Only today would be different because Iris wouldn't be there when the waffles popped and the juice sloshed into the glass. By then, she'd be adventuring on her own.

It had taken three tries to get the note how she wanted it. The first one looked too scribbled, and the words weren't just right. The second draft looked too neat, like she'd labored over the cursive S's for hours, which she had. Maisy would know for sure if what was written was contrived. The last note struck the perfect balance between scrawl and ramble, just neat enough to be legible and clear enough to be understood by most but not many.

Hi Maisy,

Don't forget. Today is that thing at school where that show is coming that everyone watches. I don't really dance, but it would probably be a good idea if I stay. I think there is going to be catering, like chips and soda and maybe a table of sandwiches. It won't be over until at least after dinner. Don't call, because they will get mad and yell if phones are ringing during the taping.

Grace Is Gone

See you when it's all over,

Iris

P.S. I don't know what happened to the car.

The note was impeccable, the tiny dots above each "i" pressed with a dark blot of emphasis. Maisy would know it was sincere, and it would buy Iris at least four extra hours of travel time. Iris could be halfway through one of the Carolinas before Maisy even noticed. Without the car, what could she do besides accept the plan? It was foolproof.

Iris walked like a stick bug, standing erect and measuring the inches back to the front door with creeping steps. It was too risky to stretch out her legs, to chance tripping for the thousandth time over a foot, and end up face first into a wall or crashing to the floor.

She planted her chin on Oscar's head, instructing him to watch over Maisy as she slept, and leaned out through the front door like she was blowing kisses from a cable car in a musical from the old days. She wasn't. She ducked and crouched, pressing the door shut like a soon-to-be fired spy unfit for clandestine operations. She was clumsy and every movement was dictated by guilt in lieu of stealth. All grace was lost in the lumbered effort of doubtful muscles unsure of the mission ahead.

The blueberry turtle lay dormant in the driveway, resting peacefully like its master. It always looked so small driving down the street, but it loomed like Gamera from the Godzilla movies, a menacing and huge beast. Would it squeal for its master when she pulled the door open? Or would it refuse to move for her? She wasn't the turtle whisperer, Maisy was.

The small rounded car looked like a piece of candy when she saw it in that showroom. Now it seemed like a monster. She talked to it, or to herself depending on who was interpreting the situation. Murph said the key to everything was interpreting the situation. Her disconnect was interpreting. That empty place where she didn't understand words and people were confused by her blinking, that dead place just before the itching started was called the disconnect. She needed to connect to the blueberry turtle. She needed to make it understand her so she could be its master.

"I'm going to do this now, blueberry, so be nice to me, okay? I'm going to sit in the front. I know I sit in the back usually, but it's going to be okay. I'll be in a different seat, so that just means the position has changed, not the act of sitting, or even your existence as a car, or mine as a person."

Defining all this made it easier for the turtle to be tamed and for the sounds in her mind to become clear. Why she'd thought of blueberry as a behemoth suddenly made no sense. It was cramped in the front seat. The wheel felt like it was pinching through her skin and muscles all the way to her skeleton. The gluey scent of tacky vinyl heating in the sun warmed her nose, so she instinctively reached to her right to crack the window even though it was no longer there. Everything was different. The words seeped in like hot oil, so she opened and closed her hands, fanning away the thought. She would lean to the left, and it would be okay. The window cranked just the same as any other, and though her heart had quickened, she was still breathing. No catastrophe had occurred.

"Check overhead mirror. Check. Side mirror. Check. Seatbelt in order. Check. Put on seatbelt. Check." As she did so, she gave herself a squeeze, letting the belt pull tight against her. The pressure was good. She felt like a balloon sometimes, too full with air when the stress kicked in. Just one tight squeeze got some of the air out. Sometimes she could hear the hiss of it leaving her, flying out of her ears in a thick stream. It was never all of it but just enough to make her head stop buzzing.

"Emergency brake, where is the emergency brake?" The monster had become a cubby that had shrunk down to the size of a rabbit hole. Maisy's biggest expenditure in the past five years had been this earth-friendly car. It was great on gas and, through diligent care, it still retained some of that new car smell.

When they'd walked into the showroom, the lights were so bright they hurt Iris' eyes. The salesman had practically run to them, flashing overly large teeth and a strange tan. His name? She didn't remember his name. His suit was green with gray reflections when he turned in the sun, and his shoes squeaked. He opened the door on Maisy's side by pulling something down under the seat. Down under the seat!

"Ah ha!" She squinted her eyes tight and pulled the emergency lever, foot pushing the brake so hard she expected the car to hurtle off into space if she let it go.

She kept it there long enough to forget time. It was hard to tell how many minutes passed as she sat chewing her fingers. It made her nervous to think of what could have happened if it hadn't gone right, so she let the skin on her fingers do its job. She bit and chewed until her jaw worked the lightning bolts out of her face and the blood bloomed fresh on the soft underside of her hands. She wasn't supposed to chew anymore, but stealing a car was stressful work.

She didn't know how much time had passed but knew that it was time. She rubbed her hands on her legs and pulled the key from its hiding place. She took a breath and thrust the key into the turtle in one motion. It clicked into place with a chirp. She cringed, gave it a turn, and pushed the start button as if the car would give out an incriminating roar. Her mind knew the blueberry was quiet.

It was a perk of such a friendly little car. The motor ran more quietly than Oscar's purring. She had to organize her documents just in case. There was an insurance card in the glove compartment and a registration paper as well. She knew that from countless times Maisy searched in there for loose change. She pulled down the visor so the sun wouldn't hurt her eyes. She had sunblock for her arms, because she'd read sunburn was common in cars.

Her license was cool under her raw fingertips and as fresh and smooth as cream. Her face smiled back at her, a reasonable facsimile for the real-life version. It was as perfect and seamless as her plan. She planted her hands at ten and two and tried to remain calm as she settled her foot on the gas. *It is going to be okay.* She repeated it like a prayer, as she pulled away from the driveway.

It was important to remember the goal at hand. The house was shrinking behind her. Iris felt a strange tingle from the top of her scalp to the nail beds on both of her big toes. She tried not to worry about the facts: that Maisy would eventually see the driveway was empty; that this eventuality was inevitable; and that Iris was only 15-years-old.

Chapter 3

Where Are You Going?

It was a straight shot down the parkway, but she had to get there first. It's not that it was hard to drive the turtle. It was much like the bumper cars on the boardwalk, just a matter of consistent pressure. When she had first driven bumper cars years ago, it had taken some doing to get the hang of the gas pedal. If she wanted to, she could close her eyes and conjure it all up like a spell, the distinct scent of hot burning oil, the dirty diesel smell mixed in with grilled onions and seared meats, all with a hint of cotton candy. The smell hung in a cloud over the bells and whistles of the amusement pier. She lurched and stopped for two summers before getting it just right. All of that came in handy now.

She steadied her nerves. Gently. She pressed her foot down evenly. She wasn't stealing a car. She was driving the bumper car in a smooth clean circle around the loop, avoiding all obstacles, watching where she turned. Iris quieted her mind and transported herself into the living room, playing a sweet lullaby with long notes. Go easy on the pedal. Like a long, slow, delicate note, she eased her foot down and held it, humming a wordless familiar tune to drown out the morning sun and the prying eyes of passersby.

It was three hills and two intersections to get out of town, which meant stoplights. They might as well be called spotlights. Woodrow was the kind of town where Iris was invisible normally or rather politely ignored. On days like today, it seemed like there were laser beacons shooting from the car and a siren announcing her approach to everyone around her. The blueberry seemed to attract the attention of pedestrians and crossing guards. The dogs even pricked their noses and raised their tails as she puttered by.

She ducked in the front seat, pulling her wooly further down on her forehead so that it tickled her eyebrows and wiggled on her head when she scrunched up her face. By the time she hit the light by the bank, she was bent and crunched as far as she could go, like a C noodle that had sat too long in the alphabet soup. Iris was a snail hiding in a shell. Her movements solidified this idea like drying glue. She dared not push the speedometer over twenty-five on the boulevard, and, though the pace was agonizing, it eliminated the possibility of any interaction that would in-

volve having to show her convincing, yet altogether coun-
terfeited license.

The radio served as a distraction for most people. Fiddling with the dial and pressing buttons somehow brought
comfort to the average driver. The black buttons peered
at Iris like spider eyes, daring her to press and prod. She
wouldn't give in by looking their way, it was too risky. If
she chose number one, she'd have to follow with two and
three, and then four and five, cycling back to the beginning again. She'd be caught in the web until she'd done
the whole thing three times so all the buttons were back
where they started.

It didn't matter what was on the stations, whether it
was a howling woman yelping like a dolphin over a lost
love or a scratchy-voiced man singing over dated guitars.
Pushing buttons brought the same kind of relief she found
by squeezing potato chip bags or peeling refrigerator dough
labels on shiny cans. There was a sublime moment of ecsta-
sy just before the pop, not unlike the bliss that came along
with things like bubble wrap. The radio wasn't as simple.
When one button was pushed, the car felt lopsided, off balance, like it would careen off the road. Just thinking of it
made her feel like something terrible would happen. She'd
find herself searching for the phantom train that would
undoubtedly squish her. She couldn't explain why, but, as
long as one button was down, an uneasy feeling would
burn in her belly like bad meat. That feeling would remain

there until she restored the buttons to their starting places. The terrible thing about the buttons is they begged, even when the radio wasn't on. They begged to be pushed. She'd thought about taping over the whole radio with electrical tape before she'd left, but it would've taken too much time, and, besides she couldn't find any.

Luckily, the lights had changed before the pressure became too much. The desire to push the buttons built inside her like popcorn on the stove. She couldn't take it any longer. Just as she was reaching across the dash, that burning eye turned green, moving her mind and car to the bigger things that lay ahead. The highway entrance was at the bottom of a long, steep hill. One left turn, and she'd be there. Highways were fast, but for the most part, straight. All she had to do was wait her turn and then go.

It was just like talking to people. She just had to wait her turn. Most of the time, Iris was quiet. She liked to keep her mind still when she was around other people. When a group was talking, it sounded like a hornets' nest, a giant tangle of loud buzzing in her ears that didn't make sense, so she would stay in her mind where it was quiet. Sometimes, something would break through the cloud, so it would stick in Iris' brain like a dart. One word or phrase would ring true and clear and bring her out of where she was hiding. When that happened, it was like her mouth got filled with electricity, so all the words coursed out of her like a current she had to let go, until it was all used up. It was usually when someone mentioned something she really liked, like baking or fish. Iris never meant to butt people out of the way or blurt over conversations, but she would when they mentioned the South, or baked goods, whiskey or history, ants—certain things she couldn't resist. The words filled her up like a giant balloon. If she didn't speak them, she felt like she would burst. It never dawned on her that someone else might want to finish what they'd said.

She settled herself at the highway entrance with both hands squeezing the steering wheel, ignoring the line of cars behind her. She reached into her backpack and pulled out the cassette player, laying it flat on the driver's seat. It felt like an ice block in her hands, cool and heavy, so it calmed her in that way, soothing the parts of her that burned under the skin. The buttons were as old and blocky as they'd always been and stuck down as she pressed the one she needed into place. There was a click, then a faint scratching sound as the familiar voice of Dave Matthews washed over her. He asked the crowd if they were ready to have a good time, and they were. So was she. He said it was all right, so she knew it was going to be. The saxophone flitted through the air like her own pet butterfly as the band came in behind, weaving a tapestry of sound. It filled her head with colors and swirling shapes and overflowed out of her ears and into the car. Warmth washed down over her skin to her hands on the wheel. It made the electrical feeling that hurt her go away, just like it did when she sang to herself all those times she wanted to interrupt a teacher or doctor. She hummed and her hands felt gentle. The tingling in her lips went away. She didn't have to scrunch her face and pick her head to make the twitches go away. All she had to do was let the music be honey in her mouth. She let it sit there to still her mind.

Now was the tail end of the morning rush, but this was New Jersey, and this particular area boasted 3,884 people per square mile. She wondered if they were all driving right now. The highway looked like rushing water, cars speeding by like silver fish in the sun. They zoomed by in a steady stream.

A clunky dump truck brought with it some luck in the form of rocks and gravel that flew from the back. The other drivers were giving it lots of room as it lumbered in the slow lane. Not even the most harried commuter would risk a windshield to save time. Iris decided to follow behind the truck. She popped into traffic right behind it and gave a silent apology to the turtle for any injury it might soon suffer. She patted the steering wheel reassuringly, hoping no errant stones would ding or scratch Maisy's most prized possession.

Once she eased in there, it was easier to breathe, despite the plumes of exhaust that trailed the truck like a stinky tail. There was no pressure in following behind. She'd left plenty of room for falling debris with confidence no one would dare sneak into the space between her turtle and that whale. Any impatient driver was in another lane speeding away. No one tried to get into the slow lane. She would stay in the shadow of the giant and ride it until she had no choice but to turn.

"Where you headed?" A red-faced man in the toll booth had leaned down handing her change. The entrance to the parkway rose at her left. The map was unfolded on the passenger seat like a pirate's prize. She blinked at the blue and red lines.

Everyone thought she was older than she was. This had been a curse for as long as she could remember. At four, she looked seven and now at fifteen, she could pass for a legal voter, a drinker even, if she slicked on the lip stuff in the bathroom drawer and took her hat off. She wasn't worried that he would know she was, by all accounts, a child. She was worried more by the question and where it was supposed to go. What did people get out of these small conversations? Would it affect the outcome of his day at all to know where indeed she was headed? She knew this was just courtesy, as silly as it seemed. *Connect.*

"I'm heading down south, sir." She tried to make her voice go up and down like a ball toy on a string and thought of the words like honey so they flowed together. When she was nervous, her voice went into a raised flat monotone that sounded more like coughing than speaking. She'd been told but she never understood until Maisy showed her by pushing one note on the piano over and over again.

Baking for Dave

Leave space, but not too much space. Two words, then one word. Pause. Sounding like a dog barking or shooting the words out like a gun would make him look at her more closely, which she desperately needed to avoid.

"To meet up with friends," she said, attempting a smile. It wasn't a lie, really. There would be hundreds of fellow bakers at the Little Dough Showdown. Friends were people who shared common interests or goals, so she would be meeting a lot of people like that when she got there.

The old gent nodded and smiled, waving her on her way, confirming any notion she had about common courtesy. No one ever wanted a long story, not really. That's why people got so nervous when she talked. Most of the time, the questions weren't begging for answers. These were the simple ways people passed time when there were a few moments of silence, just like the buttons on the radio dial.

Chapter 4

Policeman

It was an easy drive, even without the dump truck clearing the way. She drove slowly, checking her seatbelt now and again to make sure it was taut against her skin. The map lay next to her like a flattened passenger, but she could find her destination without it. New Jersey made it easy. The parkway cut through it like an incision, ending where land hit water. It wasn't the most convenient way to get south.

Most people took the turnpike, but that road was infamous. Each exit presented a different repugnant surprise. The paper factory before the airport put off a mustard smell. The oil refineries were further down and the highway reeked of pickled rubber and burnt chicken soup. Then there were the delivery trucks and tourist buses spewing exhaust, like bad advice for miles. Beyond that were bridges and merges, giant sections of construction and concrete-thick traffic.

Taking the turnpike would be a bad idea. She would take the ferry when the parkway stopped. The salt air and water would make her mind happy, and, if she were lucky she might see some cool fish.

Part of the reason Maisy had gone for the blueberry in the first place was gas efficiency, and she'd made a wise choice. Iris filled up at the rest stop, where the shore signs had turned to a long stretch of dry-looking pines, next to the highway. She stopped not so much because she needed to but because the gas station was closer than her tank was to empty. The ferry was close, so after that, she'd have to worry about pumping her own gas, a reality she was not ready to face. She smiled at the attendant, more grateful for his service than he knew.

When she crossed the big bridge after Atlantic City, she had to flip her tape. Then she reached instinctively for the item she had made sure was under the map, while slowly breathing over the rise and fall of the water. The emergency hammer was something she'd seen on a commercial during the morning news. It could cut clear through her seatbelt and shatter the window if she needed it to, just in case the blueberry turtle went over the bridge or if the whole thing collapsed. Preparation made her panic subside into a sweat.

Before long, the raging river that was the parkway had thinned to a mere trickle, cutting through the forgotten counties of the Garden State, the ones closer to the Mason-Dixon line than the city. It was dotted by the occasional pickup truck, but for the most part, the road had become hers. She followed it until it disappeared into traffic lights and pedestrian crossings. Locals astride cruiser bikes rode beside her, and a few old men stood where the dirt butted the pavement, pulling long strings with crab traps from the murky water of the bordering swamp. There were more dogs than she could count, every owner nodding at the car like she was in a parade. Ladies in floppy hats and a short little man with leathery skin— they all tilted their chins in greeting as she drove by. It was very different down here, to say the least. The leisurely pace was welcoming. Every twenty feet or so, she was met with a new sign leading her to the ferry, like guide markers in a theme park. That was quite fitting, because she was about to go on quite a ride.

As it turned out, it wasn't just one ferry. Several waited at the end of the expanse of black and white that stretched out before her. The lot was massive. With only a handful of visitors there, she felt silly all of a sudden, to be driving this tiny car, licensed or not. It was marked with long white stripes that split it up like a giant game board.

There was a line of cars to the left that inched slowly after a long, beige camper that looked like it had seen its fair share of summers. The line drifted forward like a dinosaur's tail. Now Iris could see the clean, bare shed with the attendant inside. A smiling lady in a navy blue hat and matching shirt was talking with the drivers ahead. Luckily, Iris was far enough back in line that the novelty of gentle conversation had worn off by the time she reached the window. The woman looked once at the ticket Iris had printed out at home. When she was instructed to pull into her travel lane, she wasted no time. It was a hard turn that crossed in front of three other lanes of waiting travelers. As luck would have it, they let her pass. Things had been falling into place around her like that all day. She was the first car in lane 14, which from this vantage, read 41. Iris couldn't help but smile.

Like most perfect moments, it didn't last. The tap on the window jolted her stiff in a quarter of a second.

"Miss?" There was a muscular man in uniform looming close to her door. She could see herself in his glasses.

Iris fumbled with the window. She was glad for the high price of automatic ones just now, because the crank added seconds between her silence and the conversation that was to come.

The policeman was, as she'd heard people on TV say, squared away, his hair trimmed to a quarter inch of his skin. His uniform was pressed into impossible pleats. His posture spoke of confidence and training, and not taking kindly to teenage liars, especially ones who absconded with other people's blueberry turtles. He was squinting at her, but his dark skin was smooth, like fudge icing on cakes and clean sheets of chocolate fondant.

"Hello, hi. Officer. Sir. Can I help you today?" She heard her voice blurt out in a strained monotone.

He looked at the girl in her thick blue wooly, head tilted. She was perplexing to him, as much as she seemed perplexed, a supermodel in awkward clothes, lanky and uncomfortable in her own skin. Her big caramel eyes reminded him of the golden retriever he left at home, the one who waited until lunchtime for the Frisbee hour when they would play in the backyard.

"Ticket please?" He asked, masking the smile that played on his lips. Her knee bounced as if it were connected to springs.

Iris swallowed hard. His badge reflected the morning sun into her eyes like an inquisitor's overhead lantern. Keep it cool, she told herself, reaching for the paper next to her, dreading his next words.

"And license?"

Iris' heart sped and halted at the same time. Was it possible to have a rapid and stopped pulse? The answer was irrelevant. All she knew was she was on the verge of collapsing or exploding. A cold wave of dread rippled under the warm folds of her winter hat and frayed her hair into angry knots that pulled at her scalp. At least it felt that way. She had to remember that it was stress, and the pains were phantom, not real. The license was as close to real as it could get.

She had to remind herself of the webinar she watched on VueClix, how she painstakingly picked out the laminate plastic, pretending municipal and state licensure were two of her new special hobbies. It wasn't a lie. None of it was. In a way the topic had become as much a fascination as molecular chemistry or colonial pastry making, or Dave Matthews himself. She needed to know all there was about making a New Jersey driver's license. It had to be foolproof.

Sergeant Belmont was no fool. She could see that in his posture and starchy clothes as well as the way his shoes reflected the sunlight when he shifted his weight from one foot to the other. He held her credentials in front of his nose. She could see the ID in his lenses, inverted like a fun house image. Upside down, her brow seemed to furrow in the license in disapproval. She made sure not to smile or frown. The motor vehicle commission had strict rules about facial expressions. It felt like days as she tried to mentally command her forehead not to sweat, as the beads gathered at the ridge of her hairline like pearls on a priceless crown.

Iris did what she knew best. She breathed and pictured gentle colors in her head. She willed her muscles not to twitch and stiffen at the sight of the lean policeman who loomed with her fate in his hands, but the will could only do so much. They were close enough that he could hear the sounds rising up from her belly. It came on suddenly, with a pop that burned like fire. She played the wince off with a half-smile, and the sound with a smack of her legs. Other people might be embarrassed, but Iris was more concerned with the cool piece of plastic in the sergeant's hands than the sounds that bubbled from within her.

"You okay, Miss?" He inquired, asking in that way people always asked, the way that implied about a hundred more questions than she was ready to answer.

"Yup." She lied. Her stomach pulled her down in the seat like a marionette at the whim of an angry child done with play for the day. The Sarge eyed her ticket, then her, and then her license as if scrutinizing every digit. The first letter stood for her last name. The next had to do with her last name. The next five were trickier, part of an encoding system for the letters in her first name and then two digits for her middle name. Then came a combination of numbers derived from the characteristics unique to her: birthday, weight, and eye color. The code wasn't as hard to crack as people made it out to be, but watching the sizable lawman scrutinize her work made her more doubtful about the whole process than she had achieved a few days before. She'd been so confident she'd forgotten what a palpable foe doubt could be. Her stomach lurched. The car was filled with a big firework sound, the kind that booms at the end of the show when the crowd is rearing up for the finale. Iris sighed over the top of it, brushing her hand over the top of the steering wheel like she was taking a casual drive.

"Something's not right here." Sergeant Belmont looked hard at her ticket and license, dropping them at his side with a look she couldn't discern, before speaking in what sounded like slow motion. "You hang tight here, and I'll be right back with you."

Before she knew it, he had disappeared out of sight back to the shed with the nice lady and the phones that called for backup and the paddy wagon that would take her away. The sweat came again in a flood that ran down her eyebrows and past her cheeks. She didn't dare take off her hat. She chewed at her fingers despite the damage it would do and sang a gentle lullaby to herself about being in too deep. It was too late to get out of this. She had to ride it like a wave.

"We have a problem." He said.

She could feel his breath as it floated into the car. She waited for the speech bubble to pop when it arrived like a bomb just beside her face. She sat forward expecting it to explode, but it didn't.

"We do?" Her eyes were wide and her one eyebrow lifted, as it always did when she was truly excited. The wooly covered her cartoonish features, though the policeman had the amused look of someone who knew what was lying underneath.

"It looks to me like you missed something here." He drummed his open palm with the paperwork in question. She wondered if the juvenile prison had a good kitchen system before turning to face the inevitable jailer.

She got the blue backdrop. She faced forward. She didn't smile. Her lines were perfectly horizontal and spaced to the millimeter. Was her shade off? In all the phrases that passed through her head as potential responses, none of them sounded like what she said when her bottom lip caught on her two front teeth.

"Merlffp?"

For the first time, Sergeant Belmont took off his mirrored glasses. He leaned into the car with her credentials in his hand with one she did not recognize. His eyes were like pirate cannonballs because he was about to shoot holes through her whole plan.

"You almost missed your coupon." The sergeant's eyes softened into globs of licorice as he smiled. "I got you two." He winked. "Each one's good for a whole meal." He slipped two pieces of glossy paper between her phony license and real ticket. They bore pictures of hot dogs and fries, sodas, cheeseburgers, and nachos "You can leave the key here and get you something to eat. Don't you worry, I'll get her aboard for you."

Iris' face was blank at times like these. At times when most people would smile or say something, she usually felt like a plain pumpkin among jack-o-lanterns, an empty space waiting for a guiding hand to help determine what picture should arise. Her eyebrow would always betray her. She could feel it popping against the thick yarned lines of her wooly. Regardless, he took her silence for reserve, as most did.

He had a lilt in his voice, like something fun was happening. "Get some food in that belly. Don't be shy!"

Her mouth pulled downward at one side, where she bit at her upper lip, eyes blinking into a hard squint. It started with a tickle on her skin that popped and scratched at the surface until it crackled like fire. By the time she realized she was doing it, she'd usually been doing it for a half of a minute.

Sergeant Belmont took it for a smile of thanks. Maybe he thought she was shrugging good-bye. Either way he walked away from the turtle with a skip in his step. Iris realized maybe she was feeling some gratitude toward the man.

In all her preparations, she had been ready for everything except Iris had forgotten to eat.

Chapter 5

Water

The ferry terminal was a marvel that gleamed like a castle carved from precious stones from far away. The glass building jutted out into the bay so the travelers inside could look out on the horizon. From the outside, visitors could watch the travelers doing so. If Iris hadn't spent the morning tensing over a steering wheel, she might have enjoyed pretending it was an icy kingdom or fortress floating in space. Instead, she counted the steps it took to get to the front door, tapping her leg each time her right foot hit the ground and chewing hard on her bottom lip. It wasn't crowded, which was a blessing, just a smattering of white-haired tourists looking to hit the outlets across the bay. Next week, when school was out, it would be different. The boats would brim with college kids and beach bums who'd stand arm-to-sweaty-arm. Thank goodness, she didn't have to think about that. All she needed was the soft padding of her feet; the sound changed to pit pats as she slipped through the sliding doors. Her feet felt free as she walked on the cool tiles past the ticket desk. Luck was still on her side.

She breezed past the souvenir shop and arcade, giving the best smile she could to the lady in the sailor suit who manned the welcome center. At the back of the building was a wall as clear as clean air, which disguised itself as an open view of the bay. There was a mini-food court here and plenty of seats, but she shimmied into the one furthest from the action so she could pretend she was out in the sea floating all alone. She set her bag beside her in the plastic booth and ripped the bagel from its wrapper, devouring it in gulps. Her belly sounds were more than nerves. She was starving and thirsty. Iris chewed ice when she was nervous. The cold made her head calm down, but there was no ice or drinks left in the turtle. She'd torn through her drinks within twenty miles of home. Her throat felt like it had been coated in peanut butter. Her plan was to buy a sandwich or two while she was here, maybe some French fries but definitely drinks for the road. Thanks to the kind policeman, she didn't need the envelope she'd set aside for spending. She just had to do it.

Iris put the contents of her bag into place, securing envelopes and baggies back into pockets so she knew they were safe. There weren't many people in the line inside. Most of the tourists liked to sit on the other side of the wall, in the courtyard that jutted out on the water like a foot. Its heel was a miniature pirate ship, a play area with climbing ropes and seats for tired parents. With school in session, there were no kids to play, just two little babies in the arcade. At the top of the foot area, where the big toe would be, an exaggerated hut sat surrounded by stools that looked like giant coconuts. It was supposed to look like an exotic getaway, but Iris knew it was really a beer shop. The old men drank whisky and the old ladies in their flowered dresses sipped wine and Iris worried that they would die sooner than they were supposed to because they were drinking alcohol, which was poison. Worry aside, she was grateful for the coconut place and the playground. The more people stayed out there, the less were in here in the snack bar line.

She wiped the back of her hand against her face, pulling a glob of cream cheese across her cheek like paint. It was always hard to tell when there was something on her skin, but it was important to keep it clean. It was important to do things like that and not to have knots in her hair. Most of the time a good hat made short work of any of that nonsense. It was also important to check her face for food, to remember to brush her teeth even if she was busy with piano lessons or baking. There were certain requirements she had to remember at all times, or the looks of strangers would be too much to take. Why anyone would care if there was a glob of bagel in her teeth was completely beyond her. It was a perfectly reasonable question for which she didn't have time. She shrugged in frustration, popping the waxed paper from her bagel into the top of her knapsack, in case she needed it later.

The snack line consisted of two old women, a man in jeans, and the young mom from the arcade. The young mother talked over her shoulder, cradling juice boxes and apples like they were buried treasure. She yessed the little kids whining for quarters from the booth behind her. The lady behind the counter was already talking to the older ladies as they approached. She was a round woman with a broad smile and a voice that carried across the blue tiles like a foghorn as she made small talk that was anything but. Iris kept her eyes on the shiny square tiles, imagining they were scarabs scuttling over ancient sand. They clicked under her feet, making music over the sizzle of cooking meats and onions. There were choices laid out in front of her not unlike the cafeteria at school, but she didn't want tuna on a seedy bun. Nor did she want a hot dog. The thought of it made her stomach tumble over itself like stinky laundry.

She found what she needed in a cooler just past the salads and grabbed two waters and a splurge, a tube of bite size ice cream nuggets dipped in chocolate. They weren't on her coupon and they weren't the kind of thing she could save for later, but the cold ice cream would feel good on her raw lips. She bit them without knowing, especially when she was stressed. The can of soda wasn't something she normally liked. The bubbles would feel like acid in her mouth, but the cool can felt glacial against her raw fingers.

The two older ladies in the line were making a meal of the weather, eating up the snack bar lady's remarks like noodles. They were all looking at each other and nodding. The round woman spoke to them of impending storms, clouds, and sun, and all the other things they could know for themselves by looking out their windows each morning, but that's what old ladies did, right? They liked to get out and talk to people. Maybe their husbands were dead or too old to travel or maybe they were hard of hearing. Iris tried to place herself in other people's minds before deciding if they were nice or not. Or, at least, she'd been trying to do that. The white-haired women were dressed for a day out and perfumed like this was a special occasion. They lapped up the round lady's attention like hungry cats. This was the conversation for some people, though it made Iris shudder. Her stomach gave a tight lurch. Her feet felt wobbly, even though she was standing on firm ground.

Snack bar lady's eyes never left the others' faces. She scanned them and soaked in their replies like a cookie would warm milk. Iris would have to remember to look up every few seconds when it was her turn, to look at that spot in the center of the snack lady's forehead. That way, she would look like she was making eye contact. She was next up and just in time. The man in the look-through window had thrown something on the grill that sputtered and hissed. It smelled like hot trash cans left out in the sun. The little kids had started a round of whack-a-something. Their whines had erupted into giggles, which morphed into sporadic screams punctuated by metallic thumps. From here, it sounded like torture she dared not investigate. The worst part of it was there was no rhythm to any of it. If there were a pattern, she could predict when to brace herself for the bang, the scream, and the dinging bell, but there wasn't so she couldn't. Instead, holding the cold can to her ear like a telephone, she planted her feet like stones.

"You okay over there, honey?" The cash lady had finished with the outlet shoppers, and the young mother had scurried back to her cubs, who were now content being cub seals, whales, or whatever small creature was popping up from the metal holes. So the eyes behind the register had Iris alone to watch.

Iris didn't look up. She turned and moved as quickly in another direction as in all those times she'd forgotten she had to go to the bathroom. "I'm fine." She shoved the bottles back into the cooler turning them so the labels were in line. "I forgot something."

Iris held her hands between the folds of her wooly and the soft warm curves of her ears and didn't look up once before she hit the water fountain. It was cooler there by the ferry entrance, a cool, clear tunnel that blew a steady flow of fresh air. Once she was on the boat, she'd have more of it and the ocean to drown out the screams and the smells of her surroundings. Satisfied she was able to steady her breathing, she pulled the empties bottles out of her knapsack. Water fountain water was free, so that was another win. She thought about the positives and half smiled. It was then, she noticed that man from the line. He had an itchy-looking beard, red like a wizard's, that curled like an old teddy bear's fur. He had a big knapsack too. He was probably some kind of serial killer, and that bag cold be filled with severed hands and bludgeoned heads. Her smile pulled tight as she closed up each bottle.

She remembered how hard this was going to be.

Chapter 6

Chris

C hris woke that morning with what-he-thought was a clear solution to the problem he knew he would inevitably need to face. Rachel deserved better, and he didn't fault her for wanting to leave. He would beat her to it. She'd never see it coming.

He loaded his duffel bag with confidence, rolling T-shirts and extra socks like loose ends he'd pack away and deal with later. He moved with an air of confidence he hadn't felt in some time. He had been driven in those hours before sunrise, compelled to do what needed to be done at any cost because, finally, he was certain. The steps he was taking were right, and he knew it.

After two hours of straight walking, his senses had become foggy, his footing not as sure. At this point, only one thing was certain. He was hurting. He'd never been tortured, but he assumed this was as close as he'd ever get.

A thick peeling sound punctuated every step, reminding him that neither of his feet agreed with this. Every time they pulled up from the ground to move forward, they protested; they would rather stay put. He tried to move, but they clung to the soles of his sandals like they'd been glued there. When he finally pried one of them free, he thought it would more closely resemble a burned grilled cheese.

The first thing he ever cooked Rachel was a grilled cheese sandwich, a burned and gooey mess that stuck to the pan like it was meant to be there forever. It wasn't that long ago really, a hard admission to make that a man in his thirties who had never lifted a finger to cook even once. When they moved into that new house, he vowed he'd do all the grown-up things and it started, which started with making Rachel that grilled cheese sandwich.

He had snuck down in the morning and tiptoed to the kitchen, a tiny square of white as new to him as she was. He saw a sugar cube set, a small stove and just enough cabinet space for their new matching dishes and sparkling wine glasses. He'd draped a linen napkin over the top of the counter with a single rose in the bottle of wine they finished the night before. He made it all perfect while the bread sizzled in the pan. Rachel drifted down the stairs like a sleepwalker, the scent of warm butter impossible to resist as it spread room-to-room.

He twirled and dipped her down like a scene from an old drive-in movie. She melted in his arms like he was the world's best lover. The smell of fresh paint filled the living room where he carried her. The carpet was soft beneath them, where he'd laid her down. They had forgotten about the sandwiches. Until the alarms went off, they were lost to the entire world but each other. Everything was new.

All that was behind him now. By his estimation, he had traveled twenty miles or so.

Two steps felt like three miles now. His pace had slowed since the early hours when he sneaked from the house like a thief, hoping to be long gone before Rachel came in staggering and smelling of alcohol. She was beautiful when her hair was pushed half out of the ponytail and cocked to one side, even when her attempt at mascara had smeared and any glint of lipstick was gone. He couldn't look her in the eyes anymore, especially when they were bloodshot slits, bleary in the morning sun.

The trouble came at sunrise, when light poured into the bedroom like water. Chris' eyes stung as much with waking as they did looking at the empty space beside him. He gulped in three deep breaths and stretched his arms against every impulse to slip back down into the depths of sleep. He had to move forward to move on, and, if he didn't do it then, he wouldn't do it ever. Instead of lulling himself on island dreams and replays of better times, he spent the better part of the next hour shoving all that mattered into an oversized rucksack from the back of the closet, the one she hated from the army surplus store. It looked tough and unassuming, and she'd never notice it was gone. Better he left before the inevitable, before she could do it first.

It was hard enough to leave Rachel behind, but leaving a man's dog takes a special kind of gumption. He'd guessed all of this would be tough, but nothing quite like this.

"Don't look at me like that" Sasquatch had waited in front of the door, head cocked, accusing and pleading all at once, blocking the entire entryway like a mythical brown bear. "I have to go." He rubbed the behemoth's head as he spoke, soothing the beast in front of him and the one within that screamed at him to stop. "Before she does."

As if in answer, the dog stepped aside with a little whine, a long string of drool dropping from his jowl, hitting the ground with a sticky thud.

It was always good to be jolted back to reality. The ground gave a heave as a delivery truck whizzed by. Four miles ago this may have scared him, but now he just leaned with it, trying not to breathe in the proverbial dust that clung to him now like lost perfume. He shielded his eyes to the blast of black exhaust and pushed to the right in its wake. This road had become familiar to him, its rhythms and sounds, its scents of diesel and pine. He had his thoughts to keep him company. Squatch was probably lying on his back, belly in a sunbeam as Rachel slept off her night shift. Would she think he was out for a run? Was she in those pink pajamas with the blue polka dots? They made him crazy. He now had a goal ahead of him that he couldn't forget. His feet throbbed in time to his heartbeat, doubling with each new step. If he could just get one mile farther, it would get better. He made those promises to himself, assuring both feet it would be okay if they could both hold on. A man was capable of some remarkable things when he was left to his own devices. It had felt like it was going to be forever, but he knew nothing lasted that long. There was a rest stop coming, and he needed the break.

Before he knew it, the sliding doors were parting and a cool blast of burger air washed over him like water. The place was clear of travelers at this hour, but the man at the back was flipping burgers with a heavy-handled spatula, with such quick precision he looked like a machine. Sizzling and percolating sounds blended with the dog-whistle screams of high-velocity hand dryers. There was no small talk or human sound but for the slow pit pats of orthopedic shoes just ahead of him.

"Good morning." Half the woman's face was covered in a of pair sunglasses that looked more like a windshield tinted pink. Her white hair radiated from her head like a wish flower, a perfect dandelion bubble. "It's chilly in here." She turned to Christopher like they were old friends, grabbing his elbow with her bird-bone hand. "Walk an old lady to her seat?"

It had only been hours since he'd spoken to another person but it felt like a whole life had passed. "Sure." He cleared his throat, smiling at the little lady, who swam in her cardigan like a young child.

"I'm Madeline." Her feet shuffled on the floor. Her voice was light and scratchy like an old record, which was not completely unpleasant. "My friends call me Maddie." She shot him a look like she'd just met her new best friend. "I come here every day for the coffee. The bus picks me up and drops me right here. It takes me home too. You think they only have burgers at this joint, but the coffee is 37 cents and fresh. You want a cup?" She leaned her head expectantly and smiled.

"Chris."

"Ah, Christopher." She pressed her hands together like she'd just figured something out. "The traveler." She looked up as if making a note. "So you want a cup?" Her lipstick was smeared way out of the lines of her lips, but it didn't look foolish. It was familiar, somehow reassuring.

"Eh, sure. Why not?" He knew where he was going, but it's not like he had a deadline. Not anymore. He followed his new friend through the metal maze that lead to the burger place, which at, ten in the morning, did have some surprisingly fresh coffee.

"Traveler?"

The little woman's shoulders looked like round pillows under the fluff of her sweater. They lifted slightly when he asked and her voice followed suit when she answered. "Saint? Big in the 60s?" She flipped her hand like a mosquito was circling. "You'd remember if you'd go to mass once in a while."

"How did you?"

She touched his wrist with a hand that felt ice cold and as warm as day all at once. He needed sleep and to sit down or, at least, to get those sandals peeled off. "Lucky guess. Got that guilty look my boys get when I call them on the carpet." She gave his hand a pat.

If he were on that carpet, he wouldn't be able to answer. Mass? It seemed foreign to him by now. He and Rachel had married at a justice of the peace, a quick few words and forever had been sealed without setting foot in a church. It was a point of contention with her parents that turned into a sweeping discussion that included advice and comments from godparents, aunts, and long-lost cousins from miles around. It was a long drawn-out argument only family can have, but the two of them had faced it together.

"Two, Bud," she pointed at the man behind the counter who had hers in hand as they approached. "So, kid. What are you doing? Are you some kind of end-of-the-world nut or something?" She flicked her wrist at the beat-up rucksack bulging from his side, tilting her head at him thoughtfully. "You don't look crazy to me."

"I don't?" He smiled, liking Maddie more by the minute.

"Nah, you look like a nice fella. A handsome fella. You single, Chrissy?" He helped her into a hard plastic chair and sat down across from her. He could see himself in the table, which had been polished like someone's treasure. He looked back at himself, fuzzy eyed and dirt stained, haggard from the road. He looked like a serial killer. "Ah, you good-looking types never are." She took a good, long slurp of her coffee, leaving two red smudges on the side of her Styrofoam cup. Her eyes were watery blue behind her glasses, two round gems sparkling behind a pink veil. She studied him without scrutiny but wondered, the creases in her eyes moving upward as she smiled at him. He wanted to tell her everything. "Can I tell you something, Maddie?"

She dipped her head mischievously, like they were about to share a secret. "That's what I'm here for."

Maddie leaned in as if to hear every word as he told her things he hadn't told anyone, but himself in the past hours. The reasoning sounded better out loud than it had in his head for these past miles.

"So you see, I had to leave."

The old woman leaned back and drained her coffee, lifting her chin to Bud, who automatically filled the next cup.

"Before she does, right?"

She didn't speak but tapped her fingers together, her eyes never leaving him. A crescent moon smile crept over her face, one side of her face crinkling like paper. "It seems like you have to do what you have to do, but this vision quest of yours, this walking to…" She squinted. "What was it, honey?" She stood abruptly.

"Virginia, D.C. actually. It's more of a hike." He sounded doubtful, but not because of his answer but because the woman had made her way to Bud so effortlessly, he had to question his own eyes.

"Thanks, Bud. Another, honey?"

"No, thanks." He rubbed at his face.

"Get Lonnie on the horn, Bud. He should be on his way by now. Let's see if we can't get this kid a lift down that way." Recognition crossed the counterman's face, so he moved as deftly to the phone that hung on the wall as he did flipping burgers. "Chrissy, you're taking the ferry and from there, you can hike wherever you want. We're buying your dogs some time, 'cause honey, they're barking."

His feet were red and swollen beneath the straps of his sandals. He'd have liked to protest, but in moments he found himself waiting for Bud's nephew Lonnie, who pulled up in a beat-up old truck. It had great raised wheels and a custom paint job that was part camouflage and part modern art.

Lonnie worked for one of the big commercial fisheries down by the bay. He pulled crab traps on the side, which was probably why his truck smelled like an old beach pail, briny and fetid, with a hint of spearmint that came from the ice tea bottle he held close to his chin. He spit there periodically, not full-fledged loogies, but polite pops from lips pursed tight from trumpet playing. It turned out under his rough exterior, he was quite the personable fellow, quite knowledgeable in all things aviary, specifically local wetland birds.

"S'cuse me," he dipped his head with lowered eyes. "Habit. Beats smokin' though." He'd say it each time, when the conversation was interrupted by the unsubtle plop, between remarking on the wingspan of the egret and complimenting Chris' rucksack. He had apologetic eyes, murky green like swamp water, but kind like a child's. They lit up when he spoke about his birds.

It wasn't odd in this area to see cars pulled off to the side of a highway as if abandoned, only to find six or seven people sitting barefoot on the guardrail dangling fishing poles into the back bay or men in pants rolled up to the knee pulling wire cages from the muddy water. Lonnie slowed when he saw a few guys he knew and saluted with an index finger or thumbs up, or the other one, depending on the particular guys standing in the great pecking order of local fishermen.

There was sand on the floorboards that scratched beneath Christopher's sandals when he moved them, not much but just enough to make his sandals sound like tap shoes against the grit. Lonnie took as much pride in his truck as he did his local wildlife. It was obvious he went to great lengths to clean it. The dashboard gleamed. He'd taken care to wash those mats daily, and those tiny grains were the hardest to get. They slipped through the cracks, and they rubbed against him the whole way. He tried not to let the driver see his annoyance.

By the time they'd hit the long winding road to the ferry, he'd been told all there was to know about the endangered wetland habitat of the piping plover. By ten o'clock he'd had more honest conversations than he'd had in months and with virtual strangers. He'd shared his master plan with two of them, neither of which were Rachel.

"Good luck to you, sir."

He left the truck knowing a little more about mussels and clams and volumes more about what he was doing. When he said it all out loud, it had made more sense and that made his steps less painful as the ferry neared, where he moved further from home.

Chapter 7

Sweet

He wasn't expecting the coffee klatch at the rest stop. It had unnerved him to be talking so intimately with the old lady he'd just met. The last thing he wanted was to talk with anyone, let alone someone he barely knew. He'd let the world off his shoulders with Madeline. At least, it had felt that way. After that, he was free to shoot the breeze with a relative stranger in the same way, which felt strangely at ease. They didn't know a thing about him, and it didn't matter. That way, there was no expectation and, definitely, no let down. It was bizarre so much so, he'd forgotten his intentions in the first place. Also, during all the uncharacteristic chit chat, Chris had neglected to eat.

The scent hit his nose as soon as the doors shushed behind him of a warm meaty cloud dotted with onions and peppers, gooey cheese and ripe tomatoes. All the delicious

Baking for Dave

smells made his stomach rumble and mouth fill with wanting. He followed the smells back through the slanting lines of the new building to the food court, a clean enough place with just enough people to make it annoying. This was usually the part where he'd leave. Maybe Madeline had changed that. Two older ladies were kibitzing with the waitress behind the counter. The one wore garish red lipstick that all but screamed over her ill-fitting caps. Her companion, in a bedazzled baseball cap, spoke thirty decibels louder than necessary. The two together gave him nothing more than a reason to walk away. Normally, that was the case, but something about their mannerisms and the easy way they interacted reminded him of Madeline. He found himself staying in line behind them. They weren't all that unlike her.

They wove stories of bad sandwiches into asides about grandchildren and spoke like old friends, though they'd clearly just met the lady with the notepad, the one who punctuated her tales with orders for onion rings and well-done steaks. These women had the same desire for company as his newest acquaintance. He could see it in the way they leaned forward and how they were drawing out conversations that would be over otherwise. In this, they were all like Madeline. However, these women seemed less attentive when the others spoke, like each of them was waiting her next turn to speak. Yes, that was it. Madeline wasn't looking for a spotlight. She was always listening.

Sweet

The guy behind the grill could have been Bud's long-lost brother. He had the same white T-shirt and folded paper hat, and his posture was one of attention and grace. He flipped food on the grill with precision, in a rhythm that seemed part of him, an automatic motion fueled by pride. It surfaced when he dinged the order-up bell with a flip of the spatula and a gleam in his eye. Christopher couldn't remember the last time he had looked at anything that way.

A mother was just behind them. In another world, she might have been attractive, but in this one she wore the heavy-lidded gaze of a woman just about to peter out. The two children with her alternated squirming with shouting. While one whined, the other yelled. When the loud one quieted, the other demanded something new. It wore on her as clearly as her faded T-shirt and frayed cargo shorts. Her voice was thin but firm as the two young children circled her like puppies, excited about a trip to grandma's house and a trip to an aquarium. They were definitely going through some kind of repeat-everything phase. It seemed as though every phrase either of the children said, they'd repeat it six or seven times. Their mother had taken on the look of someone about to jump ship. He knew that look all too well.

Sandwiches and burgers were the standard fare here. There was a cooler with pre-wrapped salads and sandwiches to go. They even had a nacho station with a bin of loose beef and a mystery tub of orange nacho goo. He made a round through the offerings, scanning spreads and pita chips, sliced veggies and bowls of fruit, though none of that was necessary. Bud's long-lost twin was an artist with a bacon cheeseburger. Christopher knew what he wanted with his first step.

That's when he saw her, the strange girl who'd taken his place in line. She looked like a supermodel, tall and thin, with precise features and big, faraway eyes the color of caramel that matched her hair. She must be someone artsy or famous because those types dressed that way. He saw them all the time back at the college in their scarves and beaded necklaces, their suspenders and bowties. She was in beat-up jeans cut off so the pockets jutted out the bottom and a green camisole over another camisole, peach? She topped it with a zip-up hoodie, and cowboy boots with knee-high socks. Even though it was June, she wore a knit cap for winter, the kind that ties around the chin, fashioned to look like a raccoon. In short, she was dressed like she didn't give a darn.

Something had her very nervous, worried on the brink of trembling. She focused on the people ahead of her, then on the cooler of drinks, then on the chilled sandwiches like each pained her more to look at than the next. Then she paused like a statue, a beautiful stone in the center of the snack area, but she was more. He knew this move because he found himself doing it more and more lately. She was breathing. The young girl stood as if she were by herself, eyes closed, hands laid at her sides, breathing. She took one breath after the other, long and slow, as if convincing her heart not to explode. He did this himself when things were bad, when he found himself on the brink of panic.

She paced from the sandwiches to the drinks, pausing in front of the salads as if she were deciding something. He thought she may speak or call out to someone, but, instead, when she drew her hand to her mouth, she did what he didn't expect. She bit her fingers hard and chewed, like no one was watching.

It was a tough few seconds for Chris, watching from the outside. Part of him wanted to help, assure the young girl that no matter what it was, it would be okay. He knew better than anyone this was a lie. Nonetheless, he wanted to help. He wanted to jump into action and help pull her away from whatever pain had struck. Just as he was about to step in with his words, she'd moved to action. She was gone. He had wanted to reach out and help, to be there, but she moved too quickly. He wasn't much use to anyone.

He scarfed his sandwich down, with his back to the crowd, alone in a corner like a punished schoolboy. He listened as the biddies finished a conversation about pinochle and the little ones convinced their exhausted mother to buy not one but two bags of cotton candy and a pair of souvenir pirate ships for the boat ride to grandmas. All the while, he wondered if the girl would be alright. He hated feeling helpless and the familiar disappointment of figuring things out too late.

If fate was a real thing, he had found his chance for redemption. The young girl stood before the boarding tunnel, as if transfixed by the water fountain.

The fountain water tasted like blood. Were her fingers bleeding again? Maisy would tell her if she'd been chewing, but Maisy wasn't here. The stupid snack bar had made her so anxious, she'd forgotten things like time and biting. Chewing felt good when the world made her nervous. She didn't realize she was doing it. The soft parts of her fingers had been worn away, raw and calloused, healed over from months and months of trying not to bite. They seemed to be intact. No blood had been drawn. That iron taste was from hard water and nothing more. Maisy would be proud.

As quickly as she realized that had been the case, she made her move. The thirst was overwhelming, because the blood taste coated her throat like tacky paint. She was emboldened by her own strength now. She could do this. She hadn't chewed her fingers. She hadn't panicked or chirped. She had made it all this way, so giving up was not an option. Small places were almost as bad as loud noises and just as bad a choice. She put her head down and shot through the boarding tunnel like a bullet. Iris worked hard not to think about the tunnel as she scurried onto the boat, as if death itself were chasing her.

Sweet

When she was little, she was afraid of fire. She'd wake screaming with nightmares of burning houses and smoke-filled rooms with no hope of escape. In a way, she was thankful not to be afraid of water. It was everywhere here. Water and air and sky surrounded her like an angel's hands, and it was heavenly. As soon as she set foot on the ferry, it was like a hunk of concrete had been lifted off her back. The first deck was open and airy, filled with cars that sat dormant. No horns or idling engines stirred or shook the ground beneath her feet. It was like walking through a life-size model of collectible cars. If she could, she would stay on this deck, but that wasn't allowed.

The commuter level had a wraparound deck she could walk for the whole trip if she wanted. So many people were leisurely strolling out there, no one would question a girl walking in circles. There was a clear view of the bay, the sky, rock formations, and the lighthouse in the distance. She smelled the salt in the air, and she leaned on the railing, hoping to see a dolphin in the water. She'd have been content out there, if not for the thirst. It was overwhelming.

Inside was a snack area, not unlike the one in the big glass building but tiny. A lady in a cruise ship blazer manned a register next to a microwave, a small cooler, and a coffee machine. It wasn't as crowded here. With the ship rocking now, she had something to distract her from the hum of the machines and the overhead lights. She'd spent too much time out on the deck. There was a line two families deep including the four-year-old from before that was clinging to a pirate ship he banged every once and again against the rack of potato chips. How could those kids be everywhere? He was yelling again. Grandma, this. Fishy that. The sibling, the bigger one, was telling him there would be a big fish or whale. Neck hurt. He said it again. Whale. Fish.

It was like rubbing fiberglass insulation all over her skin. She turned to shield herself from the sound, but there was an older lady with spider-web hair right behind her, who smelled like too much fabric softener mixed with dried flowers. Iris had picked up her water in hand and a cup of ice cream nuggets. The cold made her forget for a moment the world around her. She breathed in the cold, shutting out the wrong words and heavy smells.

Just then all she could think about were comic books, all those stories about losing one sense to strengthen others. They were far more accurate than the little boy who insisted mammals were fish.

She closed her eyes to breathe and, like hornets, the buzzing crawled into her ears, boring holes into her head. Even with her eyes closed, she could see the flickering of the overhead lights, like a black-and-white kaleidoscope on her eyelids. Those fluorescent bulbs whined like hungry cats. She wanted this so badly, not just the water or the ice cream—but to be able to push through, but she couldn't bring herself to do it. She threw her items back, not even bothering to straighten out the containers she knocked over.

She almost knocked down the itchy-looking guy with the dirty-looking beard, the guy with the big bag from the snack bar before. She didn't care. She needed to find her quiet.

It was easy when she knew where to look. The silence on deck was like cold water. The rush of air over her fingertips felt like icy silk. It calmed the burning where she'd chewed through the skin. That last episode had proven to be too much. She could hear Murph lecturing her about impulses and controlling her body. She could hear Maisy saying, *"It was too much today."* It was so frustrating when they were right. She never knew when she was chewing, not until the blood flowed, and then it was too late.

She wiggled her fingers in the cold and sea air, as if they were gloves protecting her from the elements she didn't enjoy.

Her eyes were trained on the horizon as she watched the ups and downs of the long straight line in front of her. It didn't make her sick to watch the rocking. Rocking made her feel better, so she went with it. Here, outside, it wouldn't be such a big deal, not now with most of the passengers inside eating microwave pizza or playing bingo machines. As soon as the boat started moving, most of the travelers who had been out here earlier had walked away. How fickle people were, walking away from an ocean view.

Iris could never tire of the quiet, the gentle sway, or the sound of the sea. It was so vast, and the blue invited her in like a dream, deep and tranquil. It was broken only by the spray of three surfacing dolphins that raced next to the ferry. Once when she was four, Maisy had taken her to Delaware, and a pod of dolphins had followed in their wake like nosy neighbors. She knew they would come. They danced in the waves doing barrel rolls, surfing, and showing off for Iris, as they had when she was small. In their acrobatics, she'd forgotten how awful she'd been feeling, how scary the world could be.

She mouthed the words to a song that made her feel better. The notes tickled her throat and smoothed away the stingers inside. It felt like needles getting sucked through a straw that went straight to her belly button and out from her fingertips. When the lights were too bright or the noise was too loud, she got the bad feeling that made her face wriggle and her eyes twitch. Strong smells and crowds were never good. Even sometimes, when none of that was present she felt her lips pulling to the side and her nose sliding off toward her ears.

The wrong words made her teeth shred. She could feel them cracking in her mouth before the sting took over. Sometimes the needle place found her even in the quiet of her own bedroom. Maisy tried to put her statues back exactly as they were, but Iris always knew when they weren't. When that was the case, the bees and hornets came, stinging her face and fingers, flying down her throat, cutting her teeth in two. Iris hated that bad place, but she'd been working hard with Murph and Doc Gentry, so she hummed.

The notes were like a salve on her skin that warmed her soul like soup. The notes danced on her lips, bouncing off the water. She let her head roll with the sound from shoulder to shoulder, and she told a story to the dolphins she knew would come. She wove the words in between phrases of the song. A mother dolphin and her pups were off to fight the evils of a dark sea king. It fit amid the verses and the chorus. Dave always left room for the audience to breathe, to fill in the gaps between the words he was singing. It was like this moment was meant for his song and Iris' tale. The small dolphin was afraid of the fight ahead. It was too much for him. She could see it in the way he followed close behind the bigger one. The middle dolphin, the sister, was brave. She'd be the one who would best the dark king. She ventured ahead of them both, and they followed behind her into the distance. Iris hummed and rocked with the waves until the sharp pulling from inside her subsided and her mind became as gentle as the calm sea ahead. All that was left was the song in her head and the quiet rise and fall of her own breath against the rail.

"Hello."

"AAAAAAAAAAAHHHHHHHHHHCCK!" Iris jumped away from the deck rail as if it had been electrified and stood bolt upright, like a deer caught in front of a truck's high beams.

The scream rattled around him and the girl panted, eyes wide like cartoons. At once Christopher could see that, for one, she was no supermodel and, for another, she was just a kid. She looked like a fourth grader who'd seen a real-life boogeyman.

"I, I'm sorry. Would you like these?" He held out the bottle of water and the container of nuggets limply, in a peace offering. She'd been eyeing them inside, but it had seemed painful for her, so, when she'd scurried off for the third time, he'd stepped in to save the day. If this was supposed to be his heroic deed, he was failing miserably. She was panting, face pulled far enough back into her shoulders that it looked like it was trying to escape her head. Her eyes didn't blink but were unfocused, like they were watching a film no one else could see, and it was terrifying.

"I just thought." He chose his words carefully, changing tactics. "I bought way too much. I drank my whole water, and now I'm stuck with this one." He held up the cup of Choco-Ice Nuggets. "I don't even know what I was thinking with these. They're completely sealed. They're not half-eaten. I haven't even touched 'em." Her shoulders lowered just a touch, eyes darting to the water for a split second. "Truth be told, you looked like you were having some trouble in there. I just want to help."

Sweet

Her gaze narrowed. He could feel her focus shift and settle right in the center of his forehead like a mystical third eye. Her head moved to a more natural angle, and slowly, like a cautious animal, she reached out and took the water from his hands.

It was the big, heavy bottle she wanted, the five dollar one on the top shelf. Iris drank it greedily, realizing only then how thirsty she'd been. Her throat felt better immediately, blood taste melting like fresh snow. The air had looked blurry before, which she only realized now that it had come into focus, like her TV after a storm. She took another sip. The water was sweet like summer corn. The dull sting in her gut calmed more with each taste. She guzzled it now in gulps, forgetting the lights and the rails and the fact that she'd run away with Maisy's car. She forgot the dolphins and the ocean and even Dave, until she looked up, and realized the bearded man was still there, nuggets in hand. He'd taken her away from the bad feeling and had saved her from the blood. She said the only thing she could at a time like this.

"Are you a serial killer?"

Chapter 8

Maisy

In her dreams, Maisy remained calm and clear-headed. She got do-overs of the dreams when she wasn't, even when she had the worst nightmares, which came less frequently now, but still often enough. This one, in particular, was her least favorite. They all had a similar focus: Iris on the opposite side of a rickety bridge that snapped; Iris floating away in a flood; Iris lost her balance at the top of a tall building. The turmoil was as real in all of them as it would feel in real life. This was one about Iris in a hallway, and she hated it the most.

Iris was at the end of a long corridor—younger, six or seven—running ahead as always, excited about a new contraption she'd made out of cardboard and leftover pieces from a building set. It was in the first grade she started building that way—repurposing things from the garbage, building new toys from discarded food containers and thrown-aside clothes. It was this version of the little girl who always stood at the end of the narrow tunnel in the dream. If she could see her face, she'd see tiny blobs of modeling clay dotting her hands and face like perfectly round rainbow measles. In this dream, Maisy couldn't see her face. It was only the back of Iris' head, hair hanging like a veil to her shoulders. It swung this way and that, as she skipped/ran too far ahead. Maisy called out to her to slow down. She shouted at her to wait and, finally, begged her not to open the door at the end of the hall, but the young girl never listened. Maisy's body tensed now knowing what came next. Dream Iris would run full speed down the hallway, rushing through the door without looking. Just like always, she would fall into the great hole beneath. That is, of course, until Maisy decided not to let that happen.

"Nope!"

The shout startled Oscar, who jumped when Maisy yelled and landed with a thud, and bounded away as gracefully as one would imagine a cat with a club foot should. He half-scowled from just outside the door.

"Sorry, sir. You'd think you'd be used to it by now." She appealed to his sensibilities. He was a reasonable fellow, but it didn't mean he liked getting flung off the bed any better. "I'll make it up to you." She rubbed him once in the deep folds just behind his head. His inability to walk like other cats did not lesson his appetite. "You want some breakfast, my squishy boy?"

Maisy

It was 8:30 already and, by the looks of it, Iris had gotten to school without incident. There were checklists in the hall by the front door, one in the kitchen, and one on the outside of the closet. Maisy surveyed them one-by-one to make sure Iris hadn't cut corners. *Brush teeth*, it said in the bathroom. Scrawled underneath the print were messy and familiar handwritten words. *Really brush them. Don't just run it under water.* There was another just like it in Iris' bedroom with reminders to wear socks (clean socks) and to wear sweatshirts over T-shirts (not the other way around). The boxes were checked in thick pencil lines. Bulky carpenter's pencils were Iris' favorite, so Maisy had several stuffed into a tall souvenir cup she kept on desk, sharpened to exact points.

Maisy worked her way through all the lists, ticking off the numbers one-by-one. "She got her socks, her shoes. Good." The list was a song she and the cat shared each morning. "Hoodie. Good. It's chilly in the morning and #$@&%*.

She bit down on the last syllables peeling the plastic block from the bottom of her foot. In its place, four perfect circles stood as reminders of the injury, like tribal scars. "At least, I didn't curse." The cat seemed amused. The big pickle jar by the phone was by now brimming with #$@&%* pennies and #$@&%* nickels for each swear word she uttered. A really bad swear word would be worth at least a dollar. Maisy had her own habits and rituals, one of which was the ritual of cursing like a drunken longshoreman in times of stress or searing pain. Iris hated the angry words. They made her nervous and stressful, which led to the look that broke Maisy's heart. She was trying her best to adapt. Change was hard for everyone, but she was trying. She sighed in relief when she heard the beep from the kitchen. Number 14 on the kitchen list. *Set coffee timer.*

By now, Iris would be sitting in homeroom. The school hadn't called yet, so that was a good sign. The phone wasn't blinking, so there were no forgotten books or emergencies. Maisy should stop expecting that by now. It had been months without incident, but some habits were just part of her. She found herself more often than not waking for phantom emergencies that never came. Routines were hard to break for everyone.

Oscar pushed his head against her leg, revving his old motor as she filled his bowl. She punched the numbers in without looking at the receiver. Eric's voice was unsurprised, if not expectant.

"You're supposed to be sleeping, Maisy."

"She get there okay, Eric?"

"Yeah, she did good. Took her a little bit to get the order, but she's getting better." She could hear the bustle of a breakfast rush but he spoke to her easily, as if they were chatting over a cup of tea. "You know, she can do this," he added, as if he'd heard her stomach drop. "She's going to do just fine."

"The store's okay? It sounds busy. You need me to come back?"

"It is fine, Maisy." Eric sounded like he was smiling.

"You moved the sign on the counter, right? Did you get fives and twenties? You're going to need them for the lunch rush. Just in—"

"I got 'em Maisy." Eric had been there as long as she had and never once had he forgotten to get change, but that never stopped her from asking.

"You have to pay attention to these things, Eric. You have to act like you care." She was harsh because she hadn't slept. The night shift did funny things to people. Eric would get so punchy that he became a great big fifth grader, giggling at packages of hot dogs, forgetting to do simple things like wrap food or lock doors. Maisy, however, got fresh when she was overtired. He knew it, and worse, so did she. "Sorry, I know you do; I don't know why I said that."

Not once did he ever show a sliver of offense any of the times she'd bitten his head off over counter signs or dollars in the change tray, because he knew she'd catch herself before he could say a word. Plus, he didn't mind. It was Eric's way. "Did you see we're getting a new batch of that salmon? You have to make sure it goes in the walk-in." Her voice drifted. She had started putting the emphasis on the wrong syllables, like a toy running out of batteries. Walk-in sounded more like the actor and less like the place they kept cold cheeses. By now, she had devolved into almost gibberish.

"That's classified information, ma'am, not available for civilians lacking at least six hours of sleep who can't actually speak like human beings." His official sounding government-man imitation and joke was lost on the non-human being on the other end of the phone, who hadn't heard a word of it.

"Cause it's fish, and you'll kill someone." It sounded like a song. "That would be bad." She leaned her cheek furthest from the phone onto her hand, so she sounded like she was miles away. "She's going to dance to." She lost a second there, maybe a minute. Eric would never tell.

"Dave Matthews." His amusement colored his words. "With all due respect, Ms. Heller, it sounds like you need your coffee, and then you need to rest." There was a muffled sound. "Hey bud, the line's there. You gotta wait just like everybody." He sounded closer to her when he spoke again. "Not like you're gonna listen to me." Maisy couldn't remember the last time she was able to sleep for more than a few hours at a time. She was her own best alarm clock.

"I will, Eric. I'm here, if you need me. Just let me know, because I don't mind."

"Maisy," he interrupted.

"Yes?"

"Go back to sleep."

She would, after her coffee. She'd drink two cups while sifting through yesterday's paper, then settle in for a few hours drifting off to her favorite show before waking for the day. It wouldn't make sense to anyone else, but it made her feel normal, a habit most people wouldn't understand. It helped her feel regular, like the people with real sleep patterns, ones who hadn't rolled out bagels until four in the morning.

This time when she closed her eyes, she dreamed she was in the circus. No, she was at the circus, chosen from the crowd to perform a juggling act in the center ring. *I don't know how to juggle.* Before she could formulate the words, the barker announced it was time for the main attraction, a high-wire act. It was Iris. This was new. She was ten, still wearing that top-of-the-head ponytail she used to love so much before things changed. The girl waved from an impossible height that defied the proportions of the tent and any law of physics Maisy could remember.

She took her first step and the wire bent at a cartoon angle beneath her, the whole thing wavering side-to-side as Iris' eyes went into the wide look that never failed in sending a wave of panic through Maisy. She could feel her chest tightening. Iris leaned one way and then overcompensated by throwing all her weight the other way. There's no way gravity would stand for any of it. Maisy lunged toward the teetering wire but was glued where she stood. The breath came harder and faster now, but no voice followed, just the helpless pantomime of nightmares where no one can hear. Screaming was futile, so no one moved to help the falling girl. *That's it.*

"Nope!"

She sat up in a sweat. "Not doing it."

It was lunchtime by now, but there were no calls, again. If Iris had called for a last-minute request for soup, she had not left a message. For the best portion of a semester, the guidance office had left her alone. All of this was good. Like a sleepwalker, she floated into the bedroom across the hall, checking on the two tanks on the dresser. All the fish had been fed according to the list decorated with sparkly bubble stickers. The setups were intact: bridge and ponies still poised at the ready for when Iris returned. She hadn't snuck any of them into her book bag to take to school.

Maisy picked out a new garbage bag, taking out some more of the incidentals Iris had hidden away. It felt cowardly to do this on the sly, to hope the girl who noticed everything would let the loss of a few treasures slip by. Maisy had to hope. There were lots of things Maisy had learned to do, that at first felt cruel, but she had to. If not, the room would overflow with candy foils from the street, pieces of cardboard boxes, and remnants of meals Iris couldn't part with. They were priceless to Iris, but the smell alone could be overwhelming.

It wasn't that she was a messy girl. There was order to it, to Iris. She would know if the tiniest gum wrapper had been removed from a pile of ripped construction paper and small sticks. *That's a comic book for Sir Laugh's a Lot.* She'd explain how the toy knight had a broken heart because the Pumpkin Princess took his sister away, holding up the doll princess with the Halloween wind-up toy for a head. *He needed a laugh, Maisy, and you took it away.*

There was the set of mini-furniture Iris sculpted from found items: a tiny throne and foot stool, even a shrunken side table, a candelabra, all of which lined the bookshelf next to her bed. Iris crafted them from Oscar's old cat food cans. The shiny metal had inspired her, so she went to that place between madness and inspiration, that quiet place she disappeared to sometimes, and, when she emerged, she'd created something beautiful from a handful of tin cans. However, she would neglect to clean any of them out. The smell was like sick mixed with rot. Maisy would never consider chucking them, so she took a handful of cotton swabs and lemon oil and worked with Iris into the night to make them spotless and fresh. Some things were worth the compromise.

The kitchen counter doubled as an office, just as Iris' room doubled as an art studio, a science lab, and a make-shift dance studio. Maisy's laptop buzzed next to a stack of papers, with as much anticipation as she did waiting for a page to load. She punched in the name and the passcode, as she had every day at just this time and waited to be let into room 1061B. This time she wouldn't be sleepily answering a discussion question or adding input to a group.

The names were laid out in a grid, ID numbers tacked on like kite tails. Maisy traced her finger down the list to her own and took a breath before moving across the row to the italicized word that blinked just above her cursor: Final. She rubbed at the letter, half-believing it would disappear under her finger. It was warm there and, much to her surprise, it wasn't going anywhere.

Her hands moved automatically to the phone, smile widening as a slew of words she'd promised not to say flowed out in a happy, yet explicit current. She'd promised Iris she'd work on the cursing, but extreme times, even joyous ones, called for the right words.

His voice cut off hers expectantly. "So?"

"It's official."

"Passed?"

"Not passed." Saying it out loud fueled a short burst of exclamations Iris would not approve. "A+." The magnitude of it all hit Maisy at once. "Eric, I did it."

Eric had a whole face that smiled when he was happy: eyes that sparkled and teeth that shined, cheeks that rose up like ripe apples even when he was slightly amused. It was his voice that smiled. His was grinning. Maisy could hear it.

"Yeah, you did."

"I never thought I'd be able to do it."

There were beeping and clatter sounds and a crackling of waxed paper before he gave a sort of sigh and laugh. "I knew you could."

Maisy

"I can't wait to tell Iris."

She had to let him go before he was devoured by the lunch mob, so she tried to distract herself with all the chores it took to get to 3 p.m. There was no way she'd get any more sleep today, not with all there was to celebrate now. Iris had asked her not to watch *Dance America*, and Maisy had promised, but nothing said, she couldn't stand in the hallway to watch Iris dance to Dave's music.

She was going to be surprised.

Chapter 9

You and Me

The girl looked at him, face inscrutably frozen with one eyebrow raised.

"I'm not a serial killer," Chris insisted for the third time. "I'm a teacher."

No change registered to indicate that his words had made any dent. Her fingertip was wedged firmly between her two front teeth. Tension tightened around the features on her right side. That cheek and side of her mouth pulled up and back as if yanked by invisible thread; the rest of her face was as serene and calm as pudding, as she chewed away like her finger was a small smoked turkey leg.

"Honest," he pleaded, holding up his hand like a middle-age scout. He looked around the boat and gripped his hands together the way people do when they are nervous. His brow wrinkled up like something hurt him as he insisted again. "Not a killer."

He didn't understand what was happening. This was what Maisy would call "the look" if she were here. The girl looked as if she was wearing a well-crafted mask. All the details were there. Her nose and lips were in proportion. It's not that she didn't look real, but there was an eerie stillness in her eyes, but not lifeless like a mannequin. It was like looking at a candle behind a screen, until it wasn't anymore. Her face tilted back to center as if a switch had been flipped. She blinked her eyes as if awakening from a nap.

"Of course, you're not." The voice came from the slit of her lips, the rest of her face expressionless, head tilted almost imperceptibly and her right eyebrow arched upward independent of the other, as if drawn onto her face.

"You're not lying," she said, blinking as if she'd just awakened from a nap. She craned her neck forward so that her face was uncomfortably close to his, inspecting him from brow line to chin.

"Definitely not." She seemed satisfied and unfolded the contents of a small paper bag she'd extracted from her backpack. She counted out five raisins and then, as if compelled, reached in for one more before tucking it away once again. Her attention was now focused like a laser on his face.

"That's good to know…" His voice went up like there was more to what he was going to say. He dipped his face down as if he expected something. Iris was not giving up her raisins. "I'm Chris." He held out the hand without the nuggets. She didn't take either. Instead, she nodded her head once and spoke as if she were reciting a child's rhyme.

"You have the same phone as me, Christopher. The Supernova 7." His attempt to get a word in was futile. "Only yours has a green cover and a crack in the top right corner. Mine has a purple cover. You like the Supernova 7, and you're not a liar, so pleased to meet you." She held out her hand halfway. Then second guessing yanked it back. "I'm Iris." Then, in a half mumble, she sputtered words that sounded melodic, a one-note tune set in rhythm. "But please don't call me Irish. The Irish are a fine people, and I am half-Irish, though it's hard to tell. That's not my proper name."

Her head looked as if it moved independently from the rest of her body, jolting side-to-side when she spoke. She was expressive in a way that made him think of the Japanese comics of his youth, all wide smiles and pulled faces. The rest of her body stayed motionless, bottom in the seat like she was an animatronics robot that only half-worked.

"My proper name is Iris Rose, confirmed Iris Rose Cecelia, if you count a confirmation name as a name. Catholics like to add a name at a certain age. I am that, and Irish, in descent, just not in name, because it's Iris, not Irish."

Not one for lacking words, he found himself grasping for a better way to describe this strange girl beside him. "You are something else, Iris, aren't you?"

"Iris Rose Cecelia." Her hand darted so quickly now to the ice cream, so he didn't have a chance to react to her taking it.

"Yes, I get that a lot."

She crammed half the container of the ice cream bites into her mouth, crunching down on bits of chocolate and ice like they were the same. "Foo mo wanno kee me ewe schnap me."

He shrugged. Most people couldn't understand Iris when she spoke while eating. She swallowed the half-chewed hunks so she could speak again and the words came in rapid fire. "You don't want to kill me or kidnap me, so why are you giving me ice cream? Are you a fugitive? Are you looking for some sort of hostage?" She paused, thinking. "Are you making up for some terrible thing you did in your life?" She eyed his backpack and his shoes. "Are you running away?"

"I'm not a fugitive," he added under his breath, "if that's what you're asking." She was using his words as an opportunity to eat another handful of nuggets. She shook the container to break them apart, picking them off one-by-one, licking at her fingers like a snapping turtle. "I saw you just outside, at the concession. And you were." The look on the girl's face had stopped him and, for the second time this morning, he had found himself wanting to talk to a complete stranger - "You were having." She had the look of tightened chests and impending panic, that blood-draining look that means the anxiety has won out. It was a terrifying, powerless look, the look that meant all hope was gone.

He cleared his throat the way people do when they are uncomfortable. He didn't hum or rock, but he felt nervous about something. Iris could tell.

"Are you having a stress problem, Christopher?" She asked it as one would ask about weather or a coming weekend, with an easy, almost haphazard air. Though Iris would never notice, his muscles tensed. "You're in trouble?"

"You were having a bit of trouble," he smiled. It was his explicit goal not to notice people normally, to avoid having to talk to random strangers about things like weather and sporting events. This girl, like his coffee friend Maddie, was different. "I just wanted to help."

"My therapist says when you have a stress problem, you need to make your body calm so your mind can face it. I call her Murph, but her real name is Rebecca Swanson McMurphy. She married a man from Ireland with a brogue, which is an accent. She showed me this." She lifted her hands palms up. "You take a deep breath i-i-i-n." She tilted her head, pulling air into her nose, and sat there for a moment with a surprised look on her face, before she leaned forward and blew like there was an invisible birthday cake in front of her. "Make your lips like this." She made a tiny 'O' of her lips like she was holding a piece of raw spaghetti there. "Now, blow it out your mouth." She nodded toward the cake no one could see. "Out goes the air, and out goes the stresssssss." It was like she hadn't heard a word he'd said.

Christopher knew a trick or two himself.

"I thought you might like the snacks." He motioned to goodies he'd brought, as she kept deep breathing, lifting her head for him to join in. "I'm not stressed."

Iris didn't answer but sat gobbling a mix of raisins and ice cream. For a second, there was only chewing.

"Is it okay if I stay here?" He patted the seat next to hers like it was sacred territory. From what he could gather, space seemed important.

She stopped her puckering long enough to answer. "You can sit wherever you want." Though he was still look-ing at her, she turned in her seat to look straight ahead at the water, her face going completely still, which stayed that way for a matter of minutes.

"So, where you headed?"

Her lips were moving almost imperceptibly, but enough to give Christopher the impression she was responding to him. "Sorry, what was that?" It was hard to make out her face under the woolen hat, especially with the ear flaps down, so he couldn't tell that she was not speaking at all but mulling to herself, a practice that made Iris much more comfortable than talking to people.

"Iris?"

"What?" She turned, alarmed, and studied him. "Are we talking?" Her forehead wrinkled. Her nose darted upward like she'd suddenly smelled something strange. "I didn't know we were talking." Stiffly, she turned, like a rod fused her back into the same angle as her seat. Her neck and shoulders didn't move and her whole body turned like a wind-up toy set in slow motion.

When she was finally still, he spoke calmly and slowly. "Where are you headed?" Her shoulder stiffened and she reached into her bag. "Not for any serial killer reason. Out of curiosity? You can't be more than..." He ventured a guess. From a distance, the girl could have passed for 21, a runway, European-type 21, thin and lithe, dressed like she'd walked off the *La Bohème* set, but up close, there were no lines in her face. If there were, they were imperceptible. The skin was marshmallow smooth, like it had been made of flower petals. It was a Snow White face, not a queen. In the sun, it was clear that Iris was very much a child.

"I'll be 16 in July." Her eyes rolled as if she'd frustrated herself as she spoke. "I know, I look older. People always say that. That runs in our family. Maisy looks *older*."

She gave no hint of speaking again, her eyes leveling on the water that stretched around them, arm wiggling in the bag in her lap as if independent from the rest of her. For the second time today, Chris found himself unloading to a virtual stranger.

"Me, I'm on a trek, an adventure, really." Her face didn't change. "I'm walking as far as my feet take me. I left the day job behind, just me and my gear and the open road. I'm living the dream." His feet were on fire, but the information superhighway that connected his muscles to his brain was clogged with screaming traffic.

"It sounds like you're having some kind of problem," she said it, without any hint of a tone that would imply criticism.

The boat lurched and pulled toward a patch of sea that looked more like marshmallow than water, white and choppy. Her eyes settled on the fizz of the churning water. Though the silence was comforting, Christopher felt like talking again.

"I don't think my wife can possibly love me anymore," he said for the second time today. "I love her, but, when she looks at me, I just know." The water rose and fell flat ahead of them, waves breaking into mist, so he kept his eyes on the steam that rose off the water as the waves broke. It gripped at his chest when he said it out loud. Then he realized he had said it out loud. "I'm sorry. Why am I telling you this?"

"I have that effect on people," she said matter-of-factly, again with no hint of annoyance or judgment. "Maisy says it's my face." She stated the simple fact of it and let it hang there before making a sound that was akin to a gasp. "It sounds like you lost your grace." She blinked once, her large caramel eyes looking like they belonged in another world, perhaps one inhabited by fairies and talking deer. "Is your Grace gone?"

You and Me

"What? No, Rachel. Her name is Rachel." Just saying her name conjured a picture in his head, holding her close after her shift was through, looking like a child in borrowed clothes, scrubs bulky on her tiny frame.

The girl either didn't hear him or didn't care because she barreled through his words like they weren't there. "Dave has a song all about this. There's a guy and he's trying to remember." She squinted. "Not remember, forget. You can tell he really is remembering because his heart is broken, which really is not true because if his heart were broken, he wouldn't be able to sing anything." Her eyes were nowhere near looking at him but she nodded in his direction. "He'd literally be dead. Figure of speech, heartbreak sounds pretty terrible. That's you, right? You're heartbroken? Your grace? Rachel? You lost her?"

Once when Christopher was a boy, he had seen a magician saw a woman clear in half, not the cheesy trick of old television shows, but, live in person, he saw a magician chainsaw a woman in half, with blood effects and gore all right before his eyes. Then with a snap of his fingers, she was put back together again. He remembered sitting with his mouth agape for a full ten seconds. Not since then had he ever been struck to such stunned silence. The shock of what she'd said had seared him from the inside out, so he sat there like a husk. The girl picked up on none of this.

"I have a dream." She stood up quickly, arm still buried in her bag. Instead of walking away, she turned to face the seat and dropped to her knees. She pulled out a half dozen plastic containers one-by-one, stacking them like multicolored blocks on the seat, humming quietly until her rainbow pyramid was almost complete. The last piece she pulled from the knapsack was a miniature take-out box embellished with pink lotus blossoms, a crowning jewel she neglected to put on top of the creation. Instead, she held it close just under her nose and gingerly pulled the flaps open to extract the treasure inside. "I make cupcakes, among other things."

She smiled, the itching in her hands subsiding for the first time all day.

Iris admired her pyramid dreamily. "Breads and cakes, desserts, candies, anything really that I can think up, I try to make." Her voice ducked down conspiratorially dropping a decibel and an octave, her monotone more pronounced at this level, like a long sad note on a bassoon.

"I'm driving to Florida. I'm going to win the Sugarworth Bake-Off."

It felt good to tell her plan to someone. He had just shared with her. That's what friendly conversations were supposed to be, give and take. They talk about something they are interested in. You talk about something you are interested in and then you share. She'd heard it so many times, but no one was ever interested in the same kind of things. Here was someone who was also on a mission.

The girl looked at ease, at least as near as he'd seen from her. She pulled from the box a rusty-colored confection he could smell from his seat. She wiped her hands on her shorts, then on her hoodie, and held the cake out to Christopher.

"I get to go to Happy World. I sent them some of my recipes that I made. They're paying for my room and everything." It had been her secret mission. Now it didn't have to be a secret any longer.

"Wanna see? Go ahead."

"What is it?" It smelled more divine than miracles, like cinnamon and long fall weekends, and holidays and home-cooked dinners. It smelled like what he had left behind. In that moment, Christopher and his plan were almost bested by a cupcake. His new friend didn't notice the tears in his eyes, and no one could feel the knot in his throat but him. He bit on his lip and pretended to scratch just above his eye until the wave of what he was missing had passed.

Iris wasn't looking at him. When she talked about something she liked, it was hard to make her see anything else. For that, her companion was grateful. Her words sped up, one after the other, as if they were trying to break through a wall.

"That's a sweet potato cake, with a spice marshmallow filling, a sugar tea buttercream, and bacon/pecan crumbles on top." It was heavy in his hands and fragrant with butter and sugar. The crumbles of candy were symmetrically placed and perfectly sized like in a cartoon drawing. The girl in front of him, still on the floor, had directed her gaze to the cupcake. Though her face remained still, her eyes looked as if a fire had been lit just behind the pupil.

"May I?"

She shot up at that. "Of course. Yes, try it please."

He peeled the paper down and two large orange crumbs fell like dive bombers to the floor. Iris swooped like a hawk to catch them, her movement a strange mix of awkward violence and delicate grace.

"You don't have to—"

She'd gotten them. Up on her feet again, she watched him.

The buttercream was the warm brown color of wet sand in the morning, just as the sun comes up. She was generous with it, without going overboard. With just a little effort, he opened his mouth wide enough to get every taste in one bite.

She watched him as if he were diffusing a bomb.

The seconds could last a hundred years if Iris were in the right mood. Right now, this Christopher man was taking an eon. He chewed with his eyes closed; his breathing settled to two breaths every 8 to 10 seconds over his previous six. It was much easier to read people from their breathing patterns, but he'd been sitting for a while. She couldn't tell. Now her skin burned at the wrists where her first watch rubbed the next.

"So?" She blurted, even though she'd been trying not to.

Christopher opened his eyes with a jolt. And sighed.

You and Me

Sighs were bad.

"It's the most delicious thing I've ever tasted."

Chapter 10

Look in the Eyes

A lot of things can happen in an hour. Life can be created or lost. A runaway baker can tell her life story to a man attempting to hike the East coast. The world can stand completely still.

"It's just you and Maisy?"

"And Oscar-the cat, and Sophie, of course, " she saddened. "My fish, I had to leave her behind. You have to do what you have to do."

He knew that too well.

"Iris, does Maisy know you're gone?"

She shrugged guiltily.

"It's a far ride to Florida." He pressed. "She's going to be worried sick."

She handed him samples of her cardamom marshmallows and saffron brittle, which were more than he'd expected. It was hard to look disapproving when they tasted like sunshine in his mouth.

"She'd try to stop me if I told her. If I can just get down there, she'll have to let me. If she tries to come get me, I'll already be there, so she'd at least have to let me try. If she knew ahead of time, she'd never let me try." She was still and spoke so quietly he almost couldn't make it out. "This is nothing like the butterflies."

"What butterflies?"

The question took him aback, as if he'd intruded on something private. "I don't like to talk about that." She pulled out another bagel.

"You like to eat, don't you?"

"Huh?"

"Never mind. Iris, what are you going to tell Maisy?"

"I didn't think that far ahead." She chewed. "She'll be sleeping 'til at least four." Iris wiped a glob of cream cheese off her face with her hand. "She thinks I'm doing a dance contest." Although the matter at hand seemed to be growing more serious by the instant, Christopher laughed, if only for a second.

Iris told him about her recipes and everything he ever needed to know about Dave Matthews. She picked off raisins and dates and crunched on granola, as she recounted her favorite set lists and songs. An hour can disappear in seconds when time decides to go quickly, but it can also be a very long time for someone who can make time last forever. The whole trip seemed to have flown by with a few blinks and stories, up until these last few minutes, if not seconds. In the past few seconds, Iris felt as though her life had been placed on pause when the ferry bobbed up and down. If it was not set on pause, it was slow motion at the least. She could feel each heartbeat as the movement pulsed through her stomach and up her chest. She did not want to throw up here, so like the panic, she choked it down.

"Iris, are you okay?"

White foam bubbled on the edges of each wave before it broke. There were probably dolphins underneath without a care of what might be happening above.

"Iris?"

The girl's blank stare broke, so she turned to Christopher with a shudder.

"What?" Her shoulders jerked up and her eyes were accusing, and the rest of her face was blank.

"You're not looking so good. Do you want to stand up? Stretch your legs?"

Her eyes searched around her and then, as usual, dropped to her bag. She touched all her items one-by-one, burying her hand deep inside. Her head dipped to the side, and she hummed. It was just two notes, one, then the other. One high note, then one low. The first two notes of the opening set of Virginia '98. Dave played on the beach, and it was beautiful.

On the horizon there were some dark clouds that were not. He could see the chop ahead. The storm was here.

"Iris, do you like to play games?"

"What?" She was doing it again. She knew she was, but she couldn't help it. That loud monotone bark when she was stressed had a life of its own. The only way she knew it happened was when she heard it herself. Even then, it was like the sound had come from someone else.

He spoke calmly, a familiar way she couldn't place. "Yes, a game. It's a good one. Do you want to try?"

She eyed him warily but answered because, whether she knew it or not, there was a comforting quality to the way he spoke.

"Fine."

"Have you ever played one of those light-up games, where you repeat the patterns?"

She knew the game well. There was one in Murph's waiting room. She'd beaten it six times. She nodded, arm still buried in her bag.

"This is just like that, only without lights. Okay?" He kept his tone even and looked at her while he spoke. "Only it's rhythm. I'm going to tap." The plastic of his chair made a sound like mice tap dancing. Iris liked it very much. "Like this. You're going to see if you can repeat it. Sound good?"

She focused on the tiny feet. They were wearing top hats and spinning their tails like canes. The rhythm shot out of her fingertips like lightning.

"I'm good at this game." The girl smiled as the boat rose and dipped over three giant waves she didn't notice.

"I think you win."

For the first time today, Chris didn't have the feeling he was doing something terribly wrong.

"Your eyes didn't dilate."

"I'm sorry?"

"When you said you weren't a serial killer," she clarified. "Your eyes were straight ahead." Hers darted from his to her lap and off toward the water, then back again as she spoke. "Not up and to the right, which would indicate a lie. Or down to the left which could mean shame. You didn't look straight down, which, in most cases, would mean you were sad." She ate a raisin before turning her attention back to him. "Pupils are the biggest lie detector in the world, even when you're lying to yourself. You looked right at me and there was no deviation in pupil size or motion, so, you weren't lying."

"Again, good to know."

She looked out on the water that had gone silky and calm.

"Thank you for playing that game with me." Her chin dipped so far into her clavicle she looked like a turtle. "It was nice." With her chin still glued there, she turned her head side-to-side while speaking, as if scratching a relentless itch. "I was about to throw up like crazy."

"I had a feeling."

"You're nice."

"But you are sad."

"What's that?"

"Your eyes." Her voice was the faintest whisper, like it came from someone else. Christopher had scrunched his face up, as people do when they are about to pretend they don't understand what's been said. She made sure to use her "conversation voice," the one she'd worked on with Murph. "They aren't serial killer eyes. They're sad."

Iris hated looking at people's eyes. It always led to disappointment, but she tried to for this new friend. Was he her friend now, this man who came out of nowhere and helped her not to projectile vomit all over the ferry?

"Why are you sad, Christopher?"

It was right there as clear as the sea in front of her, a big pocket of sad just behind the white. It watered the color and dulled the pupil. All the things people try to hide live in the eyes. He hadn't answered. He was rubbing the side of his face. Then he sighed.

"Did something bad happen?"

"We're almost docking. I'm going to get some air. You want some air?"

"We're in the air. I don't understand why." She caught herself. "Sure."

"You can beat the crowd off the boat."

Whether she was trying to stop it or not, the humming came on fast and loud as she noticed them approaching dry land. Her voice, like the boat horn, was long, loud, and monotone, cutting through the air.

"Cuuh-riiiiiiiiiiiisssss!"

She said his name to get his attention, though she may have been trying to gather her own.

He turned with a jump. Her words were darts.

"Your hike?"

"Yes?"

"Does it *have* to be a hike? Or could you, um?" She felt like a foolish little child but asked anyway. "Drive?"

The boat ride had distracted him from the blistered swelling that was the wreckage of his feet.

"I s'pose I could. Why do you ask?"

Iris' words came fast, and she barely looked up from the horizon line. "Well, considering I'm not 16 yet, and I've kinda stolen Maisy's car, and Florida is really far away—perhaps I haven't thought this out as thoroughly as I thought I had." In her head, she heard rumbling, echoes of screams, and ladies crying. "Would you drive with me?" It's scary when the stress comes. "It is at least for a little while?"

The girl's forehead smoothed and clenched. Her face was a storm beneath a smooth veil. Christopher knew so much about that, he didn't have to think.

"Of course I will, Iris. It would be my honor."

Maisy told her all the time that her face went sideways when she was happy, as if the right side got excited to celebrate, it couldn't wait for the left. She could feel that now, her right cheek lifting up like a rocket ship for the sky, relief washing over her like waterfalls.

"That's really nice of you Christopher."

"Davenport." He put out his hand formally.

"Like the couch." Iris held out hers and swung it toward his in a sideways high-five.

"Yes, exactly like the couch."

"Now we know each other." Iris' right cheek grinned.

They both got in the turtle, her new friend in the driver's seat, ready to embark on the rest of their adventure.

"Well, you're not a serial killer, but you're definitely weird."

He just wanted to help. "Why would you say that?"

Her smile took over her whole face, as if the left side had finally gotten the memo.

"You're hanging around with me, aren't you?"

Chapter 11

Gas

"It looks like we could use some gas. I'm going to pull in here, all right?" Even in this short time, Christopher had picked up on the rhythm of warnings. Iris liked a head's up, more than liked, *depended* on it. She sat with the tape player between them, playing invisible instruments that hung in the air, plucking strings he couldn't see. The map lay across her lap like a blanket, which she slid it into the door as he pulled to the right.

"Where are you going?" Her eyes, wounded and worried, burst open like a porcelain doll's that had been picked up too quickly.

"We need gas." He tried to smooth the edge off the words that had sharpened through repetition. "I just said that. I'm just going to pull in here." The convenience store sign glared in garish orange and boasted the lowest gas prices in town.

"No, you're not." If any other almost 16-year-old said these words, they would be colored with defiance or rebellion, but there was nothing audacious about the way Iris spoke. They were the word equivalents of flat tires: flat, off-center, and airless. She steadied herself with her right hand and reached her arm across him as if she were going to take the wheel, which she didn't. Instead, she pointed. "We should go there."

Across the highway on a patch of dirt and flat grass sat a large one-story building in bright white that looked like it had come from another decade. The big round sign up top made a promise that had captured Iris' eyes and held them there.

"It says they've got the best donuts, Christopher. We need to go there."

"Didn't we just get donuts at the last pee break?"

She squinted, reaching into her bag. "Those were *cronuts*, completely different. Besides, the sign says, 'They're The World's Best.' We have to stop."

She reached and pulled out a long folded sheet of notebook paper upon which she'd scrawled notes about the road and sky, snippets of songs she'd heard, and ideas for future baked things. Most importantly, it contained the neatly numbered list she consulted on back.

"We made a stop after the," she read the words 'Freshest Corn You'll Ever Taste' stand, the one with the lady wearing the straw hat. The words were clear to Chris as

Gas

they approached, 'Yeasty Donuts Made Fresh While You Watch.' Look, they have gas, too." She handed him a sandwich baggie filled with folded over dollar bills, with the word 'GAS' clearly printed in permanent marker across the front.

"I've got this one. I'll meet you inside."

The two pumps were off to the side and looked just as much like forgotten relics as the building beside it. "I guess gas is gas."

He'd grown fond of pumping his own gas. There was no forced banter or waiting awkwardly for an attendant to wipe down the windshield. He felt silly, if not ashamed, watching another man clean his windows as he watched through the glass. This was much better. For a moment, he took in the quiet and enjoyed it. Iris' questions and boundless curiosity were a welcome distraction, but so was the silence. With the sun around him in the quiet of this time capsule of a place, he almost felt at ease with the choice he'd made.

Despite its aged exterior, the Crumbly Krumb was impeccable inside. The white countertops sparkled amid stainless steel tabletops buffed to a mirror shine. The right side wall was loaded with all the standard trappings of a donut shop. Creams and sugars were arranged on an orderly table, and a cooler was filled with sports drinks and waters. It was the opposite wall that drew the eye and the nose. The scent of the place hit Chris from the side as soon as he stepped through the door. He could see why. The opposite wall was half window. Iris stood there in awe of what was happening on the other side. Shining metal arms punched perfect o's out of supple dough that looked as though it were peeled right out of a cartoon, they were carried to a conveyer belt where they traveled like soldiers through a contraption that left them golden brown. From there they took a ride on what Christopher could only think looked like a pastry ferris wheel that cooled them off and brought them onto a slide drenched in thick, sugary icing. A thin woman in a paper hat prompted any lag-behinds with a stick while she danced between trays shaking sprinkles and sugars, switching to drizzled chocolate stripes and sheets of caramel. It was like peeking into Santa's workshop. Iris was transfixed.

The regulars seemed unimpressed, as did the older woman at the register who slid out from the counter like a doll in a cuckoo clock to refill the coffee of the graying man who held out his coffee in perfect timing, never lifting his eyes from his newspaper.

"Erma, how long does the whole process take?" Iris was already on a first-name basis with the lady Chris had just noticed favored her left leg.

"From start to finish, the process takes 12 minutes, sugar. When you get them, they're still nice and warm."

"What do you do with them all? There's no one here." The place was, for the most part, empty, but for the coffee man and the girl who could be 12 or 20, who was taking selfies of her blue hair.

"Iris."

She didn't see him next to her, watching the gears of the ferris wheel click into position. "Oh, hello." When she jumped, it wasn't for effect because she moved as seamlessly from panic to calm as the fried sweets moved from the conveyor belt to the cooling tray. "You scared me. Did you see this, Christopher? Everything happens right there. That washing machine-looking thing over there mixes the dough. Then that box, the one that looks like it has eyebrows at the top? That's where the donuts rise, which can take as long as an hour depending on the humidity. She looked at her white-haired friend. "Right, Erma?" The older woman winked.

"That's right, honey, and what we don't sell here, we ship to the other stores." Erma added with a wink and an elbow to no one in particular. "We don't get many customers around here and that's why we ship to other stores." She smiled at the girl in the way that grandmas smile at their grandchildren and spoke in a conspiratorial tone for only Chris to hear. "She's very smart."

People always thought Iris was smart. What they underestimated was her hearing.

"I have a high IQ, at least that's what they tell me. I don't know about all that. There are things that are very easy for me to understand, like light refraction and breeding betta fish, the lifespan of a star, the dietary needs of a koala. But, then, I don't understand banking. Where does the money *go*?"

The gears from the sweet factory whirred, clicked, and hissed. They banged and clunked, but Iris could still hear the man chewing three tables behind her.

"I also have super senses," she shrugged, as the grown-ups looked on.

Iris ate two donuts as Chris drained coffees one after the other. She chatted with Erma. Her voice was as easy and level as it had been all day, but her eyes never left the bakery next door.

"Shelley's doing a great job out there." She had thick cream filling in her fingertips. She looked at Christopher's coffee cup. "That's her daughter. This place has been in their family for years." The girl had plunked the last bit of donut into her mouth, so her voice drifted away with the rest of her, as she moved back to the window.

She stood there unblinking and the room went quiet, with Erma back into the steady rhythm of wiping down tables and refilling coffees, the man with his paper flipping pages, and the girl admiring her wild hair in the reflection of her phone. The steam hissed as the dough hit the oil, and the gears clunked in place. Iris had begun to tap her fingers on the window in time to the sounds.

The pages flipped. The coffee cup clinked against a table, so Iris began tapping her feet.

Gas

Hiss. Clink. Clunk. Flip. She tapped fingers and toes. Now her lips smacked together in a combination of pops and smacks. Christopher had never heard anything like it, but it was familiar. He couldn't place the beat until the humming came with it.

It was a familiar song from the 1990s, but so different. It sounded vaguely like a jam band anthem from his college days, but she didn't sound like that guy singing about bugs. She didn't sing those words. She was the instrument—if not the whole orchestra—tying together the familiar sounds to make them extraordinary. She sang not words but ooh's and ah's, primal sounds she somehow made transcendent, like notes that came not just from her throat but from all of her. She tapped and clicked in perfect time to the mechanized rhythm around her. Then, whether Iris knew it or not, she was singing like an angel, words that were never part of the original lyrics.

If anyone asked, he would have had no way to communicate this moment.

Even the man with the paper paused from his funnies to take in the sound no one could describe. Erma's eyes brightened, and the girl with the phone turned her lens away from herself.

When Iris had finished, it was like she'd come out of a daydream, looking around like she'd forgotten something she wanted to say.

"How do you do that?"

"Do what?"

"You, your, that thing you were just doing." Iris' eyebrow lifted in confusion tinged with worry, so Christopher reassessed his approach. "You get the people here to tell you their life stories. You touch people, Iris. You make them feel comfortable, but meanwhile on the boat." He didn't know how to proceed.

"I was scared to death?"

He held his coffee up in agreement. "Precisely."

"Most people scare me. Some people don't."

Chapter 12

Called Out

"I think that girl was taping you." Christopher mused as the big donut shrunk behind them.

"Who?"

"The girl with the blue hair." He smiled wryly. "Didn't you see her back there?" She had that phone flipped on you. That was some trick you did back there. You're gonna end up on VueClix."

Iris adjusted her baggies and fiddled with the buckle of her backpack. "I have no idea what you're talking about." She really didn't. When Iris made music, she wasn't doing it for clicks on a website. Most of the time, she wasn't aware it happened. She did know that, for a brief period, she felt at ease with herself and the world around her. The tightness that almost always grips her muscles melted away like a pool of butter, and all the electricity that was under her skin drifts up out of her into the sky like vapor.

"I don't see how that would happen," she said as a matter-of-fact. "VueClix is not for people like me. It's for Maisy to watch *Ghostbrother* gag reels. It's for pet care, unboxing videos. Old Dave sets." She rattled off a number of videos she watched daily, none of which included teenage girls in donut shops who may or may not have been singing.

"I call it mouth-music."

"What's that?"

"That trick I do. If that's what happened, like you're saying it did. That's what I call it." She looked out his window. "I don't think I did." Iris hated when she lost time.

She remembered standing in front of that window watching the donuts move forward one-by-one, enjoying the light scent of sugar from behind the glass. The steam sound from the coffee hurt her ears, like a snake. When the mixing machine thudded, the hiss was more like a snare drum. They had come together at the right moment to hit the perfect one-two beat. The paper sound from the grumpy man, the one with the coffee, was grating. It sounded like a cheese grater on cement, and when Erma moved the coffee beans, they shook like maracas so that paper was transformed. It made a cha-cha-cha sound, and the machine went "whir." The lights above were buzzing. Like insects, they invaded her ears. The sound zipped down her ear canal under her skin creating that tingly feeling that she hated. In that moment—anywhere else—she would be ready to explode, but she had this beautiful machine making music, so that lightning feeling wasn't lightning any longer. It was light, and she was floating over the world. It was Dave, his voice with the band jamming, and she was there with them in the crowd. She was happy.

"Maybe I did." Her chin found that special dip in her collar bone and rested there. "No one would watch that."

Iris went to her quiet place, watching the landscape change from urban sprawl and highways to long narrow country roads splitting cow pastures and chicken farms.

"The map says we're in Delmarva. That makes no sense. Is it Delaware or is it Maryland? It's not Virginia."

She squinted her eyes to make out the word and then opened them wide in shock when she saw what Christopher was doing.

"Why are you looking at your phone?" Her breathing sped, and her voice took on a more guttural sound. "While you are driving?"

Christopher dropped the phone immediately. It bounced off the tape player, sliding the map off the seat to the floor.

"Oh, oh, no, no. No. No. No." Iris' hands shot out from her sides gathering the map in her panicked fist. She continued the chant until things were exactly as they were before, give or take a few new wrinkles and divots. She looked at him accusingly. "You are NOT supposed to do that."

"I'm sorry, Iris. I shouldn't have looked at my phone."

"Or taken your hand off the wheel."

He repeated her statement but slowly, methodically to show he understood.

She whispered to herself, "Hands at two and ten, two and ten always." She got her breathing back to normal. "Why were you looking at your phone?"

"I'm sorry. I know, Iris, it was very irresponsible and very unsafe. I won't do it again."

"No, *why*? What are you waiting to hear?" She was thoughtful. "The thing that makes you sad?"

He hadn't thought about it, but, in a way, he had thought she would call. Rachel checked in around lunch just about every day. It was how they made her nights on third shift bearable. But there were no messages. Not yet. That call would come. And he wasn't wondering so much about what she would ask, but more how he would explain. He didn't think he could.

"I guess I'm expecting someone."

He wasn't saying anything else, but he could feel her expectation.

"Okay, Iris. How can I put this?" It made better sense in his head when he was walking last night, when he packed his bag, and a week ago when he decided his course of action. The words he said barely sounded like they made sense together: "It's complicated."

The girl spoke as if she were describing a neck tie in a men's clothing catalog. "Doesn't sound complicated at all."

"Really?" This is coming from the girl who just literally lost her mind over a piece of paper. He wouldn't say that out loud. He would not say something hurtful to her.

Iris didn't pick up on irony. "Sounds like you're in crisis." She was too busy picking at the truth.

"Huh?"

"Not crisis mode. Crisis mode is when things get rough, and we either face it head on or we run away. Murph talks to me about that all the time. No, you are IN a crisis. It's different."

"Really?" He kept his hands at ten and two, focusing on the girl's words as much as the road.

"Maisy says anyone can have a crisis, not just me. Anybody. It doesn't have to mean a flood or emergency. Those do happen." She counted them on her hands. "You can have a creative crisis, emotional, a crisis of faith, an identity crisis. Oh!" Something had dawned on her. "How old are you?"

He arched his eyebrows. "34."

"A *midlife* crisis." She scrunched her face thinking. "There are all kinds. Anyone can have one. It's on you to fix it, once it happens. Something hits you and turns you upside down and, then, you have to figure out how to turn yourself back over again. Like, for instance, right now that little green light has been blinking on your phone for the past five seconds. You've been acting like you didn't see it. When you changed lanes just now, your eye went right to it and then you tightened your grip on the steering wheel. Your shoulder tightened right there, like you were thinking about reaching, but you didn't. I don't think that was because of me. You didn't make a move to look at it. I think it's for the same reason you're sad. Is that it, Christopher? Are you having a crisis?"

Everything she said was true, and he didn't need her pupils to know it. His eyes darted to the console next to him. He'd seen the light change to green as soon as it had happened.

"Why are you not answering your phone?"

"I'm not answering. I just missed it, that's all." He hated feeling cornered or, in this case, called out.

"After looking at it all morning, you didn't pick it up. Why?"

She buried her hand in her bag, eyes dropping to its contents.

He turned slightly. "Why do you keep looking at *your* phone?"

"Maisy's not even awake yet, but she's going to be and I am going to have to answer. She's going to be *really* upset." The magnitude of this had not struck Iris until just then. Sometimes she had trouble seeing things from other people's perspectives. What Maisy would experience when she realized that Iris had left would cause her to feel heavy and dirty. "I know this is going to hurt her a lot and I'm going to have a lot of explaining to do." She pulled her hand out of the bag. "I guess I keep looking because I'm trying to get ready."

"Are you?" Christopher asked. In the quiet, the blinking light between them seemed to have a voice of its own.

"Are *you*?"

Chapter 13

Blueberry

Despite all efforts to the contrary, Maisy had fallen into a deep sleep. It was late afternoon when she sat up with a start. Again there was no message, no blinking caller ID. They'd made it through another day with no forgotten lunches, no fainting spells or trips to the nurse. It should have been a relief. Worry nagged at Maisy as it always did, starting in the pit of her stomach and creeping up her throat like a worm until it rested behind her eyes. The headache was always there waiting. She'd take the good while it lasted, so she tried to stuff any worry as far down as she could. Dr. Gentry had told her to let go a little, which she tried to do. She took her shower without bringing the phone into the bathroom and avoided looking at it as she got ready.

She laid out the dress Iris liked the best, a fifties-style number in green with navy dots, and the navy headband with a green silk bow. It was a dress she didn't need, it was more suited for weddings and baby showers. Iris had gotten it for her last spring after winning a radio call-in contest. She used every last cent of her prize money to get Maisy the dress she "saw her looking at" in the storefront window. She even got her matching shoes.

This was Iris' special day at school and it was going to be fine, Maisy told herself as she smoothed on face lotion and brushed her teeth. *Don't forget to rinse*, the sign reminded her, printed neatly in Iris' handwriting. *Flush.* Without that, the house would smell like a subway station. There were picture panels, laid out like storyboards, taped to the wall, taking anyone who needed through the steps of doing business in there. Iris had drawn cute cartoon characters, remembering to use toilet paper and washing their cartoon hands in mounds of glistening soap bubbles. Loud noises were startling to Iris. The signs made it easier to deal with the roar of the toilet and the hiss of the sink. They reminded her that certain things had to be done, whether she liked it or not. *Did you forget your pits?* Maisy tried hard not to think about the questions, taking the time to put on what little makeup she had, blowing out her hair and brushing it into a neat twist at the top of her head. She wanted to look just right.

She had plenty of time to get a good seat at the show. If she was up too close, Iris might be too distracted. If too far, Maisy wouldn't be able to see, and that would defeat the purpose after all. Like everything else she did, this would require balance and forethought.

At any given time, Maisy could list at least five incoming storms or weather fronts, not because she was particularly interested in meteorology but because she lived with her own personal Doppler system. Iris knew all there was to know about westerly winds and arctic fronts, and according to her, there was a storm rolling in today. Iris was rarely wrong, but the sun poured in through the windows to the contrary.

"What do you think, Oscar?" She opened the front door to look up at the sky, trusting there'd be a gray cloud looming just out of view.

There was indeed a cloud.

"Where the #$@&%* is my car?" It shot out like a cannonball.

The cat looked on in disapproval. That was one for the jar. She tried to rephrase.

"Where the *ship* is my car?"

Maisy felt like a puppet controlled by a cruel child, leaning out the door to make sure the car hadn't moved itself in a game of hide and seek.

"Frockfrickshackfarmerflockcockadoodledoo."

Maisy paced from the front door to the kitchen to the front door to the kitchen and back again, before pacing back to the phone like a sleepwalker tiptoeing through molasses. Then, it finally hit her.

"Someone *stole* the globdang blueberry."

The Woodrow police department consisted of seven people. There were the old-timers who'd been on the force since Maisy's parents were in school. Then there was a heavy-set lieutenant and a detective who'd seen too many forensic procedural dramas. Officer Judy was the nice lady who came to the school to talk about stranger danger. Then, there was Officer Kevin McEllroy, the one she hoped wouldn't answer when she called.

"Woodrow Police, Officer Ellroy speaking."

Maisy clutched at the silk bow on the side of her head and spoke in the most even voice she could.

"Hi, Kevin, it's Maisy Heller. I wanted to—"

"Maisy Heller? The golden star of the stage? Maisy, Maisy, Maisy. How've you been? You gonna sing something for me?"

She bit down on her lip so the nickel words would stay put.

"Uh, ha. No. Kevin, I'm not calling to sing. Actually I'm calling because my car—"

"I can still see you in that hula skirt dancing around. What was that play? Fiji?"

"*South Pacific*, Kevin. Anyway. My car—"

"Oh, Maisy. How many years ago was that? Wow, you know, you haven't changed a bit. Every time I come into your shop, I tell the guys, 'Fellas, you gotta see Maisy Heller. Still looks like she's 18.' I don't know how you do it. You always were on top of your game, if you know what I mean. You know I just ran into Meghan Albright. You remember her, from geometry class. Wow, that one really *let it go* if you know what I mean? Talk about derailing."

"I'm really sorry to hear that, Kevin." It was getting harder to hold back the money words, the ones that folded. "As I was saying."

"You know, no offense. You just, you really stayed in shape."

"Thanks, Kevin, really."

"You know, considering even."

"Kevin?"

"I don't know how you do it. Well, maybe it's because you're always moving. You always were such a mover and a shaker, you're always working and all. You know, you're the best thing in that bagel shop. Of course, there's all that running around with, you know. I—"

"KEVIN!"

She knew where the conversation was going and didn't need to hear it. On top of that, if he didn't stop talking, she was going to wear a channel between her kitchen counter and the front door if she kept pacing. She settled herself by the front door, looking through the window at the empty spot where the blueberry had been.

"Sorry, Maisy. What was it you wanted?"

"I'm calling about my car."

"The blue one, right? Little fella? Looks like one of them clown cars, right?"

Maisy was glad she'd learned so much about breathing and relaxing. It kept her from biting Kevin Ellroy's head off through the phone. Instead, she ran her hand down the wood grain of the secretary desk in the hall. She felt the ridges under her fingers as he repeated the digits of her license plate and gave his opinion on foreign-made cars. She felt her hands moving automatically like they were functioning independently from the part of her that had to listen to his story.

The lid creaked open and the treasures beneath peeked at her like reassuring friends. Greeting cards and Iris' treasures were tucked into several of the cubbies. She kept her keys in the small square drawer up top that slipped open with the slightest touch. It was stuffed full with something distinctly, but *not* her keys.

Kevin droned on about his old Chevelle.

"Now that's a car. Still running you know? We had some times in that, didn't we?"

It was one date, a decade and a half ago. She had more important things to think about.

She read the note three times before what had happened came close to computing, but that didn't mean any of it made sense.

P.S. I have no idea what happened to the car.

"Maisy?"

She'd not realized the white noise had stopped. She was too busy trying to figure out how she'd ever get enough money to make up for what was about to happen.

Kevin made a strange noise on the other end of the line that sounded very much like a gasp.

"Maisy? Are you okay?"

She pictured an island with a tree standing in the sun, lapping waves, and imagined the smell of coconut; it was supposed to be relaxing, but she was gritting her teeth so hard, her jaw hurt.

"Who me? Yes. I'm fine Kevin. How are you?"

He sounded tentative and calm, more like a policeman now than minutes before, when he was the guy from geometry with the Black Sabbath sticker on his notebook.

"What was it you wanted to report about your car?"

She measured her next words and did her best impression of a girl from a romantic comedy.

"Oh, silly me, Kevin. You know I thought I had a big scratch on my car. You know as if it had been keyed? Wouldn't you know, as I'm looking at it in the sun, it's just a big smudge."

He was still in full cop mode, cynicism cutting through his words. "A smudge?"

"Yup, isn't that silly?"

"Silly?"

"Yup, silly me. You know how airheaded I can get, especially when I'm doing a million things at once. I looked out there, and I swore there was a big old scratch, and I just panicked." She laid on the sweetness like honey and this time he bit.

"Ha, yup. Just like a woman."

The veins in her neck strained. "Yup, that's me." She did some acting for Kevin after all.

Oscar had picked up the change and paced alongside Maisy from the door back to the kitchen. When she slunk to the floor, he stayed there nestled beside her.

"Iris, what have you done now?"

Chapter 14

Maisy on Bike

Maisy stood in the kitchen staring like a statue, one hand hovering over the phone, until her mind clicked into place, and she snatched the phone off the cradle like a snake. Oscar, not used to seeing such a display, lowered his tail through her legs and ran to Iris' room.

"She's not in there, Oscar. Stupid cat."

Nothing was moving quickly enough, so before the first ring was through, she'd slammed the phone back down so hard the battery pack cracked out of the back like a pistachio nut.

"I'll get that later," she said, as if there were someone there to help. She opened the front door but doubled back after the first step, crumpling a twenty into the swear jar.

"That oughta cover it."

Then she ran out almost too quickly for the door to shut behind her.

Baking for Dave

The cobwebs covering the shed were usually the stuff of night terrors, so a trip out there for garden shears required a hat, gloves, long pants, boots, or a radiation suit. But panic does a funny thing to people, especially Maisy. She ripped the door open and barreled through the cobweb seal, with no second thought to the eight-legged inhabitants that created it. The spider webs stuck like cotton candy to her new dress, but she picked them off like dead leaves.

"I had my freak-out today." She reminded her mind, and her body responded, her breathing slowing to a less frenzied pace, even though her mind was still racing, but slower now. It wasn't because she had special powers, she had had years of training. In their house, Maisy's rule was set in stone: *one freak-out a day.* This meant that whoever needed to freak out at any given time was allowed to do so, but only once. For Iris, it was a guideline, to try to reign in the emotions when her senses got the best of her. For Maisy, it had become a physical reality. Once she lost her buggers, there weren't any buggers left to lose. After something terrible, she usually achieved a certain serenity that carried her for the rest of the day. After that emotional storm, she dropped into a tranquil calm and sailed in a placid state that most closely resembled autopilot.

So the shed would have to wait for another day to give her the heebie-jeebies. It seemed Maisy had none left.

Underneath the scarecrow and behind the big wooden tombstone from Halloween, she found what she was looking for. She squeezed by the lawnmower and pulled the bike out with a yank that defied any spiders, wasps, or critters who had anything to say about it. It was dusty, and the tires were half-flat, but it would do.

In hindsight, she should have taken off her new navy polka dot pumps, but that would take away from the sight of her peddling uphill in all her color-coordinated glory like that mean old lady who threatened poor Toto in *The Wizard of Oz*. She couldn't help but hum the wicked witch theme in spite of herself.

"#$@&%* These hills won't kill me." Her little bow flopped in the wind on the downhill. At the bottom, she dialed Iris. One ring. Two. Then voicemail. "#$@&%*, #$@&%*, #$@&%*." At this rate, she was going to run out of money. She dialed Eric on the next climb.

"Eric, did Iris say anything weird today?"

That was a loaded question, but he answered her with his own.

"What's the matter with you? Maisy, why are you panting?" He had been playing the newest whack-a-mole game on his phone, but he'd laid his new toy aside.

She couldn't answer. She wasn't a kid anymore, coasting up and down the Woodrow hills like she was on an amusement park ride. This was work. She needed both hands not to careen to sudden doom.

By the time she blew through the door to the shop, half her twist had unraveled, and the cute little bow on her headband rested across her forehead like a ninja star.

"Save it, Eric. Is she here?"

"Who here? Maisy, what're you talking about?"

She blew past two customers like they weren't there, looking past the breads and baked goods to the far wall.

"That little rat. Where is she, Eric? She here? What'd she say to you this morning?"

Wayward hairs flew into her face as she moved through the store like a storm. At worst, Maisy was impatient when it came to bad songs on the radio. At best, she was the most tolerant person Eric knew, with customers and in everyday life. He'd only even seen one thing that could work Maisy into this kind of frenzy.

"Has Iris run away?"

She didn't answer but walked behind the counter, opening coolers and the walk-in freezer, half expecting Iris to be there. Sometimes this year when the start to high school felt like too much, she'd end up here nestled in with the bags of lettuce and tubs of cream cheese. The boxes were untouched, as neatly placed as she'd left them early this morning. There was nothing here but the cold.

She'd shut the door tight to keep it that way. She had strict rules about things like that, keeping the store room neat, stacking things neat and tidy, so they could always be found. Maisy had lots of rules to make sense of things. Right now she was breaking her biggest one.

Maisy on Bike

Eric could hear her screams from outside the reinforced door, but he waited for her to come out on her own.

"She's not here, Mais." Eric's voice wasn't gruff. It was the quiet voice he used when things were hard, the one normally reserved for the girl in question. "You want to tell me what happened?"

The story of the note, the shed, Kevin Ellroy, and the rusty cruiser bike came in the form of one long sentence punctuated at the end by dollars, dimes, and nickels while she dialed the phone. A surge of electricity prickled through the big guy. It was the sickening half-chill that rolled from his head, down his spine to the bottom of his feet when he replayed this morning's events back in his head.

"Pick up, Iris, pick up. Pick up." She chanted to no avail, for the first time focusing on Eric with pleading eyes. "I can't call the police on her." Her voice lowered. "Not again."

Chapter 15

Storm

"How many does that make?"

"Seven."

Iris crouched in her seat with the phone next to her opposite ear, but Christopher could still hear the voice on the message.

"Are you going to call back?"

"I sent a detailed text."

"How's that? I've been sitting right here. You hit like two buttons."

Iris read it back, clearly satisfied. "It's me. I'm alive." She smiled. "Okay?" Christopher's face was frozen in disapproval. She sighed and spoke the words slowly as she added, "Don't wo-rr-y. Better, you think?"

He'd learned to be diplomatic while teaching at the community college. There were students of all types and ages. Some grasped things easily, while others needed repetition. He was a naturally tactful and understanding person, but it was hard to keep his voice even.

"I think that's very far from okay. I think there's going to be an Amber Alert put out for you, and I am going to be in prison if you don't call soon."

Her response was sure. "Maisy's not going to call the police."

His voice was just as sure of something else. "You know, I think she will."

Despite the growing edge in Christopher's voice, Iris spoke calmly, like a mother reading a fairy tale, but she told her own story. "The cops had to come and get me once. Maisy didn't like it. It was the beginning of this year. I have bio in a real bio lab. I never had a class in a lab before. There were all kinds of dead things in jars: frogs and bird eggs, larvae, bugs. There were these dragonflies pinned onto hard pieces of paper plastered to the wall." Her eyes focused out the window. Fog was rolling in, so it was hard to see where the marsh ended and the water began. The storm was coming. She could tell. "In the same room we had butterflies. Well, almost butterflies. Right with all that dead stuff there were chrysalises, little baby butterflies getting ready to be in the world, and the first thing they would see were a bunch of dead things."

Iris watched the area where the long grass met the water's edge as it drifted by like a long green zipper and she stopped speaking all together. The gentle voice pulled her from it.

Storm

"You okay?"

"Huh?"

"If you keep chewing like that, you're not going to have any fingers left."

The metal taste was in her mouth faster than the words made sense of the sting in her red raw fingertips.

"Sorry." She opened and closed her hands around the invisible ball she imagined gripping. Ten times right hand. Ten times left hand, and two breaths in-between. She had to finish once she started. "The lab was on the third floor, where all grade nine classes were. It's not my fault it was so high."

"Iris? I'm not following."

"I didn't want to jump. I wanted to free the butterflies."

Her eyes, like the sky, were threatening to break open and pour. "It was an accident." Christopher remained even and steady.

"What happened, Iris?"

"I picked the locks when everyone went to lunch. It was a simple pin and tumbler. If they were really trying to keep people out of the lab, they should have invested in a more complicated mechanism. I opened the cage and let them out. When they flew out the windows, I followed them."

"It *was an accident*."

He let the words float between them and asked the inevitable.

"Were you hurt?"

She looked at him incredulously as if he'd said something shocking. "How could I get hurt standing on a ledge? I was balancing. No one would let me explain. They just called the police before Maisy could even get there. They took me away for three days, because they thought I was going to hurt myself. I was *on a ledge*."

It was making sense to him now, at least as much as it could.

"I got to ride in an ambulance." She brightened momentarily. "They wouldn't turn off the siren."

The sky outside was growing dark as if heaven itself agreed with her.

"The doctors kept asking me why I wanted to hurt myself. I wasn't trying to hurt myself. I was helping the butterflies. I stood on the ledge. I didn't jump. I just wanted to see them fly." She laid her hand flat against the window. She liked the vibration of the wind against the glass. "No matter what I said, it was like they didn't understand, like I was crazy."

"I understand."

"You do?"

"That's a horrible feeling," he nodded, knowing better than he'd like to admit.

"When I got back, they had a big meeting. They made Murph come, even Dr. Gentry. They had to prove I was *okay* to stay at school. Then, when I got back, all the people at school started calling me Spider-Man. You know, because I was hanging on to the wall for so long. I'm not a man. It doesn't make any sense."

She turned the phone over in her hand, like she was inspecting a jewel.

"Are you going to call her back?"

"Maisy would never call the cops on me."

The light winked green then black at her, like a clever cat.

When Iris opened her mouth, it wasn't her voice she heard but a thunderous crack from thirty yards away. The sky lit like a candle, and within seconds, opened like a giant eye ready to weep.

The girl bounced at least five inches from her seat, almost hitting her head on the car ceiling. In the short time he'd known her, Christopher had surmised there was order to everything Iris did, but lightning didn't play by rules.

"Oh, oh, oh. No. No. No." Her hands fluttered near her face in spasms, as if the shocks from the bolt outside had shot through her. She opened her eyes wide, then shut them so tightly, it appeared her whole face was blinking. All the while, she repeated one syllable.

"Iris, it's okay." He tried to speak softly.

"Huuuuuuum. Huuuuuuum." The sound drowned him out and alternated with gasping breaths as she began hitting her head on the seat, not hard as he'd seen in the movies, but tilting in a backward nod, as if to show how strongly her whole being disagreed with this shock to her system.

Christopher spoke calmly and narrated what was happening so the two of them could be sure no surprises would come from inside the car. "Iris, I'm going to pull over here, okay? You're going to feel the car move to the side and then stop. Are you with me, Iris?"

It was hard to tell what she heard and what she didn't with her eyes shut now. She panted like a woman in labor and had shifted her weight toward the car door so that she banged the side of her head on the cool window. It was an act of repetition, not force, thankfully. The hits weren't hard enough to injure her, but still, the thud of skull on glass was disconcerting.

There was no shoulder on this stretch of highway, just marshland on either side. He pulled to the first sandy patch he could find and, instead of stopping, he made a hard right so they were looking toward the water. Rain dumped down in sheets, and, then buckets. The storm was unpredictable, but it wasn't violent. It was shocking at worst, but it was no threat. At the rate it was going, it would blow out soon enough. It already seemed to be moving.

"It can't hurt us in here."

Her eyes seemed more focused, yet they weren't looking at anything in particular. The head banging stopped. It was replaced with knee-knocking, which switched to toe tapping within seconds. It was like the current was moving through her to the ground. He tried to break the circuit.

"Iris, can you hear me?"

Her chin was pressed hard against her chest like she was trying to bury herself there. The blueberry rocked with the storm outside. The fog was lifting enough now to get a clear view of the water.

"Iris, look at the water. Do you see there where the bubbles come up from the rain? Each drop is like an explosion. Each drop makes its own ripples, but they drift out into the rest of the water, where it all goes smooth again. The rain's letting up a little. Look." He spoke softly but directly, intent on making the connection. The wind and lightning picked up, but the rain was slowing. Storms like this couldn't last.

She was humming softly, mouthing words to herself, biting her fingers so hard they crunched.

"Iris?" His tone never deviated. He never raised or lowered his voice though things were changing rapidly in front of his eyes. What Iris spoke had the cadence and rhythm of words, but they were no language he ever heard, and it connected in one long thread, which only broke for breath. None of it shook him. The windows rattled, but Christopher was steadfast.

"You know, I never really listened to Dave Matthews. The way you sang that song before, I may be a fan. He pressed "play" so the music played low behind him, and it felt like a pressure valve had been released. Iris' shoulders dropped and her eyes closed. Her face was no longer clenched in a ball of anxiety but went smooth. The only visible lines were the streaks where the tears had fallen freely.

"Do you like this song, Iris?"

Strings played over a catchy beat. He remembered this one from his younger days, hearing it out of boom boxes on the college green or at parties sung by frat boys wearing backward hats. She didn't sing the words. Iris began humming and sung the melodies like her voice was its own instrument. She, by no means, sang along. Singing along was for someone along for the ride. Iris was adding to this, making it better. There was a break in the tape. After two clicks, the car went quiet.

He didn't know what he was doing this morning, but he knew what he needed to do now.

"Iris, I'll take you to Florida."

The girl looked as if she'd returned from somewhere else, her eyes resting on the water.

"What about your hike?"

"It can wait."

She bit her lip, fighting with something.

"Iris, I left for an adventure. What's more adventurous than this? My plans aren't changing. They're getting better."

Relief washed over Iris immediately. She knew he wasn't lying. In a way, Christopher felt it too. He focused on what was in front of them. Gnats settled, then pulled away from the surface, and a fish broke through. Iris looked settled.

It was all happy thoughts and quiet things for both of them until the water went still.

Chapter 16

Fog

The fog had lifted. On this stretch of road, it looked like they could see for miles. A comfortable quiet had settled in, so the hum of the road played backup to the scratchy tape keeping time. Iris had calmed. She had even dialed Maisy not once but three times in succession since the downpour. The girl looked content. With the road ahead Christopher couldn't remember when things had been so clear.

"She must be somewhere," Iris snapped, remembering. "The dance thing." Her voice tensed. 'She promised she wasn't going to go." Her posture changed as she repeated it to herself half silently.

"You're not saying you're mad at her? Are you? For going to a dance show you're not really at?" Iris didn't shrug at this. To say she shrugged would imply that her shoulders lifted and dropped. When Iris did it, it was like her whole body took part in the action. Her eyes, face, lungs, and feet all widened, scrunched, swelled, and lifted in conjunction with her shoulders' action. It was a whole body, whole spirited shrug that left no doubt as to what she was feeling.

"I'll try again." She began the call but stopped abruptly. "Virginia." She read the sign as they passed it. This one, in particular, was meaningful to Iris. "That's where it all happened, Christopher." She calculated quietly, just above a mutter and spoke quickly. "You're going 75. You should probably slow down but it's not raining anymore and the flow of traffic seems to be continuing at the same rate. So with wind. Deviation. Give or take. Carry. Move that over here. That makes."

He could feel the vibrations as she bounced in her seat.

"We're close to where it happened." Her eyes widened and her smile followed. "It all started in Virginia."

Iris had told him the entire history of the Dave Matthews Band.

"Can I ask you something, Iris?" He'd started prefacing most of his questions and comments, just after the second corn stand. She nodded appreciatively. "What is it about this group?"

She looked as if she didn't comprehend. He proceeded carefully.

"I mean, to you? I know they're great." He fought to keep her from wilting. "Don't get me wrong, they are great."

Fog

Iris sat up in her seat, as if something clicked, and the words Christopher said had suddenly made sense. "It's because I'm not a bro, right?" She nodded slowly and exaggeratedly, like they were sharing an inside joke. She mimicked and put on a deep voice, "Backward hat. Beer." She made a circle around her midsection. "Belly."

"Um, to put it that way, yes." That was exactly what he'd meant.

"Dave's music appeals to a broad base of listeners that span cultures, religions, and economic backgrounds." Her voice took on a tense monotone, like a human Smith Corona typing words on the air. "Somewhere it became synonymous with the term 'bro rock.' 'Frat boys.' 'Thirty-year-old white men.' No offense."

"None taken."

Iris searched through her bag and pulled out a tape labeled in purple sharpie marker. "Ah, ha. Here we go." Bubbly guitar licks and the roar of a crowd filled the space between them. He went to speak, but she held up her hand.

"Just listen, and you'll see."

Dave greeted the crowd over a low bass line, and they moved into that anthem Chris remembered from college. It was a catchy enough tune, but the elation in Iris' face told the story of a siren's song, like she'd been touched by the divine. There was a rustle and scratching noise that interrupted the song, possibly a problem with the tape. Then a muffled voice, a young woman's said, *'Whoops.'* with a giggle.

It sounded familiar, but he couldn't place it. "Is that?"

Before he could finish, another sound had broken in that had nothing to do with the tape.

It shook in his pocket, ringing for the second time.

Iris snapped to attention, stopping the tape in its tracks. "Are you going to get that?" It rang again. She shifted in her seat. Iris did not enjoy ringing phones. "You better get that."

He picked it up but didn't answer. He stared at Rachel's picture and watched dumbly as it rang again and once more before stopping.

He didn't have to look over to know Iris was glaring at him. "Why didn't you answer your phone?" She cut him off before he could speak. "You just let it ring." He tried again to speak to no avail. "You *said* we need to let people know where we are. You *said* I have to do that. That's why I keep calling Maisy." He opened his mouth, but she got the last word. "Your phone rings and *you* don't answer it."

There was accusation in her words and indignation he'd reserve for more lofty issues.

The hurt was real. Iris wasn't doing this for show.

"How many times has she called, Christopher?" She'd taken his words and pointed them at him like a magnifying glass and, only now, let him speak for himself.

"Six." He was ashamed to admit he'd sent Rachel to voicemail five times before, afraid to hear her voice. Iris wouldn't look at him. Instead, she bit at her own knuckles. Mouth half full, she spoke the last thing she would speak for the next 23 minutes: seven words that played in Christopher's head like a scratchy bootlegged tape.

"You're going to have to answer soon."

For the next 23.2 miles, Chris had nothing but the clouds to keep him company. They rolled out and then came down to greet him in a fog, which seemed almost impassable. They cleared just in time to see the sign.

"Iris, look. It's Virginia Beach. Iris?" She had been staring at her tape deck, but this wasn't a case of the girl drifting off into her own world. She was giving him the silent treatment. It had been a standoff, and she was winning. She'd remained implacable through his futile attempts at small talk, even when he'd squealed like a little girl, moments before the fog lifted.

He had been driving slowly, but received the jolt of his life when an RV popped up right in front of the blueberry. He yanked the wheel, pulling the blueberry and all its contents so hard to the right that the contents within went sprawling. Chris' arm had flown to the side with some protective instinct to shield Iris from the flying tape player coming her way, but she didn't flinch. There was no fear, no thank you, no reaction at all, when the car came to a screeching halt. She simply picked up the phones and put them back on the console, straightened the loose contents in her backpack, and resumed her position gazing at the tape player that had gone quiet. She remained that way.

"Iris, you can't still be mad at me."

He slowed the car as much as he could without stopping just as they passed the sign that welcomed them to the state "where it all happened." Iris didn't move. A strange guilt crept over him as they passed, like he had ruined something important, so he was overcome by an impulse.

He yanked the car to the side of the road once again, not enough to jar anything loose but enough to lift the girl's eyes from the tape player. He took a deep breath. "Look, I'll call okay? I don't know what I'm going to say, but I'll call right now." He pleaded. "The sign is right there. We can go back and—"

He meant to say take a picture but didn't get a chance to finish. His promise to call Rachel was cut short because she had beaten him to it. Without looking, he snatched up the phone, hitting the answer button with a triumphant look.

The thought of his wife's voice made his body feel heavy. He didn't know what he was going to say, but he'd start with hello. Iris looked amused.

"Hello?"

"HELLO? WHO THE #$@&%* IS THIS?"

It was not Rachel's voice. This was the voice of someone new, someone familiar, someone who sounded a whole lot like Iris, only angrier.

"This is Chris."

Fog

Iris had broken her silence with a giggle holding up the phone with the distinct crack in its side as he spoke to the woman screaming on the other end to the one she'd switched for his.

"You must be Maisy."

Chapter 17

Devil You Know

"You're #$@&%* right, this is Mais—how do you know my name? Who the #$@&%* is this? Eric, there's a man in the car. Why is there a #$@&%*? You #$@&%*, whatever you did to Iris, you're not going to get away with it. I'm going to find you, and I'm going to rip your eyes out. THEN, I'm going to kill you. Eric, there's a man." Her voice was frantic and each swear word gained both speed and bite. He picked up the words, "*dead*," "*ditch*," and more distinctly, "*castrate*." She spoke to the person next to her. "She's in a ditch." Then she came back with fervor, the timber and rate of speech slow and methodical. "You tell me where Iris is you sick #$@&%*.

Iris' hand came from his periphery like a slingshot and snapped the phone away, like a frog eating a fly. Her voice was as level and monotone as it would be if she were reading from an economics book. "Maisy, I'm right here."

He couldn't make out what Maisy said, only loud muffled noises peppered with profanity.

"Stop swearing. You've been doing so well. You said you were going to try harder, that's not trying." The sky behind her was turning gray. Iris sounded like a mother, soothing her child as the storm caught up to them. "What?" She looked at him. "No, he's not a serial killer. His name is Christopher and he's from New Jersey. No, a teacher." She looked at him, as if questioning the last bit, to which he reluctantly nodded. "He's on a hike. Not a molester." Maisy's voice was not as loud, but the tone was the same. It came through the phone like a bass beat: hard, fast, and punctuated by pauses. "I know," she lowered her voice, "I know he isn't, because I looked at his eyes." There was just a muffle now coming from the phone, and there was a distant crackling in the sky above. "He's going to help me get to the, yes, Maisy, I'm going to the Bake-Off. My recipe was really good, that's why. I told you a million times that I. Yes, I can too." There was a murmur from the other end that had all the flourish of music but wasn't. "I didn't end up in a ditch. I'm in the blueberry." She looked at the map. "In Virginia."

There was quiet now on both ends, and Iris said as if it were spoken from on high, "Maisy, I can do this." Iris leaned into the door of the car so he could only see her nodding from behind, repeating "uh-huh" several times before turning around apologetically.

"She wants to talk to you."

He took the phone, and Iris looked at him like he was about to walk the plank.

All of a sudden, he felt like he was in seventh grade again, caught in the middle of a prank call gone terribly wrong. "Hello." *Did his voice just crack?*

Maisy was calm. She spoke with the air of one who has resigned herself to whatever was coming next. She no longer sounded angry. She sounded tired.

"Christopher, is it?"

"Yes, Christopher Davenport."

There was a muffled sound, as she repeated his name back to whomever was standing next to her.

"You can look me up if you like. Go to Seaview Community College. Just search my name. You can see it's all there. I promise, I'm not a serial killer." She repeated what he said to the person standing next to her. There was a second of tense silence. "Planning to hike down to Virginia, commune with nature. Do my Walden thing," he babbled. None of that had factored into anything he'd decided.

"Liberal Arts faculty?" Her voice was tight. "Guy with the bowtie, you're a college teacher?"

"Yes, that's me."

There was that uneasy feeling again in his stomach, like he was about to get in trouble. There was more murmuring and some "ums" and "hums" that sounded like assurances from the male voice. He heard bits and pieces that sounded familiar, direct quotations no doubt from the bio he'd written for the department less than a month ago.

"I'm on," he searched, leave." It wasn't leave. Leave would mean he'd let them or anyone know he was going. He hadn't. To do that, he'd have had to have a clue as to what he was doing, which he didn't. Instead, he woke this morning with the semester behind him and left the life he knew with it. "Semester break, really." He felt warm. "Gives me some time to get in touch." He felt foolish. "And, if you click on my personal link, it will take you to my number. If you want to call. There's my cell, and my home number. You can talk to my…" It felt like worms were boring into his navel, "wife."

"Uh hm."

She didn't murmur but spoke in the same simple way Iris did when stating an indisputable fact.

"You having some kind of crisis, Christopher?" He pretended not to hear. Though he was certain she saw through it. She sounded skeptical. By the sounds of it, her hand was over the receiver because it sounded as though she spoke from behind a wall. More than likely, it was to protect him from what she said. "He's having a midlife crisis."

"Rachel." He spoke more loudly than intended, to let her know he was still hanging on. "She should be awake by now. She's on rounds at the hospital. Night shift, you know how it is?" He could only imagine her shock picking up the phone. In hindsight, he might have left a note. He was trying to sound regular and at ease in an attempt to make simple conversation, though the fact remained that nothing about any of this was simple. He was in a stolen car with the kid who stole it, and, yes, he was now babbling. "You can call her if you want to check up on me. She'll assure you I'm not a serial killer or criminal mastermind. I'm just a guy who saw a kid in trouble and wanted to help."

Before she could murmur or respond, he added, "Call my school. Call. I assure you, my intentions are noble." He meant every word, especially the part about Iris. It would make things easier if someone else broke the news to Rachel.

"If you wanted to help, you would've brought her home." Maisy was shouting, but caught herself. "You would've brought her home."

She was right. That would've been the adult thing to do, but he wasn't so good at that. Rachel had told him he had the knack for saying the wrong thing at the wrong time to the wrong people.

"Have you tasted any of her stuff? It's really good. She's a got a shot at this. It's a once in a lifetime opportunity."

"Who in the #$@&%* are you? What do you know about once-in-a-lifetime? You don't even know her. What do you care about Iris? She's just a kid." Her voice had jumped up again, but a pinched sound squeezed what she said next. "She's got a lot going on."

"Would you rather she tried to drive to Florida on her own?" He spoke carefully, "with all that going on?" Iris chewed her fingers to the knuckles and absorbed his every word. He was careful here. "A 15-year-old kid?"

"Almost three months." She corrected.

"Thank you, Iris. Would you rather a 15-year-old, and almost three months, with no license drive 1,000 miles with no help at all? Do you think that would be a good idea?" He hadn't meant to raise his voice, so he took a breath.

There was silence, no muffled talking, no jostling of the phone, just the sound of thinking.

"Well." Maisy sighed. The voice next to her spoke as soothingly and softly as a voice that deep or gruff could. It had a familiar tone, like they'd done this before. When she came back to the phone, she sounded more like the girl sitting next to him. "Thank you, I guess. For making sure nothing bad happened."

He didn't want to panic Maisy now that she wasn't screaming at him, so he left out the part about Iris' panic on the ferry or the six stops for corn and the kaleidoscope of circles on her map. He kept it simple. "I was just trying to help."

She didn't cut him off or curse at him. Instead, she rubbed her face the way she did when the world felt like it was on fire. "Where are you exactly? It's going to take me a few hours to get there."

Iris smoothed out her map reciting highway, mile marker, and exit loud enough for Maisy to hear. "You can meet us?" She bounced happily in her seat.

"So I can bring you b—"

The blueberry lit up like a party, and Maisy was cut off by the giant crack that divided the sky.

"We've got some weather," he tried to explain but was overpowered.

"Ohhhhhh. Hummmmmm. Hummmmm. Hummmm." The sky was black behind Iris, and she was like a specter moaning in the darkness. Her face was a shell, expressionless but for the O of her mouth. This was a death mask, petrified by fear. The rains that plagued them a few miles back had found them once again, and Iris thrashed from side-to-side hoping to slam away the fear.

"What's that?" Maisy's voice changed. It was high and strained. Christopher knew that feeling of panic, the kind that gripped the vocal chords so tight his voice went up an octave. He balanced the phone on his shoulder, steering the blueberry through the river falling from above and tried to navigate the storm.

"It's lightning. We were trying to stay ahead of it." Iris covered her eyes and hummed one long note, pounding her head against the seat like a bass drum. Maisy tried to yell through the phone to catch Christopher's attention, so she could talk him through what was going on. Storms could be terrifying. Instead, she hung on hopelessly overhearing everything that would transpire.

Iris screamed. There was a thrashing sound. Maisy could hear the water pelting the car, or it could have been heavy breathing. She couldn't tell. Her knuckles hurt where her hand clenched around the phone. She reached for Eric with the other. She couldn't hang up. Instead, she hung on for dear life.

Chris spoke but no longer into the phone.

"Iris, can you listen to me?" He tried to keep his voice in one note, a low honey-coated tone that didn't rise or climb. He could see light ahead. There was a general store up ahead. If he could get there, he could stop. He'd have two hands, so he could concentrate more on calming Iris down and less on not crashing the little car into oncoming traffic. "I-ris." He said it like a song and tapped his hands on the steering wheel in time. "I-ris. I-ris. I-ris." He pulled into the gravel lot. It crunched under the tires, so he used that to his advantage. "I-ris." Tap. "I-ris." Tap. Crunch. Tap. "I-ris." It was a catchy, primal chant she couldn't help but repeat.

Iris did the little song adding a tap on her window. Then he repeated, adding the sound "ka-boom." He took a deep breath before speaking the first syllable and held out the boom, like it was a long choir hymn. By the time they cycled through the sequence three more times, her tears had dried.

"Better." It wasn't a question but a statement.

"Yeah." The girl seemed shocked to say it, but she smoothed her hat and smiled like she'd won something grand.

On the other end of the phone Maisy was waiting, her mouth hanging open like a fish.

"What's happening?" Eric prodded her, napkin in one hand, knife in the other, while Mrs. Renfro pretended not to listen as she waited for her "everything bagel with extra cream cheese."

"I'm. Not. Sure." Maisy's brow looked like a child's imitation of cursive, all crinkled lines and furrows, and her voice was much lower than it had been.

She leaned into the receiver conspiratorially, "How did you do that?"

Chris had forgotten the phone was there. "Do what?" Iris was already looking at her map, making a small dot where they'd stopped. Her breathing was even. She mouthed a happy tune he hadn't heard since 1998.

"That." Maisy insisted. "How did you know how to do that?"

It had been a long ride, and he had had time to adapt to the girl's ways, but that wasn't the whole story. Now he leaned into his door.

"I teach psych," he mumbled like a sitcom teen trying to get away with something, "though I'm out of practice."

"Practice what?" Iris looked up from the world of her map, eyes still damp from the storm.

"My ocarina." Christopher said without missing a beat. "Iris, why don't you get yourself cleaned up? I'm sure there's a bathroom in there, some napkins at least. See if you can get a couple of pretzels." He handed her a crumpled ten dollar bill from his pocket. The store looked promising. A bright neon sign had already piqued Iris' curiosity.

"Or a sandwich." She beamed, carefully drawing a pig face on the map, happily climbing out of the car in search of the *World's Best Virginia Ham*.

Maisy heard one door shut and then quiet. Panic rose up in her throat like hot metal. "Did you just send her out there? By herself?"

"Just into the Chuckey's, yes. Thought she could use a sandwich. She eats a lot, you know?"

A torrent of words left him feeling like he needed a shower and when Maisy came up for air, he got a word in.

"She'll be fine, Maisy."

"How do you know?"

"I just do."

"You've got a lot of nerve. You're lucky I'm not calling the cops on you. You're with her for what, two hours, and you're some kind of expert. Do you have any idea what it's like for her to be in a store? All those noises? The people? What if there's a bright light she's not expecting? It's hell.

Or if there's a lady wearing too much perfume? Do you have any idea what that could do to her?"

"I think I do."

Her voice lingered between alarm and sadness. She sniffed at him, her words sharp. "Now you're a #$@&%* doctor."

He was resigned. "Yes, actually."

"Yes, actually, what?" Maisy sounded like she wanted to reach through the phone and throttle him. He had become surer in the past moments of what he needed to say.

"Yes, actually a doctor."

Maisy repeated what he said to Eric and, then, returned with rediscovered cynicism. "I thought you were a teacher."

He tried to make as little of what he was saying as possible, while maintaining a deep lean into the driver's side door. It was a story he hated, but it was his after all. "I was. Am." He corrected. "I do teach psych at the college." There was an itchy, uncomfortable feeling in his throat. "I am a doctor, but I teach while I'm not practicing."

"*Practicing*." It made more sense now. Maisy sounded like she was attempting to crawl into the phone to better hear him.

"I took some time off after Christmas." The muffled sounds on the other end let him know Maisy was sharing this information. "I started at the college this semester."

"You're a shrink."

These words felt thick, like poorly cooked oatmeal and day-after drinking, but he pressed on. Iris didn't like surprises and, by the sound of it, neither did Maisy. "I prefer psychologist. Licensed therapist, if you like. Family and marriage counseling, mostly. Dr. Christopher Davenport, at your service." He attempted a jovial tone. It couldn't have felt less forced if he'd sung it.

"That's why I thought I could help. Why I should help. Why I had to help."

"With Iris, you mean?"

"Exactly."

"Why, because you think she's crazy." Tension hardened her words and she seemed infinitely older than moments before. More murmuring let him know Eric was being apprised of the new development.

"I didn't say that." He pressed on despite the opposition. "I have some experience with," he measured his words, "people like Iris. The routines, warnings. Planning. Anxiety." He felt none of them was making this easier, but he pressed on, testing the waters, each word more tentative than the next. "I think you should let Iris do this." He cleared his throat. "This Bake-Off."

For a minute he thought she didn't hear him, until she cleared her throat. "If you start heading north, I can be at the ferry in a few hours to pick her up."

"I'm sorry, but no."

"Excuse me."

"I said 'no.' I think this would be really good for her, and for you. She needs to know she can do this." Just this morning, Chris would have preferred leaving an entire life behind to avoid a conflict. Now he found himself digging his feet in the sand. "I think you do, too."

"That's your expert opinion?"

"Yes."

"As a doctor." He felt like a dentist recommending gum on TV.

"An avid baked goods eater." He attempted to lighten the mood. "Her stuff is really, really good." There was silence that reminded him of every conversation he'd had with Rachel in the past few weeks, the kind of silence that spans decades and chills the bones. He'd learned to count through it, at the risk of saying something worse than what he'd said before. Sometimes he'd sing a commercial jingle or fast-paced tune, he didn't have to choose this time. As if in response, Maisy made a sound that was more like a pressure cooker release than a sigh.

"I can't think about that now, Dr. Chris." The frantic edge had smoothed her words, and she spoke like a patron calling a manager over to discuss cold soup. "What I need right now is for you to get in that, Chuckey's, was it? And make sure Iris is okay. You get in there and watch out for her?"

The overreaction seemed so ludicrous to him, he almost chuckled, but, for a split second, he thought about Iris and reconsidered.

"What am I watching out for?"

Now she almost laughed. "Doc, you have no idea." There were thumps against the phone. She was talking on the move. They went quiet as her voice became very clear. "Anything can happen."

"It's just a souvenir sh—"

"Since you want to help, I'm just suggesting you get in there. She's in a new place. You don't know what's in there? Does she? No, she doesn't. You can't look away for a minute." She sounded like she was fighting with the last thing she said and exhaled from the effort. "You get in there with her, and I'm going to get my #$@&%* together." She caught herself and cursed for cursing. "#$@&%*." There was that sigh again, and she came back more composed than before. "I'm going to get my stuff together, and call you in about five minutes. Okay?"

"Of course."

"You make sure you answer your phone." Before he could assure her he would, her hand was fumbling with the phone and she was talking to the man next to her in speedy yet hushed tones. "Get in there, okay? Please make sure nothing happens to her."

Chapter 18

Chuckey's

The door had hanging bells on the back that rung out like Christmas, as her fate sealed behind her. There was no hope of going back now. Her foot had crossed the threshold, so she was here to stay. Despite the sign that glowed on top of the storefront like a sparkling crown, Chuckey's looked less like the kingdom of Virginia ham and more like purgatory. Iris had read about that place a million times when she was going through her Dante phase. Of all the otherworldly places, the middle one seemed the worst. It lacked the heavenly good things of paradise and the personality of the place below. At least the *Inferno* had flair. Chuckey's had none.

From the entranceway, it seemed an odd general store and coffee shop hybrid that was at war with its own identity. There were graying shelves filled with powder soaps and jars of mustard. There were souvenir shot glasses and snow globes with smiling pigs on the beach, oddities of all kinds for weary travelers to pick up on their way. The whole back end of the place was a grill area where men in paper hats flipped grilled cheese sandwiches and slung hash. The smell told her that long before she saw it.

It hit her nose like a punch, a gamey smell that tickled her nose like cracked pepper. She exhaled like she was blowing out a candle trying to push the smell as far away as she could. The air was different here, thick and oily, sticky air that grabbed at the dust around it and followed like a cloud even when she tried to get away. It clung to her skin and made it tacky, so she felt like flypaper, exposed. She could feel the bugs on her, ten thousand tiny mites adhering to her every pore, covering her whole body like a living suit. They were crawling there now with their exploring feet and teeth sharpened to tiny points. They would nibble her skin like an army of scarabs until there was nothing left of her but bone.

Breathe. It was hot in here, but not like the *Inferno.* It wasn't heat that burned and singed but cramped airless heat that closed in and squeezed, despite the ceiling fans that seemed to be everywhere. The blades wobbled and wavered overhead like giant leathery wings, ready to descend and feast on her brain like carnivorous wasps in the sky. She told herself to ignore them. *Look at the walls.* They were the color of old wet cardboard, and every few feet there was a sign or two she could read to distract herself from the flickering lights and the boxes that sat crookedly on their shelves. If she didn't focus, she would be tempted to touch each one of them, moving bottles and cans until all the labels faced the same way. She couldn't do that.

She put it out of her mind. She stepped across the tiles, brown to brown and green to green, skipping over the beige ones. They were the lava. *Don't step on the lava.* She made a game of it until she arrived at the back of the store where the big counter with the spinning stools sat like a throne. Waves of sound radiated in her ears. The heat sizzled her earlobes, eggs popping on grease. The metal scrape of a spatula on a flattop was enough to shred her skin to the bones.

Ignore it.

She slipped her hands up into her wooly and made circles in her hair. Three forward, three back. Scratch. Scratch. Scratch. *Breathe.*

Forks—forks scraping on plates—screamed through her body. The screeches climbed up through her and knocked on the back of her eyeballs trying to push them out. Her gums pulled back off her teeth. She could feel it. Her teeth were splitting in two.

The counter was elevated, the men back there looking like ancient priests, their white hats keeping the offering pure. A younger man chopped up steak on the grill, his spatula pulled across the hot metal like he was peeling up a scab. The older man had a moustache, thick and dusted with white like a bag of flour had exploded. His face wore the lines of years in the sun, but he had a warm voice that matched the smile behind his walrus whiskers.

"What can I git ya?" Iris should have expected the accent, but it took her off guard. She stammered and caught the glow of a knife on the counter. It sparkled like a star. A wet meat sound slapped her and stuck to her forehead. It lay there like a damp cloth.

"Ham. Ham? Ham." It didn't sound like a word and felt like flavorless gum she rolled over in her mouth. "Ham."

"Sandwich or platter, little lady?" Both sandwich and platter came with a choice of sides. Pictures of greens and sweet potatoes, French fries, fried okra, and macaroni and cheese were taped across the raised counter, like a food shrine. The high priest stood at the dais awaiting direction from a voice on high. She was miles below sucked into a vortex of Technicolor noodles and starches looking straight into the abyss. The air burned like poison fog and choked out her voice. It was lost, hidden away like a buried relic, dry and hot inside her. Her head hurt. She pressed her eyes shut and held up a finger.

"I'll come back." Her voice adrift sounded like someone else's, like it had been recorded and played back from the inside of a tin can. Even though she'd practiced a thousand times in the mirror, Iris still wasn't very good at ordering.

She tapped on her legs, breathing shallow, so that the sludge air didn't drown her. There was a caterpillar video game machine beeping to the left. There, on the right, was hope. If she could make it there, it would be all right. The whoosh sounds from the soda machines were waterfalls and dragon sneezes. A cold cup of lemon-lime soda would be bubbly and delicious. Iris pulled her hat as far down as she could without covering up her eyes and focused on the tiles and the sounds of her feet. She held her fist up next to her mouth as if she were going to cough, but, really, she was smelling her own hand, biting into the soft flesh between her knuckle and thumb.

She didn't notice the two ladies shopping or the young man eating fries at the table she was headed straight for. In her defense, he hadn't noticed either. His gaze remained firmly fixed to his phone, even as she almost knocked his table over. It was only for the brief second before the table moved, when he had to save his tipping fries, that he glanced at her and then looked again, with the faintest look of recognition, as if they'd met before. She was probably imagining that. She'd sometimes think people are angry when they aren't or, worse, that people were being nice just because they were smiling. The nuances of facial expressions were almost as troubling to Iris as the people who wore them. Either way, the guy had dropped his attention back to what was at hand, his fingers moving soundlessly.

The fountain drinks smelled like caramel and sugar, punched with ripened fruits and lemons. Should she get the sweet tea? The label boasted it was southern made, which was a "thing," a specialty. Choosing was almost as hard as getting there.

Each beverage had its own neon sign, they boasted like Las Vegas lights. One alone was blinding, but there had to be at least a dozen here. The red elf man in one sign shouted with a blinking orange bulb to drink Fruit Twist, while the CocoLoco Soda dancers gleamed in golden piña colada yellows to *Sip and Savor the Island Flavor*. Iris concentrated on the metal grates underneath the spigots. The basin underneath kept the spills at bay by funneling all the lost drinks like a soda river to some unknown magical place. With the cool metal under her fingers, she felt better She traced the grates and followed them down the row of drinks like a lifeline, where they ended at a tower of cups in the dispenser. She pulled one loose with a pop, a large red cup that was cool and waxy like a giant ladybug. It was smooth in her hands.

She pushed the button to get her island flavor and changed her mind to go with the elf man and found the dispensers made different sounds. One gave a 'shoosh' while the other gave a 'tsssss'. Perhaps it had less carbonation? Maybe it was a density issue. Whatever it was, Iris liked it.

"Hmmmm."

She grabbed another cup and set it down with a thunk, then hit the drink button that made a swoosh sound. No one seemed to care, not that she was looking. She grabbed two more cups and plunked them bottom up on the counter, tapping them lightly with a straw. It had a nice crisp sound like mice tap dancing. The meat air seemed to thin out, and the air felt cooler on her fingertips. She grabbed three more cups and laid them out the same way, this time staggering them like building blocks. Like an artist, she carefully set another row of cups on top of those. Then three more, and two more, and one until she'd made herself a pyramid of sound. She tapped from the top to the bottom, alternating beats with pushes on the soda dispenser buttons until she was playing a steady syncopated beat.

The young man with the French fries had noticed and started watching. Iris did not notice him or the shoppers or the walrus or the young fry cook who'd stepped out from behind the counter. She held her straw over what she'd built like a scepter and played a song King Tut would have loved. No scarabs or poison fog could close in on her here, not in her pyramid. She stacked and drummed her lullaby. She was Hathor, Goddess of Music, and nothing could scare her now. Iris hummed and swayed lost in the soda dispensers. The patrons of Chuckey's looked on in awe, not entirely sure what they were seeing. For Iris, the scene was clear.

The flickering lights were the warm glow of the sun reflecting off the desert. The cool drinks were the Nile, and the queen's voice rose from the waters like an ancient hymn.

Chapter 19

Song

Chris walked into Chuckey's expecting to see Iris checking out with a bag of pretzels and a soda, but he didn't see her or anyone at all. For all intents and purposes, the place looked deserted. The aisles up front were crowded with knickknacks and souvenirs surely designed to grab the eye of weary travelers pulling in for coffee or a needed rest. There weren't any travelers of which to speak. The cashier stand stood vacant, and shelves of hula girls looked out onto an empty audience, even the one that wiggled slightly, as if someone had started the show and forgotten her there. In the back of the store, the grill was abandoned, heat still radiating from the flat top. The scent of hot dogs and grilled onions lingered like a phantom. He'd seen things like this in zombie movies and old *Twilight Zone* episodes about places the world and time had forgotten. This was no Atlantis, nothing fancy like that. It was the same feeling, a place untouched but left exactly as it once stood, abandoned by its people because something giant had occurred. When he pushed past a rack of neon-colored T-shirts, he saw what it was.

A semicircle of people had formed around the fountain drinks. Two men in white paper hats stood rubbing their hands on their aprons with looks on their faces like little boys hearing their mothers sing. A handful of ladies were laying down their plastic baskets filled with knick-knacks and sundries to hold their hands to the sky, like they were hearing the Sermon on the Mount. A young woman, who by the looks of her nametag was a cashier, spit her gum in her napkin and wiped what looked like a solitary tear from her face. A young man who had been typing furiously had let his eyes drift up from his phone and watched in wonder.

They were all watching Iris.

Not just watching. Watching would imply that there was some level of control over what they were doing, as a person taking in a TV show could choose if he wanted to munch on popcorn or speak during commercials. This sight was nothing like that. They weren't watching her as much as they seemed to be part of her. She had drawn them in and kept them there in the web that was both spectacle and spell. The pyramid in splendid red stood taller than the average kindergartner rising above the soda taps and napkins. On any other day, he'd have reacted differently. On any other day, he wouldn't be standing in the middle of rural Virginia with raw hamburger blistered feet and a knapsack on his back. Christopher decided to reserve judgment and pushed closer to the soda machine.

It was a familiar tune from his college years, also known as the third song on tape two, 1998 in Iris' collection. She didn't focus on the lyrics or even the melody. Instead, she took a phrase and made it something new, drawing out notes, dipping and diving like a butterfly over the original song. Her voice, an angel voice, rang out over the small crowd and, whether they knew it or not, they had become her choir. The older women rocked and swayed to the sounds of Iris' song. Not one employee took a step to stop her. The grill men were nodding and smiling to each other. The cashier watched in silence and bit her fingernails as if in salute to the girl who was singing.

You never know what can happen.

The ladies had started to stomp in unison in time to the music and taking the cue the grill men joined by clinking spatulas with forks on the off beats. The silent cashier hummed a low tone that filled in Iris' tune like colored paints on pencil lines. The young man with the phone stood as silent and as still as Christopher, transfixed, with his phone aimed at the action like he was witnessing something mystical. For a moment, Christopher felt like he had indeed stepped into another dimension, because it was quite extraordinary.

He wanted to tell Maisy she was right, but not in a way that made her voice catch or her mouth go straight to the sewer. He wanted to tell her that, even in the darkest shadows of fear, there was the possibility of something beautiful. He didn't think that yesterday, but today wasn't yesterday.

Now, he needed to tell her.

As promised, his phone rang silently in his pocket. He hit the button and without speaking held it out toward Iris and the soda machine. He and the French fry guy shared a moment reaching out like the faithful. As the song ended, the French fry guy slid back to the video game and laid his phone down flat so he could use both hands. The clapping started slowly, and, as the shoppers joined in, the counter man whistled. Iris, with her back to them, only then realized she had an audience, and smiled with a shrug so tight it looked as though her neck had disappeared.

Chris spoke softly into the phone, "It's gonna be okay."

He clicked off with Maisy after promising (again) to check in as soon as they'd eaten. Iris was deep in a conversation with a lady in a pink and purple flowered dress about natural compost in the garden when he broke in to deliver the news.

"She's calmer now."

In a flat voice free of panic or concern, she turned her head in his direction. "She's going to kill me. Can you get me a ham sandwich?"

Song

The counter men were chipper and chatted among themselves, humming snippets of Iris' song.

"She's gonna win that Bake-Off, I'll tell you," said the stubby man flipping onions the color of warm sugar. The younger man whistled, and the both of them seemed to agree that the young girl who waited now at the counter seat could do anything she wanted, if she put her mind to it.

Iris ate her food like she'd never seen any before, slurping up her sandwich, greens, and an order of fried potatoes like they were a kid-sized snack. "Are you going to eat those?" She pointed to the onions on his sandwich as he was about to bite it. He halted the food just before it hit his lips and laid it back down on the plate.

"Uh, no." He peeled the onions from his brisket and put them on her plate. "Knock yourself out."

"I really like pickles." She added and, likewise, he transported them from his plate to hers.

"You might want to take it easy." He tried to advise her, as she inhaled the pickle and the onions as if they were an afterthought.

"Easy how?"

"Never mind."

The ladies had returned to shopping, and the counter men seemed at ease behind the grill, spatulas moving like tap shoes. For the most part, Chuckey's seemed exactly as it was before the impromptu sing-along began—except for the young guy playing the Caterpillar game. When he wasn't trying to pretend he wasn't looking this way, he was making slow circles around the perimeter, like a sedate and not-so-clever shark.

He couldn't have been much older than Iris but old enough to be too old. Christopher felt the unexplainable desire to grab him by the neck of the shirt and gently remind him where the door was. He heard himself saying, "Can I help you with something, buddy?" *Buddy?* When did he become someone's grandpa? If he'd heard anyone else talking in this strange voice coming from him or in this way, he'd get dizzy from rolling his eyes. Now he was standing and approaching this 18-year-old kid. The boy had the makings of a goatee and gripped his cellphone like a life vest. He looked like a strong gust of wind would knock him over, but still Chris heard himself again.

"You got something to say, friend?" He was all Clint Eastwood and felt his back stiffen as the boy took a step back and then forward again, toward Iris.

"You look so familiar."

"Hey." He put his hand up but, the boy spoke over him.

"I feel like I've seen you somewhere. Are you on TV or something?"

Christopher was losing patience. "All right, kid. That's enough, what are you gonna do next, ask her what's her sign?" It was like the boy didn't hear him.

"I swear I've seen you before."

Iris was unmoved by any of this. She was busy picking crumbs from the plate and licking them from her fingers.

"You must have her mixed up with someone else, kid. Move along."

Christopher hadn't felt this protective of anyone in a long time and, for a moment, understood the panic Maisy must be feeling. It was like she'd heard him from miles away. The phone was ringing again. He yanked the phone from his pocket so as not to keep her waiting a second longer. Now he was starting to understand.

"She's fine Maisy, we're just finishing up."

"Not Maisy." The voice was strained and tired, more so than usual at this hour, the way she sounded when she hadn't slept.

"Rachel. Hi."

Chapter 20

Travel

"You're going to stop at the next place you can rest and stay there." Maisy's words were so different than Rachel's had been. She was direct and driven. Her certainty reverberated through the words like drum beats. Rachel sounded like a drugged patient, unsure of anything she heard, like she was in some kind of dream. Even in her nightmare trance, she had been sure to tell him the two things she was sure of, which haunted him now. Chris couldn't read women, and he basically had no sense of humor.

"Well, we did just stop. I thought we could make it at least another state."

"Are you being funny?" Her voice contradicted the words, because Maisy didn't sound like she wanted to share a giggle with the good doctor. She sounded like she was about to bury him in the hole he'd just dug himself.

"Get to the next lodging area and you WAIT there for me." There was a pause heavy with murmuring. "Get two rooms." More murmuring. "Two. You got that, Dr. Davenport?" There was a hint of hesitation. Maisy, unlike Christopher, was a good judge of character and her call to Rachel had put at least the most important worry aside. Nevertheless, she spit it out like a change receipt. Better safe than sorry. "No, funny business."

"I wouldn't dream of it."

Maisy sounded less frantic this call, but her voice had taken on the scratchy note of concert goers who'd been screaming all night or overzealous cheerleaders the day after the game. She wasn't musical or cheery. She was worn out, and she knew it.

Christopher wanted to ease it away. "Dr. Chris."

"What?"

"My patients," former patients now—"call me Dr. Chris."

"Right." She wasn't entirely with him. He knew how that sounded, too. Half of what she said now was to herself. "She's going to need to rest, whether she knows it or not. All that driving, if she doesn't decompress, it'll be like the Hindenburg." Then, as if she'd just realized he was still on the phone, she added, "You'll make sure nothing happens to her?"

"You have my word as a doctor." Her pause had more to do with her own nervousness than it did him, but it made him want to lighten the mood nonetheless. "A teacher and a hiker."

"What?"

"And an eater of baked goods?"

Maisy's attention was finally focused on him.

"Dr. Chris, you sound like you are a little nutty."

She had a good point.

Maisy clicked off the phone and rushed from the back of the store to the front in one fluid motion, her dress flowing as if she were followed by her own gust of wind. It was like her body was under a spell that broke the moment her hand touched the cool metal of the door.

"I don't have a car."

Eric had never stopped watching. He was right behind her. He leaned on the drink cooler with his arm extended, keys in hand.

"Take mine."

"You, how are you going to? It's late when you get off. What are you, going to walk in the dark?"

Eric stood taller than most and almost as wide as the refrigerator he leaned on. A long line of linebackers in the family tree and four years of college football tend to do that to a guy. He wasn't really worried about a half mile walk up the street.

He wasn't thinking about anything but her, and she was always thinking about everything.

"Your knees, Eric? What about your knees?"

He focused on her voice, strained and tense. He let those words drop away and thought of the ones he'd spoke just this morning.

"Maisy." In the years they'd known each other, they'd never so much as shaken hands, but he put his hands on her shoulders and looked down into Maisy's eyes. "Breathe."

They were a winter sky just before a great snow. It was easy to mistake the stillness for calm. Churning beneath, turmoil was brewing.

"What am I going to do?" Her shoulders were shaking.

His voice was as calm and as measured as it would be if he were reading a poem at the library.

"First. You're going to get in my car." She nodded, taking in his words like they were a foreign language. "Then you're going to drive."

Maisy was as much a list maker as Iris. She liked to have details hammered down and double checked, plans marked as pinpoints on long slips of paper.

"That's it?"

He squeezed her shoulders just slightly, a hand hug that in any other situation he'd second guess. This was a no-brainer. He nodded smiling. "That's it."

It wasn't intricate, but it was by no means simple.

"What about your—"

"I'll use my bike for a coupla days."

Her face scrunched and released as the horror rushed in and washed away like flood water. "But your knees!"

"They'll be fine. That's what ice is for." Her head moved almost imperceptibly, the slightest hint of a disbelieving head shake. "I never stopped riding. They can handle it."

She held up her fingers like she was about to start ticking off to-do's, but he stopped her dead in her tracks. "I'll feed Oscar and Sophie and the hermit crab. I'll take in the mail. I'll even run your water so the well doesn't settle."

Before she could take a breath to remind him, he added with flourish, and I'll tape that show about the idjits and the Impala."

Maisy was settling, the curve of her brow softening so her eyes focused in front of her. Her voice went quiet. "Wear your helmet."

He gave her a thumbs-up, and finally, she smiled.

"Better?"

Her eyes looked settled, determined.

"I gotta pack a bag."

Eric was a big man. Years of football had built his body up like a fortress, his large shoulders and strong legs like cinder blocks on his solid frame. His car had to live up to that. Eric boosted her inside and Maisy felt like a mouse in the hulking utility vehicle. He still wore a strange look on his face, since the odd moment when he had put his hand out to help her in. In five years working together, they'd never so much as brushed elbows, and now, they'd had not one but two fairly close encounters. She shrugged it off with a smile. He had dimples under that beard. She could tell when he smiled.

He'd let her take his pride and joy. The interior was as fresh as it had been in the showroom, if not more pristine. It still had a new car smell, though he'd been driving Bessie for more than a year. A car tends to stay like new when it's taken for a bath every two weeks and a full makeover once a month. He had the dates marked on the dog-eared planner he got from the bank last fall, the one he kept in his back pocket. He'd pencil the dates in month-to-month like they were a newborn's doctor appointments, ones he couldn't miss. Now he'd put his baby in Maisy's hands. That took trust.

She reached for the phone to check on Iris again but then thought better of it. She was a good enough driver, but she didn't know Bessie like she knew the blueberry. Though there wasn't a whole lot of traffic, the New Jersey Turnpike wasn't known for its leisurely or easy pace. She felt slightly more comfortable with the situation now, comfortable enough not to risk smashing into a guardrail with Eric's car, not that comfort could ever explain the feeling of knowing Iris had run off. Christopher's story checked out. Right now, though she wouldn't admit it to anyone if pressed, she could use some time away from the phone.

The call to Rachel was brief, but it felt like it had spanned years. Maisy caught her just before she dialed the doctor. As he'd predicted, she was sleepy but helpful. She had a kind voice that was laced with a worry Maisy knew too well.

"What's happened to Chris?" Her voice sounded trapped, like no space in the world could give it enough room to fully express the worry held inside.

Maisy was less frantic than before, but the panic in her voice had jolted Rachel out of her sleepy state and shifted her into an alert with which Maisy was all too familiar.

"He's where? Right now?"

Rachel seemed lost not only because she'd just woken up. It had fallen on Maisy to tell this sweet, sleep-addled woman that her husband had left with no warning. In between sniffs she blamed on hay fever, Rachel had corroborated, if not reinforced, Christopher's credibility. He was, in fact, a licensed therapist and a highly published child psychologist with a long list of credentials and a history of charitable work. In a way, she was relieved it was he who found Iris standing panicked at the ferry terminal. Otherwise, there was no relief for Rachel.

"This doesn't make any sense at all. Without him telling me? Why would he do that?" Rachel's voice had shrunk down so low, she sounded as if she were a million miles away, but she wasn't so far from Maisy at all.

Maisy came as close to being calm as she could, once the doc's story had checked out. There wasn't anyone more equipped to be on this journey with Iris, other than her, that is. For that, she was thankful. At the same time, she wanted to lay a beating on the good doctor. Calm was still in the next hemisphere.

Her nerves felt like frayed wire, brittle on the edge of combustion. It wouldn't take much. Eric had developed the habit of referring to Maisy as CIA, which wasn't a bad nickname. It didn't bother her at all. In fact, she even enjoyed it. It would take torture of the third degree to get Maisy to admit she needed help with anything, that there was a problem, or that she didn't have everything there was to have squared away, checked off in a neat little box. She didn't feel squared away. She felt like the Christmas lights hidden in the attic, a knotted mess that had just begun to come undone.

A torrent of things she'd never said out loud flowed like lava. They had little to do with Christopher or the woman who sat on the other end of the phone, what she said would surely have cost her her CIA card had anyone else heard them. Rachel had sat there silently, like a confessor. Maisy had repeated her words like a song. *"Some men aren't built to stay."* She tried to help her close the wound that would hurt for years to come. Rachel's reply was the first to sound free of the hay fever with which she'd been so recently suffering.

"But some men are."

Maisy had only talked to her for a few minutes, but she liked this woman.

She knew her.

Travel

There weren't many people in the world Maisy could say that about, besides Iris. She knew that girl in her heart and soul. Now there was Rachel, this kindred spirit who put on this brave face and pushed through the conversation as if her heart hadn't just been broken. She listened to Maisy like an old, dear friend. Maisy had felt the need to comfort Rachel as much as Rachel had felt the need to comfort Maisy.

Maisy pushed the gas, and Bessie purred under her like a mighty lion. Eric took such care with this car. It was a miracle he'd let her take it. He'd tossed her those keys without her even asking, as if it didn't require a single thought. He'd just ride his motorcycle this weekend. He said it like she never saw him limping on damp days, like she'd forgotten about the accident that had shattered his knees and his football career. He said it like she didn't know him, but she did know Eric, didn't she? He stood by her for years, quiet and, for the most part, unnoticed, taking in her decisions as they unfolded, never once with a word of criticism. Her temper and her lists, they were just things he accepted as given. He was always there for her and Iris. When she was torn apart, he supported her without judgment. In a nutshell, that wall of a man never let her down.

He knew her.

The car shifted gears as she changed lanes, as if to agree.

Chapter 21

Driving

The open road was a thing of beauty and, now that the worst had happened, Chris felt as if he could almost breathe easy. The call from Rachel wasn't ideal. How could it be? He'd left her, after all, and no amount of logic could reconcile that. He hated hearing the sadness in her voice even for the few brief minutes he stayed on the phone. In the long run, all of this was better. It was better to do it now, to rip the Band-Aid off quickly than to let the poor girl suffer for years at his side.

Iris had been quiet since Chuckey's, not in the distant way that meant she'd crept into her own world but in the silent contentment of babies on the verge of deep sleep. She looked out the window with her fingers on the glass, watching trees pass by like green race cars. They'd cracked the windows, so the cool air poured in like water from the storm. He'd forgotten how good that was, not like the artificial candles that reeked of expensive stores and old lady's perfume, but real, fresh rain air. The tires hummed under them, gripping the road like grooves on a record, playing their journey out like music. Maybe this was midlife, but it didn't feel like a crisis. It felt like freedom.

Dave Matthews was talking on the tape about the sky and clouds, a vampy interlude before one of the hits, probably taken at one of those music festivals just before the natives got restless and set fire to all the portable toilets. There was boyish hope in his voice. Dave was Peter Pan. He was free, free to do anything he wanted, with no worries of the pain it may cause his friends.

"Rachel and I wanted to visit every state in the country, back in college. We hit upstate, Pennsylvania, Ohio, and Maryland." He sighed. "We never got to Virginia."

She let his words drift off. Murph had been working with her on letting other people finish their thoughts before talking. She counted beats in her head after someone's last word to make sure she wasn't cutting them off. In this case, she gave Christopher plenty of time because his words were coming more often, and he looked like he needed them, more than she did. When three bumps passed under them breaking the hum of the road into a sweet drum beat, she offered the only wisdom she had.

"We're not in Virginia anymore."

Chris' head felt heavy. "No, we're not."

Driving

The road signs had changed, and the girl was right. These back roads didn't offer much as far as rest stops or lodging, so he could feel the promise to Maisy slipping away. Another letdown he couldn't take. Plus, she'd kill him if they didn't stop soon. He couldn't see camping out in a large parking lot, not with all the bright lights and honking cars amid the gargantuan trucks and midnight people. It was well before dinner, but he'd seen enough *Unsolved Mysteries* to know a truck stop was never an option.

"What did she say?" Iris had broken the silence with words that could cut glass, so he pretended not to be wounded.

"Hmm?"

She narrowed her eyes. "Rachel." Where most people would let the expression go, she held her face there like a mask, waiting for his answer.

"Oh, that. Yes." The casual voice was unwarranted, but still he pressed on. He wore a mask too. "Well, she wasn't excited that I'd gone on this trip. I suppose a note would have helped. You know how it is. Spontaneity." He waved his hand her way forgetting about ten and two. She shuddered with a jolt. "Guess, not." The mood was not light, but he tried to make it so. It was the heaviness he was trying to avoid. The girl looked at him like she could see it there, pressing him into the ground. She would keep poking at the boulder pinning him down until it rolled away or crushed him, but he had to do something.

"Okay, Iris. You said I was weird before, and Maisy said I sounded a little nutty. In a way, you're both right. I'm," he searched for the word, "inconsistent."

There was no better way to describe the ups and downs that had plagued him his whole life, the ones that had intensified so much of late he couldn't breathe. "Rachel needs someone who's going to be even. She deserves that." Iris was still inscrutable but didn't interrupt him at all, which was amazing. She was making great progress. "I became a doctor to help people. I always wanted to help people, especially Rachel."

"So you left?" Iris' eyebrows curled like question marks.

"Iris, do you know what bipolar disorder is?"

"A brain disorder that affects mood function, more than likely attributed to the circuitry in your pre-frontal cortex," she shrugged, like the answer was simple. When she put it that way, it was.

"How do you know that?"

Her face evened and she leaned her head back on her chair, instead of halfway into his seat as she'd done before. "I have to go to therapy once a week, so I know how to 'talk to people' and not get so scared." Her voice went into a droning, annoyed sing-song as if she were repeating an old song. "So I don't climb out onto ledges or drink paint."

He sat up. "Did you drink paint?"

"I did a million and one years ago. Not really. That's hyperbole. Fifth grade, Ronnie Halloway told me it would turn me blue." Her head and voice dipped in embarrassment. "I wanted to be blue." She talked to her lap. "Anyway, I'm there a lot. Maisy comes in with me, most of the time. I read all the pamphlets while we wait for our turn. Everyone's got something, that's what Murph says, and there are a lot of pamphlets that prove it." She ticked off her areas of expertise. "Schizophrenia—that one has the lady sitting in a corner. ADHD—has the boy with the crayon. Eating Disorders—teenage girl. Oppositional Defiance—two kids screaming. You name it, I know it." Her smile was crooked, when she looked back up at him.

He knew those pamphlets. They were stacked in his waiting room exactly where he'd left them. She'd mentioned all the key points verbatim. She didn't mention the obvious. "How can I help any—"

"It's very common." She picked up as her head dropped back to her lap, like the stream of thought had never been disturbed. "There are more than three million cases diagnosed per year in the US alone."

"Yes, but how am I going to be of use to any—"

"Easily treated with medication."

"Iris." He stopped her, and she looked up at him. "I have it." He hadn't said it out loud to anyone, even though he'd known for as long as he could remember. It was why he went into psychology in the first place, to figure out what was wrong.

"What's that got to do with Rachel?"

"How can anyone depend on me when I can't depend on myself?"

Her eyes stopped darting out the window and settled on the tape player between them. Again, she stated words that seemed as plain as the nose on his face.

"I do."

It was that simple. He meant to speak: to thank her for today, for bringing out the best in him, for every moment since he'd seen her at that terminal, but he couldn't.

An oasis had risen up on the horizon. It reared up like water in the desert, just after the bright blue sign welcoming them to North Carolina. From afar, the day-glo letters shone like a nuclear rainbow, even at dusk. It called them to lodging that promised to answer their every vacation wish. A big red arrow told them that in three miles, they would be whisked away to the Tiki Oasis. Christopher held on to hope it wouldn't be the rat trap that it implied.

Chapter 22

Just in Case

It had taken Eric all of 36 seconds to find the fastest route to Iris and the good doctor. He was flummoxed by the cash register at the store and the scientific calculator she used for her classes, but on that phone of his, he was some kind of wizard. In a matter of moments, he'd found a map, taken its picture, and sent it to her phone.

"You just keep it open on the phone, Mais, like a backup, he'd said as she pulled out of the driveway. He talked her through setting the GPS and gave her some last-minute hints on how to use the cruise control and Bessie's driver assist, if she's needed.

"I'll be fine, Eric." She lied. Quite honestly, Maisy was crap for driving. She did all right herself. It was the other people she had to worry about, which she did. She hated variables. On a highway, she was in a sea of them. Maisy wasn't one for texting or net surfing or any of those other things people did while they were staring at the glowing rectangles in their hands. It only took an eighth of a second for catastrophe to strike, especially when the crazies were weaving in and out of lanes with everything from mascara wands to half-eaten sandwiches in their hands. There was no way she was going to wreck Bessie because she was fiddling with a phone.

When it came to devices, Maisy erred on the side of caution, so much so that the screen had flipped off due to inactivity. It was a screensaver, Iris had explained when picking out a set of pictures to occupy the screen when Maisy wasn't dialing or expecting a call. Iris flitted back and forth on the screen, a shot from when she was a little girl playing with a big red balloon on the front lawn. She had a gap between her front teeth that more often than not had some reminder of what she'd just eaten. The screen cycled through a bunch of shots taken on that warm summer day so closely together, the little girl seemed to glide across the screen like a cartoon. It was all well and good to see her there.

"Hey!" She punched at the middle of the steering wheel, a move that in the blueberry would've resulted in an anemic warning, a weak chirping sound that was no more menacing than an irate cricket or an offended butterfly. Bessie, however, was a different animal altogether. On contact, her hand brought from the behemoth a titan's roar that screamed at the offending party and shooed them out of the way. In this case, it was a 1993 Toyota Celica that couldn't decide if it would rather hit a guard rail or Maisy as its driver picked a song to play.

"Do not kill me," she advised through gritted teeth. She peered at the man as she floated past him like a reminder. Then muttered to herself, "That guy is gonna cause a crash."

This is where Iris would chime in. She'd interject random Dave stories at off times just because they were on her mind, or she'd spew out moments in historical Egypt and/or notes on fish species, like she was a fact fountain. It didn't matter what was happening around her. Her voice, always flat, would roll forward in a monotone, like tires on the road. Cars made her nervous, and nervousness brought out the voice that sounded more like a machine. Maisy hadn't heard that voice in a while. Maybe it was because she was in a new state? She didn't recall hearing the robotic voice tell her anything since she had gotten to the ferry.

Suddenly, Maisy felt jittery. She hadn't eaten on the ferry. It was the last thing on her mind, but she should have. Her hands were shaky on the wheel. It was dawning on her that the little lady in the GPS had been mighty shy these past couple of miles. Something was amiss.

There was a button on the steering wheel to check what was going on, so she wouldn't have to fiddle. Eric had shown it off, like a proud papa.

"GPS on." It beeped at her expectantly a little box blinking on the console. "GPS on?" She repeated it slowly and slightly louder than before. She couldn't help but think of travelers abroad screaming slowly into foreign faces as if louder made it more intelligible, but this is no foreign land. This was the realm of Eric and he assured her it would work. "GPS. Are you there? On? GPS ON?" She tapped the button again. "Resume route?" The cursor blinked at her like a puppy. "Route to Florida?" She tapped again. It blinked, blinked, blinked.

She ran through the past few hours in her head, trying to recall the last time she heard the monotone voice that kept the mile markers checked on the map. For the life of her, she couldn't remember. She'd cut the engine for the boat ride. She had to. Did her co-pilot say anything when she departed? She couldn't remember, not that it mattered what happened then. She was stuck now. The cursor blinked happily, awaiting her command. At this point, she'd have more luck if it were a puppy. A puppy, she could cuddle.

Despite her fears, she leaned into the passenger side and pulled the glove box open in search of instructions. Almost immediately, she was reminded of what a poor decision this was. The steering wheel jumped in her hands and a rumble shook the car. Again, she found herself wishing Iris were there.

"Oh." She said apologetically, although to no one. "Didn't see that." She smoothed her hands over the steering wheel like she was comforting a startled child. The surge of adrenaline went right to her hands. They were shaking worse than before, now with the added sheen of sweat.

On the side of the road, she was safe with Bessie turned off, so she leaned back into the passenger seat to pore through the book. There must be something in here. She couldn't very well stare at a cell phone the whole ride down, even if she wanted to. It seemed technology, and she remained at odds. The screensaver stayed stuck with Iris' picture frozen on the screen.

Maisy wasn't like Eric. She didn't look at it as if it were a tool and couldn't navigate through screens as effortlessly as he did. In fact, she was more prone to call it a smart butt than a smartphone. It had mocked her by sending a message to the whole PTA she'd intended just for one. Jokes about the principal looking like a turtle go over more smoothly when addressed to just one person. It had embarrassed her, sending an email via "reply all." Now it had gobbled up the backup map to Iris.

She'd have to pull off the protective cover and pull the stupid battery out. At this rate, she wouldn't get to them until tomorrow.

"Stupid. #$@&%*." The words stuck in her mouth, as she pried the cover away from the phone with a fingernail, half of which was sacrificed to the cover in the process. It flipped up in her hand like a nut popping from a shell, she jumped not because it had done so but because she hadn't expected it to ring.

"Hello?"

"You okay there, Maisy?" The voice wasn't Iris but it calmed her frantic heart just a beat. She attempted not to sound frazzled.

"Are you calling to check up on me? Or the car?" Her intent was to sound cool and collected, but she always had a hard time balancing cool with callous. The words came out with bite.

"Come on." He played it off well but the slight was there just the same. She had to stop doing that. "I wanted to make sure you were okay. How was the ferry? You make it in time?"

"Straight shot down the line. No problem there." She didn't have to try so hard to sound relaxed. Her hands had already stopped feeling clammy. "GPS barely said anything."

"You didn't need your map?"

"Nope."

"Boat was okay?"

She had to pull his baby, a boat in her own right, over the narrow ramp onto the ferry and then zig-zag her through a set of cones of cars to get her set just right. Okay was not precisely how it felt, she lied.

"Smooth sailing." Lied again. Eric let out a noise that sounded like a laugh shoved back inside with a cork.

"Really?" The word hooked up high at the end like it was climbing a rollercoaster. He knew about the storm. He had to. "Weather Bub said there was a pretty good storm. I thought you might've hit some weather."

"You look up what I ate for lunch on that thing too?" Again. She didn't want to bite his head off. In fact, she would've felt a whole lot better if they were talking face to face. Then he'd know, like he always did, how hard this all was for her. Like always, he wouldn't say a thing about it. That way she wouldn't have to explain what happened on the boat, but he wasn't here. He couldn't see the way she tucked her hair behind her ears or how she bit her bottom lip. He couldn't read the "tells" he called her out on, time and time again, so she would have to say something. For that, she could kill him.

"I threw up, okay?"

"What?"

Her voice went quiet and her words were a different animal now, one that lacked claws and bite, one that was meek like a kitten. "I threw up, on the boat. The water was much rougher than I thought it would be."

"Oh, the storm. Should've know you were gonna hit some swells." He said it like that kind of thing was common knowledge. "Weather bot said it was going to be rough until at least this afternoon. Midrange swells. Winds are coming in at 30 mph." There was a pause, and she could tell the big man didn't know what else to say. "Did you make it to…?" He let that hang there like he didn't know how to finish it.

"The bathroom. Yes, but I did grab a barf bag just in case."

After that, everything came at once, all the things she'd never admit to anyone, her trouble navigating, the GPS, "this stupid phone."

He talked her through resetting the lady in the console who, as it turned out, gets a little miffed when she's not turned back on.

"I should've told you that. There's a little button that says resume. See it there on your right?" He was too polite. It was the size of a grown man's thumb. It was red and marked in large while letters that all but screamed at her to RESUME NAVIGATION, her mind was between the voice and the phone, and not hurting someone else's baby.

"Now, what's the problem with the phone?"

"It's not going to be a problem for you. You know everything there is to know about these things. You're Mr. Supernova 8000." She was trying to be playful, but her nerves were showing. "You know, you won't buy yourself new sneakers, and your T-shirt is just about see-through but you have a zillion dollar phone. You eat, sleep, and breathe that thing."

She felt silly and childish, and he knew it.

"The phone, Maisy."

"You're going to think I'm so stupid."

"I'd never think that."

He wouldn't, and he wouldn't bite her head off or criticize her so relentlessly, like she did him.

"Listen, you restart the stupid thing and, in the meantime, I'll find where you're at exactly, and I'll tell you where to look on the map."

"What map?" She took a deep breath before speaking, feeling the frustration fighting to get out of her. "I mean, I just said, the map is gone. The stupid phone is frozen."

Eric's voice had a way of smiling. She could hear it. "Not that map. Is your phone open?"

"Yes, I just cracked open the stupid phone."

"Flip it over."

Wedged in between the phone and its protective cover was a piece of paper folded into a neat square, taped neatly to the back. When she opened it, she saw Eric had printed out her exact driving route, highlighting stops for gas, lodging, and rest breaks.

"Looks like there's only a few places in that area they'll be able to stay. I'll get cracking on the possibilities and see what I find."

"You looked all that up?"

He laughed. "Yes, on my stupid phone."

"Hey, Eric, I'm really sor—"

"Don't worry about it." Eric wasn't one to interrupt, he also wasn't one for things getting all serious either. I thought maybe it would be good to have a backup for all the stuff I sent you."

She flipped the color-coded map and read the words he'd scratched on the back as he said them out loud.

"Just in case."

Maisy's face grew warm and, for once, it wasn't because of stress.

"All right, I gotcha. I pinged your location. "You know you should shut that off."

Eric paused thoughtfully. "I'll show you how when you get back." He had every detail for her. It was like having a co-pilot, even though he was another state away. "There's a place coming up that makes homemade donuts," he said, "Reviews say they make them right there." His voice had the distant sound of a multitasker and, when she listened hard enough, she could hear his fingers tapping the front of his screen.

"Oh, that's new." His voice changed. It became alert suddenly. "This wasn't here this morning."

"What?"

"Video, hang on." Maisy could hear tapping and the muffled sound of playback. "Looks like someone's created a video of this place."

"What is it with these people? Why would someone video themselves eating a donut?" Technology had just helped her get her degree, but it made her head hurt sometimes.

"You're going to want to see it. Trust me."

"Why's that?"

He could feel her anxiety crackling through the phone like electricity. Her voice sounded brittle, threatening to break. It was so different than the voice that drifted up out of his phone like a ghost.

"You know what? Never mind." Eric made an executive decision. "Stupid phone." He'd keep that information classified, for now. "You said you're gonna catch them in North Carolina?"

"Mmm hmmm." She rubbed her eyes in hopes of keeping the migraine that threatened at bay. It pushed against her temples like a swelling storm cloud.

"Okay, so you're close to. Wait a minute. North Carol— Maisy, how fast are you driving?"

The silence of her shame spoke volumes.

He let out a sigh. She could hear him working feverishly all the while crinkled paper and murmuring voices punctuated with the clang of bells let her know he was holding down the fort just fine on his own.

"All right, then it looks like there's a Green Acre Lodge." He was reading out loud. His voice traced the ups and downs of the map he surely followed with his eyes. "That looks like it's closed for renovations and scheduled to open in a few weeks for summer. Here, there's a Penny Landing." He drifted between periods of reading to himself and reporting out loud. "Nope, that's booked. Convention."

"Eric?"

"Yeah?" He tried to keep his voice engaged but she could tell he was still reading.

"You're doing a good job."

His voice leveled and he spoke like there was nothing on earth that could draw his attention away again.

"Thanks, Maisy."

For a second, thunder rumbled in the distance through the sky. Something was brewing, all right.

His voice had changed slightly enough that the customers would never hear it, but Maisy knew him well enough to know his voice was smiling. Maybe it was because he found what he was looking for after all.

"Here we go. Looks like there's only one place they can go."

"Where's that?" Maisy's day brightened just then as the sky broke for the first time.

"Here's this place called The Tiki Oasis."

Chapter 23

Oasis

Chris pulled the blueberry into the large lot lined with gravel the color of sand. The Tiki Oasis lived up to its name, rising up out of an otherwise blank landscape like a dream. It was a strange place to find in the middle of a long country road, at least for him. Iris didn't seem to think so. She pressed her head into the window to see it better, the large hut with palm frond roof, and the miniature out buildings tucked up on the hill, and the long rectangular surf shack boasting the best rack of ribs this side of the Pacific. She pressed so hard against the glass, it left a mark on her forehead when she pulled away.

It was an incongruous place that didn't fit into its surroundings, but even more, seemed to be from some other time. With its palm trees and totem poles, it could be an ancient place, a magical land where medicine men and mystics called to the ocean gods to bring on the rain. The main building was the king, a beast among the smaller huts in the distance. They were covered in palm fronds woven with twine and bits of dune grass, and they varied in color from sandy browns to the deep mahogany of rich wet soil.

Two tall totems flanked the big hut, baring menacing scowls and toothy grins from top to bottom. They weren't merely painted but hand-carved. Their expressions could be seen from a distance because the grooves were cut deep into the wood so they wouldn't wear away.

In front was a neon sign crafted to look like a plank nailed to a two-by-four. It let them know in bright orange letters shaped to look like bamboo that there was room at the inn.

The "beach" covered the length of the property, from the bigger hut across the way to the long rectangular shack that sat off to the side. On the left of the main hut a path was cut into the sand and dotted with round earth-colored stones that were so smooth they looked like water. They reflected the palm trees that lined the way. They reached up a curved hill where six similar but not identical huts—smaller versions of the beast out front—sat side-by-side.

"That's the rooms, I think." Iris bounced on the balls of her feet, crushing gravel beneath her heels and listening to the crunch.

Chris took in the place that was no more an island than it was an oasis and the girl whose eyes darted from small hut to totem pole. The morning had brought so many surprises.

Oasis

"I guess we should check it out."

The door sounded like a ceremonious gong that alerted natives to volcano sacrifices or incoming waves from the Kahuna gods. Iris jumped, not out of fright, but with the excitement of a cat pouncing on a bit of string that catches the light.

A rush of cool air hit them that smelled of tropical getaways and island escapes. Beside them, a floor-to-ceiling fish tank brimmed with the likes of marine life Iris only imagined in the most far-off tropical reefs. Puffers and lionfish promenaded from side-to-side while wisps of silver and tangerine darted between ridges of turquoise and aquamarine coral. There were colors she didn't think existed in nature, not in real life, and they were all here in this perfect tank. The counter was polished to a sheen and looked like the most pristine bamboo. The walls were covered in panels of deep red teak, and ukulele music floated in the small space on the sweet pineapple air. Every detail was covered from the sunset mural behind the desk to the veil of grass that hung in the doorway behind the counter. Someone loved this place enough to take care of the minute details. Iris didn't know her, but she liked Darlene long before she emerged from the grass doorway.

"Welcome to Tiki Oasis, I'm Darlene."

Her voice was high and scratchy like an old record but inviting like an old song. That's what Iris thought of as Darlene wobbled slightly toward the desk, the kind of walk that wasn't quite upright but swayed side-to-side, as if daring gravity to choose a side. She wore a bright flowered shirt with big round buttons up the middle and her hair looked like cotton candy on fire. Her lips were coated in a pink gloss, and they were as plump as the rest of her, not like balloons but like bubble letters that spelled out a greeting.

"You folks. Looking for a cottage for the night?"

Before Chris could speak, Iris had lunged forward thrusting a hand at the woman.

"Your cottages are true to surf hut tradition. Did you use real pili grass? It looks like pili grass on that one cottage. Sugar palm on the other." She turned to Christopher as if just realizing he was still standing there. "Did you notice they're all different, Christopher? They are all different, but similar. Like a pattern." Then she made a pained noise and turned to Darlene, remembering that she too was there. There were too many variables involved with conversations. That's why they were so difficult for Iris sometimes. "Nice to meet you Darlene, I am Iris and this is Christopher." Her words sounded like wooden blocks falling from the sky, the rhythm unpredictable. The tone and volume remained unchanged. Her head was tilted one way as she did the best imitation of eye contact she could muster. Iris tried, because she liked this lady's face, her kind smile, and her pretty fish, but there was a lot going on in this room that made her face start hurting. The smells, lights, and the intricate details of the décor carved lines into her face, like one of the Tiki masks.

"Do y'all like barbecue?" The lady asked and started to say something else before Iris interrupted. "We have our own smoker out at Jack's Sh—"

"We're on our way to the Sugarworth Bake-Off, and we need somewhere to stay. It's really nice here. Do your fish have names? I have a fish at home named Sophie and I miss her. Can I help you feed your fish?"

"Now Iris," Christopher wanted to slow her down, to save Iris that moment of impending awkwardness that would surely come. The girl's eyes had been darting like minnows from the polished countertop to the floor, and her lips stretched and pursed as if they were at odds with each other. He didn't have to worry because, instead of making a strange face or giving the girl an odd look as he feared, Darlene jumped into the conversation as if the ebb and flow of the girl's words were as natural as the flow of the fish in the tank.

"Of course, you can. In fact, they're about due for their dinner." Darlene had a hopeful look about her. Perhaps it was in the way her whole face seemed to sparkle or the fact that she wore the brightest smile Christopher had ever seen, but there was a faint glimmer in her eyes he recognized immediately. It was the look of kindness he saw in the selfless, of understanding he saw in the compassionate.

Maddie had it. Iris had it. Rachel had it. His stomach sank, but he pushed past it.

The woman came out from the desk and, without another word, ushered Iris to the tank against the wall. She was friendly—not in the obligatory way that business owners are friendly. Iris' eyes brightened like candles in the night as she grabbed a pinch of food. Darlene pushed on the rich teak wall next to the tank and a hinge released. She pulled the stool out from within and pushed it toward Iris.

"Neat, huh?"

"I have a fish at home named Sophie. She lives in a one-gallon tank on my dresser, nothing like this, of course, but she's colorful. She looks like she's wearing a dress. Do I just climb up here?"

The kind woman nodded, "Uh huh. Then just pull the latch. Freddie likes to eat first. You're going to want to drop those big flakes."

She dropped them in with a thud, and they splashed on the surface of the water. The lion fish darted to the surface and slurped them down in one sullen gulp.

"He always looks pouty. Don't mind him." The fish flitted away with a flourish. "He acts like he's tough, but he's a big teddy bear."

Iris giggled. "Maisy and I know someone just like that."

"Maisy?" Darlene's tone was friendly and soothing.

"Maisy. My—" Iris had felt just moments before like a lightning bolt was cutting her face in half. This was the feeling she got just before her teeth shredded, the distinct moment she hated when her nerves pulled so tight it felt like her teeth could crack in half, but she didn't feel awful now at all. At least, she knew now it wasn't the case; instead, it was only her nerves making her feel awful, but her nerves felt just fine after only a few moments in this new place. "Maisy is always with me."

Iris didn't know this woman at all, but she was just as at ease with her as Christopher was. On a normal day, this would have driven him to pacing, this small lobby with a virtual stranger and another he'd just met, but today, wasn't normal at all.

Iris stood at the top of the stool, and Darlene handed her handfuls of pellets and flakes for the various types of fish in the tank, stopping at the smallest. When the tiny silver fish had their fill and all the fish were full, she came down the ladder satisfied with a job well done.

This was a silent operation, like the sound had been sucked from the room through a big straw. They smiled and gestured with hands and chins, but not a word was exchanged. Strangely enough, neither party seemed to mind.

Darlene dusted off her hands and helped Iris off the stool. "Bake-Off, huh? What sorts of things do you like to make?" The two walked to the counter as Iris lost a hand to the inside of her bag. She pulled out a bevy of baggies and foil packages wrapped like tight silver bricks. She offered her a saffron butterscotch, the color of warm wet sand, and Darlene looked uncomfortable for the first time.

"Oh, honey, I can't." She sniffed at the candy that smelled like roasted marshmallows and adventure. "I'm watching my figure."

"Watching it do what?" Iris asked without a hint of mockery. Her hand was still extended holding the rest of the candies that Darlene looked at longingly.

"I'm trying not to gain any weight. I've been doing so well, and, you know?"

Iris' eyebrow slowly arched the way it did when she was processing someone's words, applying the tone of their voice to the vocabulary they chose, working to match both with the expression they wore at the time of speaking. It was an exhausting process, but it had been proving successful.

"You are using a figure of speech when you say you're watching your figure, aren't you? Of course you are, because how could your physical shape change in such a short period of time. It couldn't go from round to flat with one candy."

Again, there was no malice in any of her words, and Darlene's reaction was not one of offense but of understanding that outreached the circumstance. Without another word, she took a bite of the candy Christopher had tasted on the ferry, the one that tasted like sunshine and home. By the look on her face, she agreed.

Iris let out a whoop of joy that was almost animal and clapped her hands twice like she was grabbing a large group's attention. Her face pulled tight at the right, as it tended to do when she was excited, but she barely noticed. "Baking is science, and, when you get the balance right, it's just right. Right?"

Darlene's answer was muddled mid-chew but she seemed to agree. Now that the seal was broken, Iris laid an array of delicacies on the smooth counter like she was constructing an exhibit. She floated a palm over them like a game show hostess, with a lopsided smile that could rival the man in the moon's.

"Cardamom meringues with candied orange peel, strawberry tart with pink peppercorn custard. That's balsamic syrup. There's white pepper in the crust."

Darlene's face mirrored Christopher's as she moved from treat to treat, one more delicious than the next. Iris wasn't watching their smiling faces. She was looking at Freddie and his friends in the tank.

"I like to take something that doesn't fit and show the world it can be sweet. Even if it doesn't seem to follow the rules, it can fit, and it can be good."

Darlene wiped a hunk of strawberry from her lip. "It's delicious, Miss Iris. Lovely. Thank you for this."

"Your fish are swimming around like crazy. I think they're happy. They probably like looking at all the neat stuff in here." Her eyes fixed themselves on the silver tails that darted from one side of the tank to the other, moving back and forth until her face felt relaxed and even. She let out a sound like a whispered gasp before speaking again. "You're welcome."

Christopher opened his mouth to speak. It had become a habit for him to become a moderator, to talk over silences, like he was conducting an interview, but, when he did so, Darlene held up a waiting hand as if in anticipation of his words. She stood patiently, pink nail polish catching the gleam of the coconut lamp that hung overhead, and waited there until Iris spoke again.

"I have trouble with that." She explained, her voice jumping from loud to soft. "Conversations with people." She spoke those words as if they'd been taught to her or, at least, repeated in practice. "Everyday things people talk about and what they say when it's their turn. I have a whole list written down that I memorized, because, when I try to figure it out, my head hurts." She had let her eyes settle like flower petals on the counter set out with her treats. She looked up to add. "Thank you's and you're welcomes still give me a bit of trouble."

All Darlene could do was smile.

"Miss Iris, there's someone I'd really like you to meet."

Chapter 24

Check In

"First things first, you all need a room."

"Two." Chris cleared his throat correcting, "Two rooms." Darlene leaned her head back like there was something on the ceiling she'd really like to read.

"Oh, no, honey. We have *room*, available. *Room*." She repeated, turning her eyes from above and back to him. "Didn't you see the sign? The "s" isn't lit up.

Christopher sucked in air the way he did when he walked into the end table and stubbed his toe.

"Oh, it should be fine." She rustled papers next to the computer console, hidden in a box that looked like it had washed up on a beach. "The Kahuna Cottage. That's what's left after Mrs. Winters, that's one." She scanned and read half to herself following the screen with her finger. "2, 6, and 7. And the convention. Yes, the Kahuna. Number 6. Has two beds. Ironing board. Hula girl night stand. Grass woven throw rug. Volcano lamp. And, two beds. For you and your daughter." She grew pleased with herself detailing the nuts and bolts of the newest cottage the Oasis had to offer, but the man on the other side of the counter didn't seem so impressed. "What's the matter? Don't you like Hawaii?"

Iris jumped in. She liked this lady already and, more so, upon hearing the intricate details that weren't spared. "He's not my father."

"Is that right?" Darlene shot Christopher a terrible look on instinct, taking in Iris' beautiful features and childlike demeanor. Her face went instantly toxic.

"It's not what you think," Chris caught the evil eye and worked to reverse its polarity.

"Maisy knows he's with me. Dr. Chris is helping me get to my contest." She pawed under her hat, grabbing a thick clump of hair. "I don't think I'd do so well on my own." Her eyes fell to her feet, in search of something more comfortable to watch. "I kind of left without telling Maisy I was going." Darlene's eyebrow was raised, but she softened when she took in the girl who fidgeted on her feet and bit at her fingers. "She's on her way to meet us." Iris had half of her thumb knuckle wedged between her upper and lower teeth, so her words were muddled. Even so, Darlene heard every one of them.

"I didn't think I'd need this much help."

Darlene's face was so soft. It looked like flower petals, but Iris looked down at her boots.

"I'm not a bad person. And Christopher's not a weirdo." She pulled her finger from her mouth and looked at the fiery red cotton candy that crowned Darlene's head. "I just really want to bake."

"I'm just here to help." Christopher added, realizing he could make this easier. "You know, I can just stay in the car. If you don't mind, Iris?"

"Why would I mind that?"

"Right, exactly, so one room. 'Cottage,' that is. The Kahuna," he pandered. "For Iris."

Darlene's face beamed. She fancied herself a keen judge of character to the point of annoying friends and family with boasts of having 'the second sight.' She had a feeling this guy was all right. Iris, with her familiar face and her quirky way, she just knew. She felt like she knew the girl already.

"That'll do just fine."

"You can just run this." Chris peeled his credit card from his pocket, and Darlene's face crunched up like she'd tasted sour grapes.

"Oh, no. We don't have one of those." She held up her hand as if he were trying to hand her a skunk. "Our connection is down." By that, she meant the machine had broken two summers back and, without great need for it, she and Jack had spent the money on more pressing issues, like authentic Tiki masks and a smokehouse.

"That's okay." Iris leaned forward, hand elbow-deep in her bag. She pulled out a fat envelope stuffed full with bills and clinking change marked clearly in black marker *"Sleep on the Way Money."* "I have money, Christopher. I can pay."

Darlene shot Christopher another sour look and took the envelope from Iris.

"It's $88 for the night."

Iris looked to the side, mouth moving as she counted. "Well, I have $202 in there, so that's plenty."

Darlene sifted through the bills, some crumpled, some wet from the storm, some drawn on with a marker, big numbers marking the count Iris had no doubt done dozens of times. She straightened the pile, mostly ones, and her voice went smooth as butter and soft like first snow.

"Iris. What's that you said you had in here, dear?"

The girl's voice went automatic and spat the number out in three monotone beats. "202."

Darlene's look to Christopher was one he understood immediately. If Iris could read faces, the exchange would have made her face go tense. Instead, she tapped her foot happily, which made what Darlene had to say worse.

"You've got 22 here, honey."

Numbers made Iris nervous when they belonged to patterns she didn't see. Dollar patterns, with their tens and twenties and fives always gummed up in her head. They made her hands sweat, and her face feel spacey.

"Oh." she said. Tens and hundreds were always tough. "Right." Her gaze jumped away and then remained on the counter just in front of the envelope. Her hands retreated to the inside of her hat where they felt safe. "I miscounted." Iris started rifling through her bag, pulling out slips of paper, notes she'd written to herself, and a pair of crumpled socks.

The girl's eyes looked like warm brown sugar about to bubble over the pot.

Darlene sucked in a breath and smoothed a stray hair from her face. When she exhaled, she brought peace of mind to the girl with the familiar face who seemed to tap dance from one foot to the other.

"Iris, why don't we do this?"

"Do what?" Iris felt like there was molten lava beneath her skin, and it was about to crack wide open.

"I propose a deal to you. Would that be all right?" Iris' one eyebrow climbed high on her forehead like it intended to escape, but she remained focused on Darlene as she spoke. "I'll give you a room for tonight for say, 22 bucks."

"I have 22 bucks." She interrupted excitedly, but even so, Darlene's voice kept the same steady level.

"I give you the room for 22 bucks, but you have to work for me tonight back at the Shack."

"The Shack?" Christopher had seen enough scary movies in his life to sound alarmed.

"Jack's Shack." Darlene prompted. "Out back? The one with the surfboards? Our restaurant. It's not too, too busy this time of year, and with the convention, it'll be pretty jumpin' tonight." Her voice was a mix of urging and pride.

"We got a big ole' smoker last year, and Jack, well, he just loves doing up some briskets and pork." She ticked off the numbers on her round fingers. "Chicken. Sometimes we even get gator."

"It's a barbecue place?" Iris' voice was at partial shout, so the question came out like a half-baked statement of fact.

"That's right. We got a love band. Folks do some dancing and some good eating. You come around to the Shack and show my hubby some of your tricks."

"I don't do magic." She'd been working on not taking things literally. Murph told her to make a mind picture of all the things a phrase could mean. It was exhausting sometimes, but she tried. "I don't play music." She corrected, and her eyebrow furrowed.

"Not those kind of tricks, honey. I'm thinking maybe you can cook up one of those special desserts?"

Iris bounced on the balls of her feet, and her smile grew wide.

Darlene looked thoughtful. "And I'll pay you 72 bucks. We can take the room outta that. How'd that be?"

Iris froze in place, eyes wide, mouth barely moving and then she spoke rapidly, repeating what Darlene said to Christopher, as if he hadn't been standing there.

"Darlene, you're going to pay *me*? 40?" Her mouth moved and her finger danced in the air counting on an invisible abacus. "No." She pantomimed a number she'd forgotten to carry in her calculation. "50 bucks?"

"That sounds about right. Did you want more?"

Iris wasn't good at affection. In fact, she hated it most of the time, but she lunged across the counter and stiffly grabbed Darlene in the closest imitation of a hug she could muster.

"So when do I start?"

"Right now, if you like. I told you, there's someone I want you to meet."

Chapter 25

Ryan

"You're welcome to come get some dinner too, Christopher, if you like? You want to check out the band? We've got some beers on tap."

The prospect of beer and barbecue was tempting, but there was a pressing issue at hand, more so at his feet. "That sounds great, really, but if you don't mind I'd like to wash up a little. Iris, do you mind or do you want to go first?"

"No!" She hadn't intended to shout, but the word had come out in a scream. "I." She took a breath through her nose like she practiced, settling the panic that welled in her stomach, which had climbed up her throat. "No. Thanks. You can take the first shower." Or any shower if he wanted, so long as it meant she didn't have to. "You go on. Enjoy it." The smile crept halfway up her face and was one of her more unconvincing attempts, but it didn't matter. Christopher was too excited about soaking his feet to question it. He grabbed the pineapple key ring and went trotting up the path to Kahuna. Hut number 6, as she and Darlene spilt off in the other direction.

The path to Jack's Shack was lined with found surf items, bars of surf wax, and leashes. They were spaced perfectly along both sides but sat casually enough to give the impression they were dropped by hungry surfers heading for some grub.

Darlene had passed the pair of sunglasses and flip flops before she remembered.

"Honey, you think you can give me a hand with that sign?" She looked over her shoulder at the words *ROOM AVAILABLE* and motioned to Iris, who went running to it without question. She had wanted to see it up close. Iris moved toward Darlene awaiting instruction.

"See that down there? There's that rock leaning up against the post?"

Iris touched it with her foot, but it didn't wiggle. It was solid, like a boulder, even though it was the size of a softball. "Uh, huh."

"That's not a rock. Just feel around the bottom and pop it open."

Iris was a spy. She crouched down and laid her hand on the cool, smooth stone. It felt warm in the middle, like there was fire inside or magic. Along the bottom was a ridge that gave beneath her fingers with a pop, like a chip can. A spring-loaded door revealed a collection of glowing buttons worthy of any space ship. One controlled the 's' she and Christopher had overlooked, while another controlled the rest of the sign. There was another for effects, and one that controlled how bright the lights could shine. It was a marvel she found hypnotizing.

"Can you shut off the rooms, honey? Just keep the one on with our name?" There were some missteps, where it seemed like Iris was playing her favorite waiting room game again, pressing lights and turning them back on in rhythm, but, then, she got it, after all. "Like that. There you go, dear. Thank you."

Iris caught up to Darlene on the path after shutting the secret rock up tight. She wore a grin that took up her whole face.

"Thought you might like that," Darlene grinned.

Iris smiled for the next twenty yards until the surf shack popped up before them. Darlene didn't say a word to prompt her to move along, when she stopped at each and every piece of decoration marking the way. She didn't flinch, when Iris picked up the shell from where it sat to hold next to her ear.

"You're good at this," Iris said.

"At what?"

She put the shell down after a few seconds, satisfied no mermaids would be calling today. "Not getting annoyed with me."

Darlene smiled and took a breath to speak, but Iris cut her off.

"Why?"

She helped the young girl to her feet and brushed the sand off her knee as they climbed the two rickety steps that marked the entrance to Jack's Shack.

"Let's get you inside."

Spiced air floated on the sweet strains of guitars that swelled in her ears. To most people, it was just the noisy sound of tuning up, different notes that collided in the air like fighter pilots, but to Iris, each note was its own song building into a symphony. The bass bellowed a hearty cry, and the saxophone answered like a lost love. The floors and tables looked like driftwood, weathered to a sleepy gray brown. The panels on the wall were the same but covered in travel posters: Fiji and Costa Rica, California and Cocoa Beach. Big fans, like the one in the lobby, wobbled overhead, but they didn't frighten her like giant bugs. They were octopuses and squid, playing songs for sirens and the merfolk of the sea.

"This is awesome." She spun in a slow circle taking in her surroundings. The floor gave a hollow echo under her feet, even amid the stray sounds that came from the stage.

"We're just gearing up. Wait 'til you see this place in a few hours. Come this way," Darlene urged, reaching out her hand. Iris didn't grab it, but held her hand within inches as they headed toward a big swinging door with a circle at the top like a porthole.

Ryan

"It's like a pirate ship," Iris spoke excitedly. "You guys thought of everything."

"If you like that, wait 'til you see this." Darlene smiled as the door swallowed Iris and brought her to something she could never imagine.

In the commercials on TV, the kitchens sparkled like they were touched up with the special effects software Iris used to make her driver's license and movies about her fish. This place was real life and put those places in the commercials to shame. Metal counters gleamed so brightly they reflected shelves stacked with fresh fruits, canned jams, and jellies. The walls were white tile scrubbed to a shine, like a thousand pearls. She was hit with the scent of baking bread and freshly picked herbs from a garden.

Darlene ushered her back behind the line where a tall thin man with skin the color of cinnamon was chopping a mix of mint and parsley so fine they looked like soft powder. He whistled casually as he moved the blade with surgical precision.

"Jack, honey. Jack." It had taken a few calls to get his attention. He was an artist engrossed in his work. "Jack!" She startled him, which caused him to drop the blade, so Iris couldn't help but laugh. She drew her hand up in front of her mouth to catch the giggles.

"This is Iris, Jack. She's a dessert expert. She's going to help you out today if you don't mind."

"Well, what do you know about that?" The man quickly picked up his blade and placed it in the sink, wiped his hands on his apron, and lunged forward with all the smiles of an old friend or relative. He grabbed Iris' hand and shook it. She stiffened, as was usual, but he, unlike most people, continued completely unaffected.

"It's really nice to meet you, Iris. Really nice. I can use some help back here, you know?" He had smooth skin and straight white teeth that seemed right at home in the room that looked like a big old pearl. "I got Hudson, over there. He helps with all the heavy lifting. Hey, Hudson!" He called down the line to a stout man peeling sweet potatoes, who looked up, nodded, and went right back to work. "As you can see, Mr. Hudson loves his work." He looked down to the opposite end of the line where the rolls were kept in a big warming drawer. She hadn't noticed the chair sitting there when she was on the other side. "There's Ryan, o' course. Hey, Ry! Say hello!"

Darlene touched Iris' elbow ever so slightly, not enough to cause her to jump, just enough to walk her down to the young man at the end of the kitchen. He was a slouchy, young man, heavier than the average boy in her high school, but about the same age.

"This is my nephew, Ryan." Darlene's eyes brimmed with something. Iris couldn't tell if they were tears or the sparkles reflecting back off the counter. The boy's eyes remained focused on the rectangle in his hands. "His mom, well his mom, struggled. He lives with us." Darlene lifted her hand as if to tussle his floppy hair, but, instead, she held it there just above his head. It fell in a wave across his forehead, hair the color of sand at sunrise, flecks of yellow mixing with light brown. With his sky-blue shirt and that mussed hair, he looked like he belonged on a beach somewhere.

The lights of the tablet spread colors across his cheeks.

"He don't talk much. But he's got buttons on the tablet, so he can say what's on his mind. He loves his electronics." She watched the boy move his hands feverishly over the screen.

"He's the one wired that sign." Darlene swelled like a mother hen. "He does all the sound for the bands." She forgot herself and rested her hand on his shoulder, immediately realizing what she'd done, pulling it away with a snap. "He just likes things a little different." She made a sound that was half sigh, bringing her hands together under her chin so she'd have something to do with them that wouldn't throw the boy off. "You know what I mean, Iris?"

Iris looked at Ryan and at Darlene, who fought every urge to hug or touch him. Iris had such a hard time talking with most people, but this had been a different day from the start.

"I understand."

Iris moved to Ryan's side, giving him a good two feet of personal space and dipped her head into his field of vision so she looked like a velociraptor eyeing its prey. She did her best to use her introducing voice. Murph told her to dip her voice up and down and to make her voice soft without whispering and loud enough to be heard without shouting.

"Hello Ryan, I'm Iris. Iris Rose Cecelia Heller. I'm glad to meet you." The hair hanging in his face made it easier. She didn't have to pretend to look into his eyes. She could see them, like two shards of ice behind the sandy curtain. The boy, with one look at her, did something Darlene never expected him to do.

He looked up from his tablet and smiled.

"Would you look at that?" Darlene was trying not to speak loudly. Iris knew what this sounded like, but she was doing a terrible job of it. Her first word was spoken like she was on a rollercoaster, and then she caught the other ones and tried to make them sound like they were spoken somewhere else, like a department store. Iris did that all the time. She was better at it than Darlene. The older woman sounded like she was trying to stuff a jack-in-the-box back down in a container that was too small. Nevertheless, she seemed happy, and Iris liked it when she smiled. Her cheeks looked like cartoon apples.

Ryan was the least impressed by the exchange. His eyes had drifted back to his tablet, fingers floating over the screen, dipping and touching the surface like mosquitoes.

"Now that you've all met, I'll go check on the front of the house." She was expecting a nice little rush with the convention and all. Iris was still attempting to appear casual, but her smile bubbled over her lips as she darted from the room on bouncy heels.

"So kid, wash up. Take this." Jack threw her what looked like a grass skirt and coconut bikini. "We got them made special. Try it on."

The apron was printed with a hula girl in front, so she looked like an island maiden. She giggled to see the tall slip of a man put on the male counterpart. His spindly arms jutted out from the musclebound apron like pipe cleaners.

"What's that you're making?"

"I got some chicken here for tonight's special." He chopped the meat into hunks sprinkling salt over the pieces and setting them aside. A startled noise came from the other side of the room. "It's okay, Ry-Ry, I'm almost done, okay?" He spoke soothingly to the boy on the tablet, who until now, had remained so quiet Iris had forgotten he was there. "He doesn't like the sound." Jack moved slowly on the next attempt so the boy had more time to prepare for the sound he hated. "One more Ry, and then it's done." He was soothing and patient and seemed so much like someone Iris knew already.

"There, see? All done." Jack washed up and pulled over a thick gray tub filled with a sweet-smelling brown goo. "In here, I've got brown sugar, garlic, and salt." He rubbed at the salt and pepper whiskers on his chin. "Vinegar. My secret spices. What's this here, sauce?" He tilted the

Worcestershire at her with a playful smile. His eyes lit up looking down into the tub at the magical brew. "All the good things that make my chicken happy."

He got a devilish look on his face and reached under the counter, pulling up a jug of spiced rum that was larger than the average toddler.

"It's like I say all the time. If you can put it in a drink, I can put it in my chicken. I get that bird all kinds of boozy."

"Rum? Like the pirates drink?"

He had a scratchy laugh that shook his body when it got going. "That's right. Yeah! I like that. We're gonna call this Pirate Chicken." He poured a quarter of the bottle into the tub, giving it a stir with a heavy wood spoon, and sniffed it, still unsatisfied. He stood thoughtful for a moment and disappeared to the back without a word.

Ryan sat at the other end of the kitchen as silent as before, but his eyes weren't as firmly glued to his tablet. They watched carefully. Every moment or so, he lifted his eyes to Iris, where they stayed until he realized she was looking.

"You like cooking? You don't like the noise, right?" Iris, asked the boy, not expecting a reply. She didn't mind. It made it easier to know when to talk and when to listen. "I like baking but not the numbers. A lot of people think they're the same, with all the measurements and all, but they're not really. Not if you find a way around it." Her eyes searched the kitchen. There were stacks of clean dishes on shelves and enough ingredients here to make a masterpiece.

Ryan

"Baking makes my mind gentle." She approached him slowly, as she would anyone, but, unlike most people, Ryan didn't look at her strangely when she did so. "There's not much to figure out, so long as you don't get gummed up in the numbers. It's science. You like science?" He looked up just then, and Iris didn't make a big deal out of it, because to Iris it wasn't.

"I thought so." She grabbed a few stray dishes that sat stacked on the metal shelves on the wall, some plates, a tall glass, and a long narrow boat that was used for dips and gravies. "What I do is I look. I can see a half or a whole. That's easy." She filled the different cups halfway up and three quarters, some with just a drop or two. "I find a way around the thing that makes me upset."

Iris had been humming as she clinked glasses side-by-side comparing the contents she filled. "When I cook it's about proportions. How things stack up."

Ryan hadn't looked back down at his tablet for the last minute. His eyes remained on the girl in the funny hat, the one who liked to sing.

And then she had an idea.

"You like making things, right?"

The boy didn't answer, but his eyes hadn't left hers either.

Iris took a large serving plate, turned it upside down, and from there, she stacked a collection of cups, saucers, gravy boats, and dishes until they sat balanced in a large tower. She topped it with a stout coffee mug that looked like a pineapple.

Ryan had given up on his tablet. He'd flipped it toward Iris so it could see what she did next.

She filled a pitcher with water and grabbed an empty vegetable crate she pulled over so she could climb to the tower's peak. Then she filled the pineapple slowly, and the water trickled down like a fountain. She tapped her fingers on the table, and they made a noise similar to the one Jack had made with the chicken, but it didn't upset the boy anymore. She played a soft rhythm to which she hummed as the water dripped from plate to cup like a fountain.

Jack returned with a jug of pineapple juice and a can of coconut milk. He thought the piña colada Pirate Chicken would be the big surprise of the day. But in the kitchen, the girl stood singing a song, and Ryan was moving his feet, swaying his tablet, like it was a musical instrument.

He dared not interrupt. He backed out of the room and waved to Darlene, whose eyes sparkled more than usual when she took in the sight.

Iris' voice rose and dipped as she refilled the cup again and again. Ryan's eyes grew bright, smile widening in recognition.

Darlene moved in closer to the boy but dared not take his hand. She let her hand drift close enough so he knew she was there and then retreated, leaving it on the back of the chair she'd assumed he'd return to, when the song was done.

Ryan

Ryan didn't sink back into the seat. His eyes drifted from Iris and down to his tablet as his fingers searched for the phrase he wanted to say. He tapped one but changed his mind. Then another. It wouldn't do.

Ryan looked up in what Darlene assumed was frustration.

"What is it, honey?"

He looked at his tablet and then back at the girl with the funny hat, the one who loved to sing, and did what no one thought he'd do. Ryan spoke.

"Angel."

Chapter 26

Maisy's Drive

Maisy's eyes felt bleary, sticky and half-shut from the lack of sleep and stress. She'd been running around like a madwoman and had forgotten to eat or drink anything but a few sips of coffee at the last pee break. It was easier now driving because of the route Eric mapped out. By now, she was confident enough in the GPS and her backup map to loosen her grip on the steering wheel. Her knuckles were still sore from the first few hours on the road. What she lacked in navigation, she made up for with speed.

She smiled to herself as she passed a sign beckoning travelers to visit Virginia Beach. If Iris were in the car, she'd be popping out Dave facts like bubbles. It was hard to know what you were going to get on a long car ride with Iris. Sometimes it was silence or quiet humming. Other times, it could be bouts of car sickness so violent Maisy had to stop driving. *She brought the tape player. She should be fine.* Worrying wasn't going to make her get there any faster. She needed to get on with it and keep moving forward. It was the only way.

If only her bladder understood that.

She'd have to stop again, whether she liked it or not. There wasn't much choice as to where. These Chuckey stores seemed to be everywhere. Though she'd give her left big toe for a large, double organic blended mocha from Queequeg's, this country catch-all would have to do. Plus, it might be nice not to spend six dollars on a cup of coffee.

Maisy made sure the emergency brake was on, turned the car off and got out. She hit the keychain twice. It beeped and turned Bessie's alarm on, then she checked and double-checked to make sure the doors were locked. It didn't seem like the kind of place where your car would get lifted, but she could never be too safe. For a late afternoon, the place was jumping, filled with pickup trucks and small sedans, teenagers who were just getting out of school, and tourists picking up cheap Hawaiian shirts and souvenirs. There were racks of them in the front and sundries for weary travelers, none of which piqued her interest. It was the smell that wafted toward her from the side that lifted her chin like a ghost hand in an old cartoon.

"Coffee."

There wasn't much as far as choice. Here it was Caff or DeCaf, but it was surprisingly fine with her. She filled the largest cup they had and went over the list of things rolling through her head like closing credits. *Eric will feed the fish. Dr. Chris is a trained professional. Not a serial killer. Not a serial killer.* It was like the loop had gotten stuck and she dared not move it along because every other item on her worry list was even more frightening than that.

This morning there had only been one item on the list. *What if Iris ran away?* After all, it had always been the biggest worry in Maisy's life, except the wave of blind panic that could strike at any moment, and send Iris running into oncoming traffic, or a ledge, or to the center of a train track, frozen in fear. These were the thoughts that kept Maisy up at night. They cinched her insides so she didn't want to eat, and they kept her as close to home as possible on any given day. Iris hadn't had a panic attack in some time, but that didn't mean the threat wasn't always lurking under the surface. *What if it happened now and she wasn't there?* As hard as she tried to put the thought out of her mind, it chilled Maisy, despite the hot coffee scalding her mouth. When Iris panicked, she took off like a deer, swiftly and without warning, with no real clue as to where she would go. Maisy was always there to find her, but what could she do from here?

Most of the time, she felt like she was trying to be superhuman. This, if any occasion required her to do more than try. This was a DEFCON 1, and Maisy was still a state away.

The best she could do was get through here as quickly as possible, but there was a long road ahead, and as soon as the coffee hit her stomach, a slow churning grumble reminded her it was important for regular human beings to eat.

The counter in back was lined with pictures of "famous" ham sandwiches and salty looking French fries cooked deep golden brown. Maisy's stomach roared when hit with the combination of images and smells, so she took her place behind an older gentlemen who seemed torn between a side of coleslaw or mashed potatoes.

This was the kind of decision that could cripple Iris. They practiced at home lining up dishes on the table. Iris would stand on one side, Maisy on the other, with a handwritten menu taped to the refrigerator. Even when the choices were slim, it could take Iris an hour to decide what condiments should go on her burger or what toppings would look best on her hot dog. Choosing the perfect side dish could be agonizing for her, who loved details as much as she loved her fish, her family, and Dave. They'd learned to be prepared for any decision. On the off chance that they'd ever travel, Maisy would spend weeks looking up places on the way to their destination. She'd find menus and stops along the way, so there were no surprises. They'd prepare together for the possible choices Iris would face, but now she was doing it alone. Maisy's jaw clenched on one side. She could feel the vein on her forehead pulsing in time to the twitch that plagued her when she had little sleep and less food in her belly.

She did what she practiced with Iris. She opened her mouth slightly like she was deep in thought and took a long breath that she held. She waited two ticks to let it out her nose, trying to get her nerves under control. It was so hard. Everywhere she looked, she saw things that could potentially send Iris into a tizzy. These stores dotted the highway like pimples on a gangly teenager. There was so much going on here. There were loud Hawaiian shirts hanging in clumps, and noisy wind chimes that looked like flying pigs. There were sparkly visors and hats, windbreakers that swished when touched, and the smell of this food was intoxicating, not to mention the sounds. The girls behind her were like two chattering myna birds, chatting and giggling about something that became a steady rhythm of repeated phrases: *Look* and *OMG*, as they stared down at their phones. In a way, she was relieved that Iris was one of the few kids in existence not tethered to a device in some way. Were they pumping music through a sound system now? She swore she could hear Iris singing along to this music.

"What'll it be, ma'am?"

The man behind the counter was a kindly man in a white apron and matching paper hat.

"Um, I'm sorry?" She wasn't prepared. The menu was an extensive list of sandwiches and platters prepared to order, at which she had neglected to look. "I'll have, um."

The girls had gone quiet so she could think. "Just a special, please."

"On the side."

"Whatever is fine."

The music lifted up now so that it was clear, a bell-like clanking and a familiar beat. It sounded like Dave, and then a voice rose up beyond it like an angel over the clouds that sounded like heaven.

It was Iris'.

Chapter 27

Floozy

Chris felt the day peel off of him under the hot water, stress running down the drain. For now, he wouldn't think about Rachel or the sound of her voice, or Sasquatch. He could hear the big lug in the background when she called. She said his name, and the dog came running to the phone sniffing like he could lick his "daddy" through the phone.

He couldn't think about this right now, so he wouldn't. Instead, he watched the soapy water swirl at his feet, and he thought about barbecue and a cold beer. He had to take those stupid pills on a full stomach. At least now, he could fill it with something good, and he wouldn't have to hide where no one could see.

Shame crept up his back like a chill, but he chased it away with steamy spray. It was for the best.

Toweled and fresh, he was a new man. The shadow of this morning was at his back, so he pushed ahead to the sounds of blues and the smell of smoked ribs that floated off Jack's Shack in a silvery ribbon.

Inside, the place was jumping. It had been empty when he'd gone to the hut. He didn't think he'd been gone for so long, but, when he looked at his watch, he saw he'd in fact, been in there for an hour. The dreaded *hour shower*. That's what Rachel called it when he did that. He'd go to hide there when he got overwhelmed or felt tension mounting. When he didn't want her to see him at his worst, he'd retreat to the running water where he could sort things out for himself. He'd come out with his fingers like prunes. Whatever discussion they were having would be long over. He always denied the shower was his thing, but deep down he knew the power of the hour shower was real, and so did Rachel.

He could barely see the cut of the wood floors as patrons and servers shuffled from table to table. The music swelled on ribbons of smokehouse air that breezed from the back kitchen to the front of the house. Darlene beamed at him from the hostess stand, making her way through a gaggle of sporting goods salesmen who wore funny hats and T-shirts with silly sayings about fish and game.

"This convention is something else, Doc," she said patting Christopher on the shoulder. "Thought we lost you for a while there."

The woman was pleasant before, but now her spirits were so high, they seemed to glow from within like someone had turned on a lamp inside.

"Wait 'til you see what Iris has got," she said, holding his elbow and bringing him to a wooden booth near the wall.

"The place is packed." He nodded to the crowded bar, where a woman with golden hair and glossy lips nodded back, mistaking the gesture for a hello.

"We get a lot of new," Darlene started taking note of the lady who eyed him like a steak, "bodies, this time of year. Conventions, end of school. Lots of folks traveling to Happy World." She fixed a menu in front of him, moving her eyes from the bar to his left hand.

"You going to be okay, Doc?"

One of Rachel's biggest complaints about him, besides his badly timed sense of humor, was his ability to be oblivious to the world around him.

"I think so. The ribs look great. Can I get some ribs, Darlene?" He flattened his menu out and spread the napkin on his lap, feeling more at ease by the second.

"Sure, and to drink?"

"How about a beer?"

Darlene was well practiced and proud of their collection of craft brews. The Shack boasted the biggest selection in the county.

"We've got Big Bear, Kahuna Brew (made just for us,) also..."

As she rattled off the list, Chris' eyes drifted to the bar where the impressive taps lined the back wall. This time, there was no mistaking the lady with the golden hair and the cropped shirt, who practically leaned off her stool to see the handsome doctor.

"You know, what? I'll go get it myself, Darlene. Thanks."

When Iris was sure her masterpiece was complete, she got Jack's blessing to join the hungry crowd out front. She saluted Ryan with a half-bow, and he returned the gesture with the hint of a smile. Out front, the place had filled up and the sweet smell of tonight's Pirate Chicken added to the tropical atmosphere. With the mix of muscular sporting goods people and long-haired rock and rollers the place could have passed for Tortuga, rich with swashbucklers and buccaneers. The band was jamming and women at the bar swayed like palm trees to the beat. A few families with small children feasted on messy ribs and burgers. There at the far corner, across from the bar, Christopher sat alone with a tall drink.

"Is that beer?" Iris' voice rose loud over the music, much louder than it needed to be.

"It is in—"

"I didn't know this was a beer shop." The words shot like loud monotone bullets.

"Deed." He finished with a sip, crisp with a hint of coconut. The Kahuna Brew was as refreshing as it sounded. "A lot of restaurants serve beer, Iris."

"It's poison, you know."

Floozy

He leaned back and stretched his hands, rubbing his face, before leaning toward the girl in the booth. He would have said something, if he'd gotten the chance.

"That's why you get drunk. It's your body telling you it's been poisoned. That's why you get sick if you drink too much. Did you know that?"

She stared at his drink like it was going to bite her.

"I assure you, Iris, I'm not going to drink enough to get sick."

"Then why do you drink it?"

"Hmm. Well, for one it tastes good."

"Nope." She clarified.

"Well, it tastes good to me. And it helps." He weighed his words carefully. "Some people relax a little."

She still looked horrified.

"I promise you, Iris, I won't get poisoned."

That seemed to placate Iris, as she settled down across from him.

"We cooked up something special. I think you're going to like it." She looked proud, smiling ear to ear, leaning her chin on her hands, content to listen to the music, picking on the homemade chips and pickles on the table.

"Why do you keep looking over there?"

His eyes had drifted to his new friend at the bar, who had picked a cherry from her drink.

"Looking where?"

"There." Iris' eyebrow lifted. "At that lady, the one eating that cherry all weird."

"Oh, that's just someone I was chatting with at the bar. I think her name is Suzie. She comes here on Thursday to hear the band. I th—"

"You want to sideways kiss her?"

"What?"

Iris regarded him warily, one eyebrow arched sharply. "I know how that stuff works. I see you looking over there. She's dressed weird, with her belly button sticking out of her shorts, and she's eating that cherry like she's trying to tie a knot in it while she's staring over here. That means she wants to sideways kiss you." She leaned forward, and there was accusation in her lowered voice.

"Do you want to sideways kiss *her*?"

She was attractive. There was no doubt about that, and she definitely was not averse to the prospect of kissing him. She had made that very clear. She was a bit too giggly for his taste, and there was also the matter of much greater importance.

"What about Rachel?"

Christopher tipped his head back and his beer with it, sighing heavily. He was relieved to see Darlene coming with a large tray brimming with food. She laid a bowl of cornbread and biscuits down, which slid on the glossy table as if it were on an air hockey rink, until it rested in the center.

Floozy

"It's all in the wrist," she smiled, Iris looking on in admiration. As quickly as she smiled, she'd returned to giving the look to the man who sat in front of her.

"What's this all about?" Darlene spoke, as she piled ribs, brisket, and every side on the menu between them, ending with a big bowl of the Pirate Chicken for them to share. Chunks of pineapple peeked out of the bowl laden with hunks of golden chicken covered in sweet, sticky sauce.

Before he could speak, Iris had crossed, uncrossed, and re-crossed her arms before interrupting him yet again.

"Christopher likes that lady."

Darlene clucked her teeth and kept him focused on the sights of the dirty look he'd gotten used to.

"Before you can say anything, I do not like that lady." He felt like he was in seventh grade. "We were just talking."

"Suzie, over there?" Darlene craned her neck. "She talks to a lot of fellas here, Doc. Watch yourself."

"I assure you. I'm not interested."

She straightened their plates with the hint of a smile.

"Really. We were just talking. I'm not interested in that."

"I'm not saying you are, but either way, be careful, " she repeated. "You're a nice fella, Doc. I'd hate to see that change. Just watch yourself." She touched a finger to the tip of Iris' nose. "And you watch him for me."

Iris took Darlene at her word, keeping one eye firmly glued to Christopher as she loaded her plate with meats, beans, buttered cornbread, and a thick buttermilk biscuit.

It was hard to scowl with mouthfuls of Pirate Chicken that was just as delicious as Jack promised. It felt like a Caribbean party in her mouth, with touches of ginger and cinnamon spice exploding in a sweet, rum coconut sauce.

"The drink stuff made the chicken really tender." Her words were warbled over the mouth full of food, but he deciphered them easily, having taste buds himself. Iris' mood softened the more she ate, and in a few minutes, the scowl had all but melted, even though Suzie had buzzed the table like a hungry bird more than once. The music changed. Iris slurped at bits of barbecue sauce that had fallen from a hunk of brisket, using her cornbread like a sponge. She looked at him triumphantly, and he felt guilty all of a sudden.

"Iris, about that lady."

"Why are you talking about *her*?"

"I just, I don't want you to think." He took a sip of water and wiped his hands. "I'm not like that. I wouldn't do that to Rachel." Her eyes had not returned to a full scowl but they narrowed on him as her gaze moved from him to the bar and back again. "It's just." How could he explain it? "It was nice to have someone talk to me like that. She looked at me, talked to me, like I was just some guy." He was telling himself as much as he was telling her. "Some regular guy just getting a drink. She didn't look at me like I was about to break into a million pieces." He caught himself with the revelation. "I guess that felt good for a minute."

Iris understood the feeling he described. It came with knowing someone was really worried, and that worry came from you. Maisy was always worried and always watching like something terrible was about to happen. Sometimes she'd catch Maisy when she didn't know Iris was watching, and she was looking with such troubled eyes. It made Iris' stomach hurt. She hated that watched feeling because it meant no matter what she did, she made Maisy's life hard.

"Iris?"

"Yes."

"Are you with me?"

"Yes, of course I am." When she looked at him, she realized she'd replaced her cornbread with her thumb. She was chewing on her fingers so hard, they throbbed between her lips. "Sorry." He watched, but he didn't have an anxious look. He waited for her to pull her hands away and adjust the plate she'd knocked askew. She liked that he waited. He was patient like Eric in that way. It made things easier, so she didn't mind asking.

"Why do people stand like that?"

"Like what?"

"Like that Suzie lady? Why does she stand so close? The girls at school do the same thing. I know they can hear the boys just fine. They speak so loudly for the world to hear, but the girls lean in like they can't hear. It doesn't make any sense. Do you like that or something?"

Christopher rubbed his chin, thinking of the best way to answer. Iris looked uncomfortable as soon as she'd asked. "

I don't ask Maisy about boy/girl things because I know it would make her nervous." Her voice dropped. "I don't get it."

Christopher took a few minutes to explain the practice of flirting to the girl in as succinct and concrete a way as possible.

"So it's all for show?"

"So-to-speak."

"Sometimes people will act all weird with someone else, even if they're not interested." He nodded. "Because they like to, not because they like them?"

He nodded yes.

"Sometimes people will even let someone do a bunch of nice things for them, even when they know they're not interested in them at all?"

He shrugged. It sounded sadder when she put it that way.

There was quiet while she fished a hunk of pineapple from the bowl.

"The frigate bird has a kidney-shaped sack on the front of his chest."

Christopher tilted his head. She elaborated because the words lulled her nerves. "The male fills it up when female birds are near. He doubles in size with this giant red balloon in front of him. It's ridiculous looking and I'm pretty sure the females know it's all air, but they play along." Her voice moved like it was making calculations. "Hot air? Is that why they say someone is full of hot air?"

"Maybe," he answered but his answer wasn't necessary. She was on a roll.

"Worker bees climb all over each other for a chance to be near the queen. It's kind of like the boys at school at gym time. Pretty much in both cases. They're more like birds and—" she sat upright as if she'd been electrified "—birds and bees! I get it!"

He smiled.

The girl sat back, finishing off the remains of her chicken without a care in the world. She listened to the band play a full song before speaking.

"Rachel worries about you."

It took Christopher a second to process what she'd said, so hot on the heels of air bladders and bees, but it made sense in more ways than the girl could know.

"That would be an understatement. Rachel worries about a lot of things, about the world and the unfair things that happen to people. About all the sick children. She worries about when we're going to have kids of our own. She wants a baby. Did you know that?" His voice was sad. "She does. Which is the problem." He reached into his pocket looking for something. "Rachel has enough to worry about." His eyes changed so quickly, Iris couldn't look.

The darkness there made her too sad. "She doesn't need to be worrying about me." He extracted the yellow bottle and popped out two pills. "Speaking of which, time for the meds," he said with a hint of bitterness. Iris did not catch it, he sighed as he swallowed them down. "I'm supposed to be someone's father, not some helpless kid."

"You're not a kid. You're not helpless at all. You help a lot of people." She'd have to remember to tell Murph that being literal was useful sometimes.

"Without these, my mind goes a little cloudy."

"So?"

"What do you mean 'so'? I want to be the man Rachel needs. Give her a family. How can I do that now?"

"How can't you?"

"Kids look at dads like they're superheroes. Like they're perfect. They're supposed to learn from them. What can I teach them?"

Iris was thoughtful. "That it's perfect to be not perfect." She picked up a string bean and chewed it, eyes drifting for a moment. "One of the best things a kid can know is that they can ask for help when they need it." She chewed again, still not finished. "I think you're going to be a great dad."

"Why's that?"

"Look what you're doing for me."

Just suddenly, she popped up from the table like a chicken timer. "I'm gonna go get something." She breezed by Christopher, giving a narrow look to the bar,

Floozy

disappearing through the split bamboo doors that led to the kitchen.

Darlene was busy calling orders to the line cooks, three more than had been there just a few hours ago.

"Where's Ryan?"

"It gets too loud back here for him when we're busy. He's in his room upstairs, playing on that tablet thing of his. He loves it." Her words drifted, as people's words did when there was a lost cause at hand.

"Are they ready?" Iris called to Jack, who grabbed two cakes off the cooling tray. They were perfectly golden and smelled like toasted sugar.

"All cooled for you. It's on you to dress 'em up all pretty."

She jumped behind the line and grabbed the sauce she'd whipped up, laying dollops of cream on the puddles she rained down on the warm cakes. "I don't understand the ladies that lean all over men. It's like they can't stand on their own. Their legs work perfectly fine." All the new information floating around her brain was threatening to short circuit her. Murph said she needed to talk more when things seemed confusing. This flirting business had made her head hurt. She talked to Darlene as she worked, never looking up from her creations.

"Well, honey, I wouldn't expect you to know anything about ladies' men and floozies."

Ladies' men, she knew. They were the guys who wore big-collared shirts and pointed at people when they talked. They were the kinds of guys Maisy said to stay away from.

"Floozies?" That was a new one.

"They circle around a man like flies. Some are looking for drinks. Some are looking for company." There wasn't malice in her words, just statement of what she saw every day, shrugging, "I suppose some of them are just lonely. Here Ginny, take this to table 9. Thanks, hon." She went back to expediting orders without a second thought to the inner working of flirting, so Iris did the same.

"Ta-dah." She tried her best to emulate Darlene's wrist flick, but the cakes hit the table with a motionless thud. Nonetheless, they were a sight to behold. She was so taken with the action that she didn't notice Christopher was not alone. The woman giggled like a girl, but there were potato chip crinkles by her eyes that told another story. There was beige powder caked inside them like pie crust, but, still, she flipped her hair and made the childlike sounds of a grown-up trying to impress a baby. Inconceivable.

"There are more in the back if you want one, she told the woman. You can order it." Loosely translated, 'You can't have any.' Iris did her best to smile cordially but the look stuck on her face like a mask.

"What is it? It looks great," said Chris.

"Jack inspired me a little. so I used some things I normally wouldn't. That's an angel cake, with a spiced rum caramel sauce. The whipped cream is flavored with

Kahuna beer." Christopher took a bite and licked his spoon approvingly. She conceded. "It's not poison."

"What do you call it?" Suzie's voice was high like pre-school teachers and girls in her school who said "aw" over everything. With all the cake talk, Iris had almost forgotten she was there.

"What?"

"The cake." The woman leaned forward like she was prompting a puppy to speak for the first time.

"I just said what it was." This conversation was tiresome.

"I think what Suzie means is, does it have a name? Like the Pirate Chicken?" Christopher did his best to make the conversation as smooth as the sauce that coated his tongue.

Iris didn't have to think. The answer was simple, and it was sitting right in front of her. "I call it the Boozy Floozy."

"What?" Suzie's face was hard to read.

"For all the ladies who fluff up their hair and drink rum and lean on people. See how the whipped cream is puffy and it slides all over the place when you move the plate? And it's boozy. See?"

There was no malice in Iris' voice. In her world, things were as matter-of-fact as what she saw in front of her. Right now, she saw Suzie making a bee line away from the table and out the front door.

Chapter 28

Fire Exits

The Tiki cottage looked much larger than it appeared from the outside, especially with all the lights off. Iris lay back on the bed and begged her muscles to listen, as she willed them to soften and relax. She reasoned with her elbows to bend into gentle curves, and she pleaded with her mind for her legs to go heavy. None of them were listening. Her limbs pressed against the cool sheet like they were made of reinforced steel, bolt straight as if she'd been zapped with an electrical current. She wanted to be happy here, to feel at ease in the tropical air. Darlene had put so much love into making this place an oasis. Yet, even with her sleep mask secured, Iris was far from serene. If tranquility were a place, she was light years away.

Outside the door, there was darkness or there was supposed to be if not for the glowing lights that marked the path. Was tripping and falling that much of a problem for weary travelers? It seemed unnecessary to make a simple walking path look like it was some kind of landing strip. Even though the neon sign was 200 yards away from her little hut, its glow seeped in through the door crack like a devil's hand. It was thin and orange, angry like a specter's, made of fire. Its slender burning fingers would get her if she closed her eyes. She pinched them shut and covered them with the lavender mask, but it did no good. She could still feel the heat of the sinister hand closing in around her neck. Fire was inescapable. There was no back door in a place like this. There was a bathroom behind a palm frond curtain but its window was too small for her body. What if she needed to escape?

Her dessert tonight had been a success. Ryan had hit the "smile," "heart," "more" buttons on his machine so many times, it had sounded like one of those party songs they played at dances at school. Darlene and Jack had showered her with accolades and assurances that the Bake-Off this year was surely already won. She asked again and again if they were kidding. Each time, they had a new reason to say it was so. She loved those reassurances as much as she loved this kind of excitement. It wasn't a nervous feeling like bugs but the fuzzy kind that covered her like a warm blanket. In all of that, she'd forgotten to ask her most important questions before retiring for the evening.

Where is the fire extinguisher?

Is there a sprinkler system?

Fire Exits

How long does it take first responders to arrive here on average?

She slipped the mask down and inspected the room with her eyes open. The place no longer undulated with heat signatures or phantoms of flames to come. It sat still, too still, quiet like a cramped little tomb, though it had felt so airy and full of cheer just moments before. The night table was practically on top of her, hiked up next to the bed like an overeager salesman. The coconut alarm clock looked like an oversized hermit crab in the dark. She could hear it moving around if she let herself, scuttling inches from her head with searching claws that could mangle her face in an instant without a second thought.

Breathe.

Murph and Dr. Gentry had said this was just the way her body worked, that at the end of the day all of her anxiety and stresses built up in her body like soda in a can that's been shaken up all day. When she closed her eyes to rest, it was like someone popped the top. As soon as she put her head down, her mind burst like fireworks, so anything that could go wrong, did—in her mind. Sometimes it replayed everything that had already gone wrong in the day, a continuous loop of things she said wrong or items in her room that were turned the wrong way. Other nights it went further than that, not only the things that had gone awry in the day, but in that month, that year, and worst, in her whole life. Other nights she had nightmare visions of the future. At home she was at least comfortable enough to know the lay of the land. She knew how to get her pets to safety. She had the house's wiring committed to memory and had a good idea of where an electrical fire would start and how quickly it would spread. Here, she had no wiring diagram of this place. She didn't know how many members made up the local fire department or if they worked on a volunteer or paid basis.

Where is the fire department?

Do they live there?

How long would it take them to get here if they had to come?

Would it be enough time?

She answered those questions with logic and reason. The sooner she realized that, yes, they were professionals, and of course, their jobs hinged on arriving in a timely fashion, the sooner her mind could move on to another impending doom.

One million dust mites could live in the average mattress. Was this mattress average? Or was it older? She had no way of knowing. Even if there were a tag it wouldn't have an expiration or a bought-on date like yogurt or a wheel of cheese, so she'd have to rely on averages, which left her with at least one million. If 1,000 dust mites could make 250,000 fecal pellets, Iris' head was swimming at the prospect the numbers presented. She could be on a bed made solely of mite poop. She tried to inhale tiny shallow breaths, imagining her nostrils as the smallest pinholes possible. There were parasites leaving thousands of invisible layers of feces on everything, and there was nothing she could do about it but breathe, but breathing would let them in. Would they nestle on her brain and build a civilization inside of her? How would she know? She could hear their tiny building tools inside her skull: hammering, sawing, building bridges on her neural pathways, taking over her mind. If she could just get to the door, Christopher was right outside. All she had to do was open the door, but it was miles away, and she couldn't move. Even if she could, she feared that, when she did, the place would be hanging in space. Logic told her it was impossible, but her heart told her the whole cottage was floating in a vast blanket of nothingness. She couldn't breathe. If she did, the mites would get in.

They had her pinned in this strange atmosphere that was both heavy and floating all at once. She was hurtling through the feces-sphere, and her head hurt. She was grinding her teeth again, wasn't she? *Breathe.* It was a strange sensation to scream in silence. No sound came out of her mouth, but she yelled in her mind to try to get a hold of herself.

She had a panic attack in school once. The first one was when she was young, so it was the one that mattered. After that one, the moments of breathlessness became common, but the first time they were playing dodge ball. The prospect of those balls flying through the air at any minute had rendered little Iris motionless, unable to breathe. The teacher assured her that no one would throw at her face, but it didn't take long. A little boy with stringy yellow hair threw the first ball of the game, and it connected with her face like a giant stinging bee that exploded like a pain grenade. It hurt her jaw, but it made her mind quiet. In a way she felt justified to panic. It hurt her jaw so bad.

STOP GRINDING! The inner scream fought over the hammering. The mites weren't hammering her head. She was chomping her own teeth. *Breathe Iris. Breathe.* Maisy's voice soothed. She imagined Maisy smoothing her hair, with her pets beside her in the house. That made so much more sense than being here.

If she were home there would be a well-worn path between the bed and the door, a path where she could pace freely and sort things out. Maisy established that early, the real Maisy, the one she'd left worrying at home. The real Maisy insisted that pacing had to stay within the house after a few sleepwalking incidents and several middle-of-the-night wake-up calls. If she were home, she could take a long shower and fall asleep with the water running over her, but she wasn't home. She was miles and miles away from anywhere safe, which was about the same as drifting in space. Her actual blanket weighed 8,000 pounds in this atmosphere so it pushed her down so she and the bed were one being. She lay motionless there, shoulders aching from tension.

Fire Exits

Maisy's eyes were stinging worse than the time she rubbed them after cutting lemons, but she was almost there. She wasn't stopping now. It had been a long enough ride already, long enough for her to figure out the nuances of Eric's car. She fought the urge to call him this late. He'd kept her company this whole way, breaking up the monotony of long roads and the confusion of road construction, even the interminable purgatory that was DC traffic.

The first time she called, she'd used her phone. After a while, she figured out the nuances of his car. He did say she should check in. She didn't want him to worry, not after all he'd done for her.

"Call Eric." She spoke to a button in the steering wheel, which, at first, had felt strange but, by now, had become second nature.

"You there?"

He picked up on the first half ring.

"Almost. I'll be pulling up in a few seconds." She was glad she got him. Her shoulders relaxed a touch. Whether she was imagining it or not her eyes felt like they were giving her a break.

"Long day, huh?" His voice didn't match the words. They were way too bright for this hour, but she wasn't complaining.

"Yes. I'll feel a lot better when I get there, that's for sure. I'd feel way worse if I didn't have you with me. Thanks for keeping me company."

"That's what I'm here for."

There was a bump on the road and a whoosh outside, while neither of them said anything.

When it came to landing big catering jobs at the store, neither one of them was an ace, because neither of them was a good closer. There was something in the quiet between them that was troubling.

"Hey, Eric. You know the weirdest thing happened before DC. I wasn't going to say anything, but I swear if I don't say something, I'm going to go nuts." She unloaded the story about the eerie Iris voice, the one that haunted her in that strange store. "So, you think I'm going crazy or what? Maybe I should have stopped for a rest. It was so real."

Eric didn't talk. He made a garbled noise that sounded like the words had changed their minds. He started to say something but had, instead, cleared his throat midway. "Yeah, that is weird."

"Why are you saying it like that?"

"Saying what like what?"

"You said weird, weird. Why are you doing that?" If Maisy had anything, she had a great BS detector. What she lacked in sales skills, she made up for in knowing when someone was trying to sell her.

There was that garbled sound again. This time it was an uncomfortable cough, a dry forced sound that was Eric's exit strategy from this call. It was too late, and she was too tired for any of this.

"You know, I think I may be coming down with something, Maisy. I better get to sleep before I go in for the night."

His voice was doing that unintentionally loud thing it did when he tried to land a corporate client, but she didn't get a chance to call him out on it, because Eric was saved by the Tiki Oasis.

"I'm here anyway." She couldn't be annoyed at him, not after everything he'd done today, and always, for that matter. "We'll talk later." There was a tiny threat hidden within in the promise.

"That sounds great." His voice sounded normal again.

"And Eric?"

"Yep."

"Thanks."

Maisy's eyes were heavy when the motel rose up on the otherwise deserted road. She wasn't lying when she said she should have stopped. The place was exactly where Eric said it would be, but it was nothing like she imagined. His description had not done it justice, nor had the throwback billboard a few miles back. With those gaudy letters, she'd imagined the place would be an outdated relic, a cheesy throwback tourist trap nestled in the middle of nowhere, but it was nothing of the sort. No wonder Iris chose this place over the big motel. It looked like an island amid tall grass and asphalt. The bigger chain hotel that was the only other choice for miles was packed full with convention attendees, but that's not the kind of thing that would draw Iris' eye. The chain motel, though clean and well attended, looked like a giant white cakebox compared to this place. This place looked like some sort of amusement park sitting off to the side of the otherwise empty road. Even this late at night, it seemed bright and alive with activity.

That might be a problem.

People were still trickling out of the surf shack that promised delicious barbecue and live music. Maisy's stomach was churning from drinking too many coffees on an empty stomach and having to drive in the DC traffic. Even so, the food smelled good, not good enough for right now, but good enough to know Iris must've eaten well this evening.

If it weren't for Eric letting her drive his vehicle, she wouldn't be there now. It was well past 1 AM and Maisy had a good idea where the cottages were. After a half day in the car, she couldn't bear to make one more stop. So, instead of parking in front of the shack for a much needed break, she hooked up the curved path that led to the collection of huts at the top of the hill, much to the objection of her screaming insides. Her bladder could wait, but Iris was in a new place that wasn't home with none of her pets or special sheets. She hadn't even brought her own pillow. Maisy stowed in a bag stuffed with an assortment of "must have's" she felt Iris was probably panicking over by now.

Maybe not. There was always the chance that today could be the day when one of the fixations subsided. She told Iris every morning when she left for school, a mantra she repeated more like a fairy tale or song, It will be okay today. Maisy wasn't a pessimist. She'd just gotten used to the way things were. With the way things were, it never hurt to be prepared for anything.

Up the curve in front of a short little hut marked number 3, she saw the outline of what could only be the blueberry. The little car was dwarfed by Eric's truck and the old man sedan parked on the other side. She peered in the window and, true to his word, Christopher was there. He leaned cockeyed from the driver's side onto the passenger seat. It couldn't be easy for a full grown man to sleep comfortably in a car built for efficiency over space.

He was a handsome man in a hipster kind of way, slim with a beard that was neither overgrown nor over-cared for, dark like the hair that fell in neat waves on his forehead while he stirred. He looked like the young professor girls would clamor to talk to after class. At least that's how Maisy imagined it would be. There wasn't much clamor in an online class—mostly discussions in a forum where the most fevered disputes were expressed in capital letters—so, anything close to flirting with a professor came through the clever use of colons and right parentheses. :)

There was no use in waking him now. He deserved what rest he could get leaning his head against the cool window with motel lights shining in his face. For all the hooting and hollering, Christopher had come through for her by keeping Iris safe. God knows what could have happened to her had she not run into the proverbial Good Samaritan. She knew. Thinking about it made her shudder almost as much as thinking about what Iris must be feeling right now. The thought of the girl alone had propelled her through the last three rest stops. Rest was for people whose minds were at ease, and that wasn't happening for Maisy anytime soon.

There was no light coming from inside, so she approached on tensed tiptoes as if a footfall could wake the sleeping girl on the other side, but, as she got closer, it was clear that wouldn't be a problem. By the sounds of it, Iris was about as sleeping as Maisy was relaxed. She didn't have to lean her face against the window as she planned to or hold her ear to the doorjamb to hear it. The humming was clear and distinct like a high voltage wire, an airy buzz that cut through the air and groaned low in a primal place that made Maisy's heart hurt to hear.

Iris hummed. The vibrations moved over her lips and made her skin on her face pop like it was covered in exploding candy. Most of the time, she didn't even know she was doing it. It was the only thing, at this point, that got her in trouble at school. There were teachers who got it and a handful of kids who didn't mind, but, in a sea of teachers and kids, that didn't amount to much. She tried to be aware of when it happened, to bite her lip when the stress got bad or to, at least, hum one of the popular songs on the radio to look like she was doing something less weird. It wasn't that she cared what people thought, but the extra attention, the pointing, and mocking was annoying. Most of the time she'd rather be left alone. Here in this room, that was the last thing she wanted. The grass curtain looked like an ominous figure, a carnivorous, eyeless alien searching for food. In the halls at school she would try to make her humming go unnoticed, but here it would ward away the carnivorous villain waiting in the dark and the thousands of flesh-eating dust mites that covered the sheets upon which she lay. She tried not to think about it, humming so all she could hear was her voice and all she could feel was the vibration of sound through her fingertips.

Until she heard something else.

The knocks had her up and gasping until she picked out the patter. There was one long knock followed by three in short succession, like the intro in one of Dave's biggest songs. Iris moved animal-like, speaking through the crack in the door.

"Who is it?"

The voice was low and muffled. It was after midnight, after all. At least, this alien was polite.

"Iris, it's me."

It knew her name. Clearly a female, this voice spoke through a guise of calm, but it was tense, probably from hunger. It was desperate to feed its young.

"Me, who?"

There was a second then. The beast was either gathering its strength to crash the door down or it was sharpening its nails to cut through the wood between them, because it took a deep breath.

"Iris, it's Maisy."

It sounded like Maisy. She didn't want to look through the peephole because the creature could easily pop her eyeball out that way. It could just stick a tentacle right through the hole, and there would go Iris' brain, sucked right out through her eye socket. She tilted to get a look without getting her face anywhere near it and spoke again.

"What's the song we sing about Oscar?"

Another pause and another breath. She braced herself for the alien claw coming through the door, but it didn't.

"What?"

"If you're who you say you are, you know it. What's the song?"

There was a quiet thud on the other side, and the voice was muffled like she'd laid a tentacle against the door and was talking from behind it.

"Grouchsleeves."

Iris smiled. She knew better than to leave it at that.

"No, you have to sing it."

"Here?" The alien was getting frustrated. It had been a long journey.

"Yes, here."

Fire Exits

Maisy rested her head against the door. It was taking all her strength to ignore her insides. She clenched her legs together and swallowed what little pride she could

She sang. "My grouch is fat."

"I can't hear you," Iris said from the other side. "You're going to have to sing louder."

Maisy cleared her throat and gave it another go, hoping it would be enough. The tune of Grouchsleeves was recognizable, and her voice wasn't half as bad as she thought it was, but this wasn't something she wanted the hut neighbors to hear.

"My grouch is fat. He is a cat. His breath smells like tuna fish sandwiches. His voice is sweet like a parakeet's. I scratch his head when it itches."

The door opened with a click, and Iris let out a small giggle.

"I knew it was you all along."

Chapter 29

In the Room

Maisy didn't realize how tight her chest had been, but the air came in a rush that bordered on overwhelming, as soon as Iris was in front of her. She looked tired and on the verge of a meltdown, but she was safe.

"I'm coming in, okay?" This was the warning Maisy used any time contact was coming. She leaned in with her hands up as if in surrender. Whether it was a hug or a bandage or a hairbrush, Iris needed fair warning, and it needed to be clear. There were odd times when she sought out human touch, most often at the most inconvenient of times. More often than not, she avoided contact like it was acid, caustic and deadly. Maisy never knew where Iris was on the scale until she issued the notice. Tonight, or, more accurately, this morning, it seemed she didn't mind as much. She let Maisy put her hands on either side of her face without tensing. As she did, Iris' eyes filled with tears she quickly blinked away.

Maisy didn't look at her eyes but at the hair that jutted out from the wool hat in a long sweaty clump.

"I'm guessing you've been wearing this all day." Maisy tugged at the hat that felt as if it had been sewn to Iris' head.

"That's all you're going to say? Aren't you going to yell? Are you going to kill me? You don't want to scream about the blueberry or punch me in the nose? Don't you want to give me the business? Where's the business?"

Maisy flattened the tangle on Iris' head, working on one long knot that looked like an intricate braid. She spoke mildly.

Maisy had planned the lecture for hours, all the places where she would pause for effect. The words had sounded so wise and disappointed, as they played through her head on a loop this whole day, but, somehow when she walked through the door, they disintegrated and fell to dust in the light of Iris' smile. Seeing her in person changed everything. She was all right, for the most part. The ripped papers all over the floor showed the trip had taken its toll, but it could have been worse. For now, Maisy had a more pressing issue.

"Oh, you'll get your business, my dear. I promise you that. But for now," she paused pulling fuzz from hair, smoothing as much of the mess as she could. "I have to pee."

Years ago, they'd taken a trip out to the chocolate factory out in Pennsylvania as a treat. Maisy thought for sure

In the Room

the girl would love to see how things worked, and the tour had been great. When they got to the hotel room—a luxury suite with a bubble bath and pillows that looked like foil wrapped chocolates—Iris panicked. At four-years-old, she was panicking about escape routes and sprinkler systems and at two in the morning, she relented and took her for a walk through the hall. They ended up piling all those pretty chocolates up high, fashioning a tent of sheets and pillows. They checked out the very next day. So this all could have gone much worse.

She spoke loudly through the cracked door, washing her hands. By the looks of the scary witch in the mirror, the trip had taken its toll on her as well.

"So the good doctor was okay? He didn't do anything that's going to make me have to hurt him, right?"

It was almost like they were home talking with Maisy washing dishes. Iris liked the sound of the water.

"No. I think he wanted to sideways kiss some lady. She had glitter on her eyes and did that weird thing with her shoulders when she walked. You know like those ladies who push out their, you know, and move all weird when they dance." Iris didn't like the word sexy. This is as close as she got to saying it. "But, he didn't." As if in an afterthought, she added "I think he just liked the attention."

Maisy felt refreshed already. She plunked herself on the corner of the bed and took in the damage to the room that in the light was far worse than it had appeared when she scurried through just moments before. It looked like a small ticker tape parade must have passed from the door to the bed and then looped back for three more shows, because three distinct lines of torn paper trails cut through the room like racing lanes. The bed itself was still made, but there was an Iris-shaped indent in the duvet, as if she'd lain there like a weight.

Iris' eyes were slits. Maisy didn't need to see them to know she hadn't slept. She patted the indent without saying any of the words she'd practiced for six hundred miles.

Iris was expecting a lecture, a tirade, even the silent treatment, but she never expected this.

"Come here, mouse. Time to sleep."

On a good day, Maisy's average request was met with six or seven questions seeking some form of clarification, always in the form of specifics. On a bad day, this could go on for an hour. In this case, Iris fell on the bed like she was a tangled puppet whose strings had finally been cut loose. When she fell, the tears came so fast and heavily, she thought she would choke. The words followed like floodwaters.

"I don't know where the fire exit is. I could have burned up and all the people next to me, and no one would even know. The rooms aren't connected. Maisy, did you see there are no adjoining doors? And who's taking care of Sophie? What if there's a fire at home? How would the fire department know to save her? Or Oscar? Is Oscar angry that I'm gone? I always give him his vitamin. I didn't think of it. There's so much I didn't think of."

The girl's body was so stiff it pressed against the covers like a lead weight.

"First of all." Maisy scooted Iris up so she could get her under the covers and smoothed and tucked them around her, like she was fixing a pot pie. "Eric's got the pets. You trust Eric, don't you?" Iris was so tense she barely had the ability to nod yes. Her shoulders were way up by her ears, but she did her best with her eyes and a short lift and drop of her chin. "He's got the 'just-in-case' key, and he's going to make sure the grouch and pretty little Sophie don't get lonely. Okay?"

Iris squeezed her eyes shut and opened them wide, repeating the process so often she looked like a mechanical doll. She went through a number of comical expressions in an attempt to make her face go calm. It wasn't a new practice, but it was more intense than Maisy had ever seen it. Blood rushed to Iris' cheeks as if she was running a race.

"In a place this small, there is no back door, but if you look in the bathroom, that window swings out if you need it to. Like an emergency exit. And the local fire department is a volunteer squad made up of fifty on-call members with an average response time of 3 minutes and 42 seconds." Iris' shoulders dropped almost imperceptibly, but Maisy always knew what to look for. "I looked it up."

She rattled off various pieces of local trivia, including the lowdown on the local sporting goods convention and even some background on her new friend, the good doctor. By the time she'd finished recounting her conversation with Rachel, Iris' legs felt more like flesh and less like cinder blocks. Maisy kept her hand on the blanket, barely putting any pressure there, but close enough that Iris knew it was there.

"You don't have to worry. I'm here." Iris finally let her head slip and fall onto her shoulder. Maisy shored up the blankets around her, making them so snug any other person would've cried uncle. "My little burrito. Do you remember that?" Maisy walked her fingers on the blanket and spoke in a quiet, song-like rhythm. "Little baby burrito, first the meat." She squeezed the blanket snug around her. "Then the cheese." She piled pillows from the bed and small loveseat on top of her. It wasn't a tent, but it would do. "And the lettuce." She lightly touched the top of her head like she was sprinkling invisible lettuce. She would talk to her tomorrow about washing her hair. What was left of tonight was for letting it all go. "We used to do this when you were a baby, remember." The tension had melted and just then the two of them could have been anywhere. "A little better?"

"Yep."

Iris turned onto her right side, as she always slept, adding one last thought before letting it happen. "But Maisy."

In the Room

"What is it?" Maisy was content that the girl was relaxed enough to finally sleep. She didn't know she had turned so Maisy wouldn't see her face was clenching again. "I'm not a baby anymore."

Chapter 30

Morning

Chris' feet burned a hole through his sleep, as the morning cracked open on the horizon. They throbbed with a sensation that was a mixture of itch and ache, more insistent than any alarm, in a perfect rhythm precise, as any Swiss watch. It had been easier to rest in the cramped car than he thought it would be, though it had been more like passing out. His head sizzled, reminding him how much beer had helped him get comfortable, though his lower body was bunched up like a pair of frog's legs and his chin was turned to a near impossible angle.

He wasn't sure if he'd ever seen the sun so bright. It was hard to see out of the car, so he held his hands over his eyes like the proverbial monkey which saw nothing. It was silent at the Oasis, save for the frogs. They sang a morning song like a green choir, and a few birds chimed in preaching gospels Christopher could never understand. He could call Rachel, he supposed. She'd would still be up and, at the end of her shift, free to talk if he wanted, but the truth was, he didn't want to. Did he? Wasn't that why he was here? He didn't want to have to explain himself or disappoint her anymore. This way was easiest. She would get over him and find someone normal, someone who could give her what she needed. No one needed this.

He missed his dog.

He shook his head, done with this line of thinking, and an involuntary sound of disgust came out of his throat that tasted like beer and regret. This was enough. He needed to move. Moving the body helped free up his mind. He told his own patients that and, for once, the physician would, at least try to heal himself.

His feet protested as soon as he stretched his legs out of the blueberry, but he would force them to walk if he had to. The grounds here were interesting, so he'd take a little tour. He'd check out the different totems and palm trees. He'd take in the froggy hymns and the songbird sermons, and he would will himself to better thoughts. He had to change his mind. People were depending on him again.

In the small room, Iris was snoring deeply after having a good cry. Once she got started, it was hard to slow her down, and it had escalated quickly. At points she was on the verge of making herself sick, but Maisy had smoothed down her hair and tucked her in tightly.

Morning

When Iris was little, she had a special weighted blanket that put pressure on all her "calm" spots and helped her at times like this. She had a tent and a noise machine, colorful lights that would project funny shapes on the wall that would twist and turn and change, focusing all her nervous energy onto one beautiful ray of light. They still had them at home. They were tucked in the back of her bedroom closet. Because they weren't home, Maisy had to improvise.

The pillows lay on top of her like a mile-high cartoon sandwich, and she'd draped a sheet over the two of them like a willowy veil. Maisy had been running on fumes, but the little coconut coffee maker had become her best friend. She'd had her third cup when the sun came up. Iris shot up in bed like a turkey thermometer. There was never any sleeping in, not even on vacations.

Good morning, it's a beautiful day." She said that every day, whether it was raining, sleeting, or a zombie apocalypse. "Oh, Maisy, your eyes look like a cat peed in them."

"Thank you, Iris. You're looking well yourself."

Iris shrugged, wiping her face, peering into the palm tree mirror across the room. "Not really. My hair has been in a hat for two days, and I have big circles under my eyes and...that was sarcasm, wasn't it?"

"Getting better, kid." Maisy winked with a tip of her coffee cup and moved to Iris, giving fair warning. "Lemme see how bad we are." She barely needed to lean in. "Whoo.

Okay. Yes. We need to do some work. You smell like a hamster cage."

Though his legs felt like a pile of crunching bones, the walk made Christopher feel better. His lungs felt clean and the weight that had been squeezing his head was letting go. Maybe he would call Rachel later, just to see how Sasquatch was holding up without him. He wondered if the big fluff missed him, but he had to put that out of his mind. He'd be better off in the long run. Too much thinking is what had gotten him up at 4 AM in the first place. That and the fact he'd been sleeping in the blueberry. He came up the winding path and did his best to leave behind thoughts of the steps he took to get there. By the time he saw the huts, his mind was clear. That is, until he heard the scream.

"Iris!" He ran, ignoring the fire that had erupted in his heels as he moved. The long moan cut through the silence of the morning and seemed to move his muscles for him. It was chilling and pained, and it wasn't letting up. "Iris, open up. Are you okay?" He beat on the door with both hands as the sound grew louder from within, which made the doctor more frantic in his attempts. He was on the verge of panic when the scream went still, which surprisingly worsened the beating in his chest. Quiet could be terrifying.

He listened to the click of metal on metal as the lock slid in place, and the door cracked open. The girl there was Iris, but not Iris. That is, it was Iris in age progression like the pictures on the milk cartons.

"You must be Christopher."

He rushed into the room expecting to see the set of a twisted horror movie. Instead, Iris sat on the bed, hair sopping wet with a towel over her face. Maisy looked as much like Iris as the face in the palm tree mirror looked like his. The eyes were different, green rather than the color of caramel. Where Iris' eyes always held the look of stormy waters, hers had a look of stillness, of steely calm.

"Okay, Iris, ready?"

"Uh huh." The girl's shoulders tensed and raised up toward her ears.

"Stay calm. Breathe. It's only few more seconds." Maisy drew the brush down through Iris' hair and the girl screamed like it was a knife cutting into her skull. "It's not that bad. Hold your towel, mouse. You can do this." She squirmed under Maisy's brush and yelped with pain like it was made of fire. "One more. And two more. And just. This. Knot." Maisy tried to untangle the last of the mammoth knots that had built up under the wool hat for the past two days, but it was going to take a good brushing. "Just hold on, Iris. This is the last one."

She yowled like an alley cat, the sound filling the small room and bouncing off the walls like super bouncy balls of sound. When it was through, she glared at Maisy, shoulders slunk down low.

"It had to be done. You *know* that." Maisy's voice was unapologetic but gentle. "You're lucky we didn't have to cut it this time."

"Ahem." Chris, feeling like the invisible man, cleared his throat for the second time, though it was the first sound they'd heard from him at all. "Does hair brushing hurt?"

"Does it hurt?" What little patience Maisy had had been used up in the effort to wash and comb out Iris' hair. "What do you think, doctor?"

His face felt warm. He didn't have to look at the palm tree mirror to know his cheeks had gone pink like he was a scolded schoolboy.

He was charming in his own way, with his messy hair and his young face. Maisy knew what to expect, having stalked his webpage and social media accounts the previous day. So she wasn't surprised by his good looks at all. Christopher couldn't say the same.

"You're Maisy?"

"That's me." She wiped her hand on her shorts and held it out.

"I thought you'd be—"

"Older?" She narrowed her eyes at Iris in a faux scowl. "Meaner?' Iris shrugged. "This one tends to talk about me like I'm some kind of swamp troll."

Iris had talked about Maisy like she bit the heads off chickens, and that hard and frantic voice from the phone didn't match up with the woman standing in front of him.

Morning

She glided smoothly over the floor, and when she talked to Iris, she seemed more like a ghost than a person, because her tone was so light. She anticipated the girl's needs before she spoke, handed her a bobby pin to clip back her hair, then the hat she held so dear. By the looks of it, it had been washed and dried overnight.

"Sorry about all that 'killing you' stuff. It's not every day Iris decides to run away from home."

Iris' eyes opened wide. "Technically, it wasn't running away from home. You knew I was in the contest. You just didn't want me to go, but you *knew*." She was jumpy, almost falling off the edge of the bed, as Maisy pulled a fuzzy from her hair. "Sort of. You knew, sort of."

Again Maisy was calm, a different person from the one he pictured when she was yelling at him on the phone. She was shorter than Iris, with darker hair she kept long, had it been down. But she had it pulled into a messy knot on the top of her head.

"I know now. And I'm here. So let's stop talking about it and hit the road."

Iris squinted hard and grabbed at her head. "I don't want to go home."

Maisy looked at Chris, and he saw something there in the still waters of those ocean eyes.

"Who said we're going home?"

Iris jumped up throwing her arms in the air. "Sugarworth?"

"We might as well, right?" She looked at him again, and he felt like he'd underestimated the impatient woman on the phone. "The doc here says you've got a shot. So let's go."

Iris squealed and danced, destroying any hair efforts that had been made, but Chris not Maisy seemed to mind. Suddenly, she stopped frozen, with a finger in the air as if stricken with a thought.

"Christopher, will you still come with us?"

Now he looked at Maisy, who seemed surprised but resigned, nodding.

"I wouldn't miss it."

Chapter 31

Reveal

I ris was up and pacing the room after only a few hours' sleep as she often did when excited for something in the near future. For her, this was sleeping in. On the first day of school, she was up in the shower at 3 AM. On Christmas, Maisy could expect a wake-up call somewhere after 3:30. She packed her things into the bag and arranged all her blankets and comfort items from home in a row by the door.

Maisy called Eric despite the hour and made sure he gave Iris the lowdown on all the pets. He even put her on the phone with Oscar and Sophie so she could say hello. Neither of them said much, but knowing they were safe made her feel warm inside. With the animal issues settled, Iris was ready to take on Sugarworth. It was nice of Eric to do so much for Maisy, and he looked at her the way little boys look at their new robot toys when they are still in the boxes. That wasn't something people could fake. It was hard for Iris to tell what people were feeling, especially when they were being fake, but the real stuff couldn't be mistaken. Eric thought Maisy was the best.

Darlene had come up the hill just before sunrise. She said it was to see how Iris had liked the hut, but the look on her face betrayed her. She was checking on her new friend. She wore the worried look of a mother hen searching for a lost chick, until she saw the girl was not alone. Maisy knew that look of relief that washed over her, and she liked Darlene immediately. Iris knew she would. Darlene was warm like her grandma's cookies when she gave hugs and she laughed easily. Iris remembered Maisy didn't laugh often, but she liked to.

"Iris seems to make friends everywhere she goes lately." Maisy's voice vibrated with a sound that was equal parts gratitude and surprise.

Darlene stood with her hands on her hips watching Iris count the bags Maisy transferred from the room to the car. Too many to count. Iris squished the coconut between her hands so it looked like a hamburger patty and hummed happily, which reminded Maisy of something she'd wanted to say before, but Iris spoke first.

"Are you sure he's okay with us taking Bessie?"

"Eric insisted we take his car. He said to leave the blueberry and take Bessie. She's got more room and GPS. He was very specific about all the things she could do that the blueberry can't. You know how he is with his car."

"Wow. That's a pretty big deal," Iris raised one eyebrow and scrunched up one side of her face to make her point.

"I know it is." Maisy twisted her hands, taking inventory of all the things they needed from the little car and moving them to the larger and, as Eric pointed out repeatedly, more capable car. Is it okay, Darlene? Can we leave the blueberry here? Is it safe?"

"It's safe and, yes, for the fiftieth time, it's okay." They loaded the car with all the things Maisy had brought to help Iris feel at home.

When they were through, Darlene had thrown in two pineapple pillows and a coconut cushion, so you don't forget us on your trip."

Iris made a squealing sound and ran to the back of the car where she pawed over her new treasures, humming with delight. Maisy perked up like a lightbulb had appeared over her head.

"So the weirdest thing happened on my way down here. I could've sworn I heard you at one of those Chuckey's places." She told them about the strange voice that floated up behind her, the young girl singing a Dave Matthews' song in the most familiar way. "But there was no one there. Just some girls looking at their phones. I swear it was Iris. Weird, right?"

"That's so weird," Darlene's response was stiff and immediate and way louder than she'd intended.

"Why is everyone saying 'weird' so weird?" Maisy's voice was incredulous.

Darlene wore a strange look on her face, like a bug had crawled up her leg. "I just. That is really strange, right? Don't you think that's strange?" She looked to Christopher for help, but he'd walked back into the hut, no doubt freshening up after his night in the blueberry.

When he emerged, Darlene had already backed her way down the hill, making the trio promise to stop in before they left.

Christopher was quietly looking up. It was a smooth kind of day where the sky looked like sea glass hanging above them. And this would bring a smile to anyone's face. Even she knew that. His forehead was pinched at the top, the way Maisy's did when she was looking at bills or a note from school.

"Do you want to go home, Christopher?"

He had been thinking about Rachel just then, the way her hair caught the sunlight on a morning like this, so it looked like it was made of gold. They often walked Squatch together on days like this, and the big lug would get so tired, they would have to carry him home. On the good days, that was the kind of thing they did, but his good days had been so few lately. It didn't seem fair to her.

"Huh?"

"You don't have to come, if you don't want to."

"That's not it at all. I was just thinking." He tried to sound light and hopped into the passenger seat. *Fake it until he could make it* as the saying he hated so much went.

"What's this?" He said, patting the bags that filled the seat behind him.

"Stuffed animals. Favorite shirt. Maisy remembered everything I forgot," which made her remember. "Wait. I forgot something."

The car had just begun to move.

"What?" Maisy tried not to sound impatient, but getting places was always hard with Iris. Getting started was usually the hardest part.

"Stop in at the desk before we go. I want to see Ryan. Don't forget."

"I wasn't going to."

"Just in case you were going to, I'm reminding you."

"Thank you, Iris."

"That was sarcasm, wasn't it?"

"Yes."

"Because you're not really thanking me."

The two reminded Chris of something he'd seen but couldn't place. Maybe it was a TV show or a movie? The unanswered question gnawed at him as much as any others that had emerged as of late.

Darlene, Jack, and Ryan were waiting outside the office, Jack with a bag of packed lunches fresh from his kitchen, Darlene with a big smile. Ryan was tapping on his tablet, holding it in front of his face so only he could see, but he moved it to the side to smile at Iris when she came to say goodbye. Then he held it down for only her to see before it rose up in front of his face again like a curtain.

She didn't know what all the hubbub was about with these video things, but she appreciated the gesture. Maisy was right. She was making new friends, and they liked her for exactly who she was. Ryan had shown her that.

Chapter 32

Angel

"The first thing we need to do is get on 95 because these back roads are not working. Eric said this next exit will take us to the highway that'll get us there. It's in the GPS. What time do we have to get there? Are we staying onsite or do we have to take a shuttle? They're putting you up. Iris? How do I not know this?"

Maisy rattled off words that scattered though the car like shotgun pellets. Christopher only caught every other question, but Iris had no trouble following. Her eyes moved like she was watching a tennis game, so she answered as if she'd been keeping score.

"I was afraid of 95 because there were so many trucks and not as many opportunities to sample regional foods, but with Eric's map and you driving that should be fine. We'll get there by this evening, with plenty of time to check into the hotel. There is a room reserved for me that, yes, was provided by the contest people. It was in my finalist packet that came in the mail last Friday. You didn't know because I kept it in my bookbag."

He realized what was so familiar about the two of them.

"The twins," he said with a hand in the air, triumphant.

"What?" Maisy and Iris questioned in unison, making the comparison all the more obvious.

Maisy gave him the side-eye but placed most of her concentration on not missing the exit.

He smiled amused, happy for a moment, because he didn't feel like he was losing his mind.

"Back at home, at my office. I used to see a pair of sisters every Tuesday afternoon. You two remind me of them, but they were twins."

Iris' eyebrow threatened to disappear beneath her hat. Maisy had a grin that matched her sideways look. It lifted halfway up her face, just like Iris' but on the opposite side.

"Did you think we were sisters?" Maisy said, overlooking the turnoff for the exit.

The weight inside the car had shifted momentarily, but it wasn't that which had thrown Christopher off balance as much as his companions' wry smiles. Iris bounced on her seat as if it were a cooktop.

"Go ahead and tell him." Maisy prompted with a dip of her shoulder.

"We're not sisters." Iris leaned forward so her head split the distance between the driver's and passenger's seat. She beamed, "Maisy is my mom."

Angel

Now with the main highway stretched out like a great straight line, Maisy looked at Christopher with a raised eyebrow that was unmistakably Iris'.

"It's true."

"She's very young for her age. We age well in our family, but Maisy had me when she wasn't much older than I am now. Sorry Maisy."

"Don't be." The older of the two smiled at the young girl, who yanked on the strings of her hat, pulling it down tight.

They spoke in a rhythm that was half tennis match, half song, finishing each other's sentences, the soft lows of Maisy's quick lilting words tempered by the slow and insistent rumble of Iris' words.

"I'm not ashamed, Maisy said with the smallest shrug. "Senior year. End of high school." A touch of irony cut through her next word. "We were sweethearts."

Iris had retreated somewhere, her eyes on the road outside the window. She was neither happy nor sad, just lost to this conversation. Her hat was pulled down almost over her eyes and she leaned her forehead against the cool glass. Christopher had seen her do this several times along the way. If not, he would have tried to get her attention.

"It's a common story. Oh look, there's an actual rest stop. Do either of you need to go? No, probably not, right?" She said all of this as if it were part of the same story she continued to tell in the next breath. "But, these things happen. What are you gonna do?" She checked the mirror, and, like all those times, Iris was exactly where she thought she'd be. Before returning her eyes to the road, as she had the other dozen times she'd done this, she let them turn to Christopher for a second. "What about you?"

"Me?" Christopher leaned in the seat that, compared to the blueberry, seemed enormous. It felt restrictive and small all of a sudden. He wanted to crack a window. "I don't have much of a story."

"Sure you don't."

If he hadn't been fiddling to get the window cracked, he would have seen how tightly Maisy's lips had pressed together as if she were about to blow a whistle.

Iris' silence was broken by the sounds of intermittent snores. She'd fallen asleep with her face pressed to the window.

"Her neck is going to be hurting," Maisy said, moving her eyes again to the road. She had an impulse to look. By now, Christopher had lost count how many times it had been. "I really do appreciate you helping her." They were gracious words, but there was something sharp underneath them that scratched her throat like tiny blades. "You know, she's not really one to ask for help or to accept it." They really were alike he thought. "So you must be at least a little okay."

"I appreciate the compliment." He would have said something witty, but Maisy kept her words moving like a train headed to a scheduled stop. She was getting some-where.

"Maisy's dad stuck around when I had her. I don't know if you got that. I wasn't like one of these girls on the TV shows. I wasn't left all alone. His family was supportive. Folks owned a few bagel shops." She laughed ironically. "I know. I'm haunted by bagels." Her voice lowered, whether it was intentional or not. "See, we weren't struggling. We had this house. He ran the shop. And then he ran."

Her eyes checked the mirror for a longer look before she spoke again.

"We always knew Iris was different. She was doing her own thing from the time she was a little toddler, so I didn't really know. Not that it mattered, because it didn't. Not to me." She smiled. "You know, she talked before she was a year old. Months even. By the time she was two, she was asking to watch cook shows and had favorite chefs. She asked for them by name."

There was that broken glass feeling in her throat again. "When the spinning, head banging and flapping started, I didn't know what we were dealing with, but I was ready to face it. When she stopped talking, I was ready to face it." She swallowed and blinked her eyes, and in a second was sitting up straighter than she had just a moment before. "He wasn't."

She shrugged like she'd been wearing a block of gran-ite on her back. "We never saw him or his family again. They sold the store, gave me a fat check, and said, see ya!"

Baking for Dave

As a therapist, this was where Chris would ask something standard like, *'How does that make you feel?'* but he wasn't a therapist, and he didn't feel the need to ask.

Iris snored loudly. The wide highway hummed beneath them for two exits before she spoke again.

"Thank you for being there for Iris." Her voice sounded like it was fighting itself. "You didn't let her down."

Chapter 33

Rest Stop

"Do you want to switch up? There's a rest stop coming up in a few miles." Maisy was a strong woman with an even stronger will, but she'd been driving all morning with no break, and Christopher was starting to feel useless again.

Without answering, she gave the mirror a look. "Iris is still sleeping. I don't want to wake her," but in that same mirror she could see her weary eyes. Coffee might do her some good. Shutting them might do even more. "But I guess we can be quiet." Her voice drifted into an almost mutter that was more for her to hear than anyone else. "If we shut the door quietly, it should be all right or we could wait it out until she wakes up." As if there were an argument going on that was about to be won, her voice gained volume and momentum until she turned to him like she'd just realized he'd been there to hear it. "Yes, let's do that."

Baking for Dave

Maisy was watching the girl in back sleeping soundly when she realized Chris had that look on his face. It was the one people gave her at parties when she packed up and left early. It was the same look moms would give her when she rolled Iris in her carriage, not on the bumpy sidewalk but on the smooth street. They didn't understand.

"It takes a lot out of her to be around people," she was explaining. Again. "She needs the rest." It was an understatement. "And to drive? You have no idea." The magnitude of Iris' little adventure hit her dead in the face like a rogue wave. She rubbed her head, letting out a sigh that was one part groan. "When Iris was little, I'd take her down to the shore for the day. She loved the water. She could play in the ocean all day, so, when she was about seven, I thought it would be a good idea to get a beach house, you know for the whole week? That way we could do the boardwalk and the rides. I was in a pinch and I had to save forever. I was eating cheese sandwiches for a month. But anyway, it didn't matter, because I got us the house. A half a block from the beach and boardwalk. It was going to be great." Her eyes drifted to the girl and back to the road. "Still out like a light. Where was I?" Her eyes hurt, and she was more tired than she let on.

"The beach house."

"Right. It was more a bungalow really, but for the two of us? It was more than we needed. We got there the first day and Iris called it our castle by the sea."

"That's great." he smiled.

Maisy made a wishy-washy sound of half-agreement. "It was great. We went to the beach the whole first day and ate big stacks of pancakes for dinner at a restaurant right on the water. Iris giggled the whole time. The next day we did the beach again. But that night I took her to the rides, despite my better judgment." Her voice had taken on a harder tone but changed in an instant. "Here it is. One mile. Rest area and food."

She watched the girl as the car pulled into the other lane. The gentle motion rocked her head on the window where it rested.

"She wanted to go on these hot rods. Bumper cars, you know? I told her I'd go with her and let me drive, but she insisted on going herself. She wanted to drive. The guy who works the ride and all these parents are looking at me like I'm the wicked witch because I won't let the kid drive the car. So I do. I give in."

"Well, the ride gets fired up and all these kids are whizzing by. And here's Iris, going about two miles an hour, driving in a perfect circle. She didn't want to bump anything, but it's bumper cars after all."

He winced in understanding.

"The more they bumped her, the more upset she got. The more upset she got, the slower she drove. She ended up stalling out. They had to stop the ride. She thought she broke it. After that, she was inconsolable. We came home the next morning. She slept for days." She took the exit at a crawl so the girl in the back barely moved with the turn. "I shouldn't have let her drive."

Maisy pulled down a slope to an area that looked like a child's toy. There was a car wash and a gas station, restaurants, and slots for trucks to pull in and get weighed. She half expected to see little plastic people with painted-on smiles working the tanks. The lot itself was large enough to be split in two. The one for cars was smattered with a few sedans and one beaten up RV. The other lot was filled, with more trucks than Maisy had ever seen in her life, let alone all together.

"Iris is going to love this." Her whisper was hardly more than breath, because, with the car stopped she tried to keep things quiet. Chris wasn't as good. In the quiet, his phone rumbled like a jungle cat purring in his pocket. Maisy's eyes narrowed as he silenced the would-be lion before it could roar.

"Was that Rachel?" Maisy mouthed the words. He nodded with pinched eyes, finger still pressed firmly on the REJECT button as if the call could creep through. "You have to call her." Her motions were so exaggerated that, in any other instance, Christopher would be amused. Instead, he felt a dull feeling in the pit of his stomach that sat like old bread. He raised a hand to fend off any further discussion. He was lucky. Iris had come to his rescue.

Rest Stop

The long sigh came from the back, like a note from an old pipe organ. It was a clear, happy note that matched the smile that grew across her face as she blinked the sleep away.

"I almost forgot you were here," Iris held up a pointing finger and aimed it at Maisy. Maisy returned the gesture with the opposite hand. In unison, they said, "Good morning, it's a beautiful day."

It was like watching a well-orchestrated dance for Christopher. For a minute, he wished he'd hit ACCEPT.

For Iris, the Truck and Rest Stop were as exciting as Maisy had predicted. The truck lot looked like a giant set-up of push cars in every color she could imagine, but these were life size, and were so clean, they sparkled in the sun as if the paint was still wet. They were all so different. By the looks of them, they were every bit as personalized as the models she painted at home. Some truckers put cool things on their tires, like silhouettes of naked ladies. Others were more creative: American eagles swooping down over fields, big tough-looking men brandishing fists ready to fight, and, her favorite by far, a pink-cabbed truck painted with candies and sweets. If it wasn't for the rumble in her stomach, she could have stayed in that lot all day, but the pink truck reminded her, she had things to do.

Inside, the doors slid shut behind her like she was entering another dimension. It was a gleaming space station with glowing signs and blinking lights all around. Rich, sweet bun smells drifted through the air, filling her nostrils with butter and clouds of powdered sugar. Somewhere in there was coffee, which she always wanted to try and never liked once she did, but the smell was intoxicating. The building was enormous and split itself into three separate sections: a shop not unlike the Chuckey's, a video game arcade where bell and whistle sounds played a chaotic symphony; and, to the left, was a set of food shops. Straight ahead were the bathrooms, where Maisy seemed to be running.

"Wait for me."

"I didn't realize," Maisy looked over her shoulder and shuffled like a quick penguin through the door, practically kicking open the stall with her bent knee. Iris spoke to her from the other side of the door, as she always did, standing so close her lips almost touched the door. Her forehead resting there on the cool painted metal, and even with her skin touching a place that would make the average person cringe, she spoke with the fast continuous pace she had when excitement met comfort.

"I forgot about your lima bean bladder. I don't know why so many women have babies if it means you can't hold your pee anymore, or why doctors haven't come up with some remedy to better keep it all in afterward. Wow. You sure had to go. It's still going."

"Iris," when relief had rushed in, she'd found the capacity to stop her in her tracks.

"Sorry."

"Do you have to go?" Maisy emerged, quickly correcting herself before Iris could speak to the contrary. "Go."

"I don't have—"

"Go."

Iris let out a sullen groan before relenting. Like Iris had stood before, Maisy waited close on the other side of the stall, listening to make sure she went and flushed. In any other situation, this would be embarrassing but it was as regular to the both of them as morning toast and model cars.

"Do I have to?'

"Wash." Maisy pointed. "We'll do it together." She turned on one faucet and, then, the adjacent faucet and counted. "One. Two," and nodded. At that, the both of them thrust their hands in the water, and they sang a ditty about soapy hands to a tune from a familiar band. "Dirt in the water. Wash in the water. Yuck in the water," Maisy sang. "And we're done." She balled up mounds of toilet tissue for Iris to dry her hands, because using the jet engine hair dryer would frighten Iris to death.

Chris waved them to the food area that promised hot coffee and hamburgers with salty fries, but the sounds of the bells and whistles from the game room were too much. Iris needed to investigate.

A rhinestone-framed doorway separated dinging and clacking games from the rest of the Truck and Rest Stop, a perfect square cut into the clear partition, possibly to keep some of the bells and whistles in. Iris bounced from pinball machines to shooting games to classic video games, not knowing what to do first. Maisy fished a dollar from her purse and fed it to the change machine, promptly following it with another without being asked.

Iris scouted the games against the back wall and, confident she wasn't in earshot, Christopher leaned on the opposite side of the change machine where Maisy had rested her head. He was still feeling a bit off balance. "You know, about Rachel. I'm going to call her. It's just complicated."

"It's not so complicated." The change clanged out of the machine. "You left." Before he could say another word, Maisy had pushed off toward the girl and her games.

After all the bright lights and even the guitar game that let her imitate her rock hero, one game had drawn Iris over as if a siren sounded. The slender crane looked like a robot hand dangling over a pile of stuffed bears and handheld game consoles, music players, and charm bracelets.

"It says it's easy to win," her eyes reflected the light that beamed inside the glass case. "I can win." She had a look that tightened Maisy's insides like shrunken socks out of the dryer. Two quarters went in the slot. Iris lined up the crane over the game console. She bent down low, so the mirrors inside the case didn't impede her vision. She could see it was a perfect shot. "I can win," she half-whispered. Down came the crane and, much to Maisy's surprise, it did, in fact, land smack dab on the console. The bony fingers reached around the slender game pack. It was unmistakably in its grasp, but, as it ascended, and as Maisy had silently predicted, that same grasp loosened just enough to let it go.

"But I had it," Iris insisted.

"That's what happens," Maisy's voice was fatally flat. There was no sugar coating here, not on a single syllable.

"Again," Iris insisted, plunking another four quarters into the slot. Just the same, she lined up the crane, this time over the same console in a different color. This one jutted up among the rest. "A sure keeper this time." Within seconds the hand had the game in its metal grasp and, just as quickly, it let it go. "Again."

"Iris, I don't have any more singles."

"Again." Her mouth had begun to slide sideways and, for the first time in almost a day, Christopher got a glimpse of the girl he had met at the ferry. He jumped into the conversation before she could do any more damage to her chewed up lip.

"I could get you some change." Maisy was mouthing something he couldn't make out. She'd abandoned the wide-mouth bass approach evidently, at least in public. He squinted at her with an upturned hand, the universal sign that he had no idea what she was saying. Maisy came close and yanked him toward a caterpillar video game that thumped and yahoo'ed every ten seconds or so to drown out the sound. "No more money. She's obsessing."

It was just a game, the kid had come close, but Maisy was tense and her fatigue was showing. Christopher assured as best he could, "I know how you must feel."

"No, you don't." She didn't issue this as a challenge but as a calm statement of fact. As she drifted back toward Iris and away from the caterpillar, she mouthed words he could easily make out. "I warned you."

He reached into his pocket, forgetting the ordeal at the Tiki Oasis that had depleted all of his funds that jingled and folded. "I can hit the ATM. I'll be back in a second."

"No." Iris' voice had the shocked quality of a prank victim, startled like she'd just realized Christopher was near. "I have some." She bent in half, reaching into the knapsack of cupcakes and strange envelopes.

Maisy attempted her breathe whisper, but in the loud arcade, it just sounded like wheezing, so Christopher shrugged.

"What?"

Maisy stood close, her whisper sounded like an agitated cat. "She's going to use up all her money."

It had to be at least fifty bucks she had from working for Darlene and Jack or seventy even, with what she had on her beforehand. He felt bad for the kid. He couldn't imagine her spending everything she had on a game that promised nothing but disappointment.

"Here we go."

What Iris held wasn't the envelope from last night. That envelope, from when they were scrambling for room money, had been battered and was almost empty. This was a pristine white envelope so full it almost popped open on its own. She'd written something on it he couldn't see. He'd definitely not seen it before.

"Iris, what is that?" Chris tried to hide his natural curiosity considering they had bartered for a room just the night before.

"It's my 'just-in-case' money, see?" She traced a finger over the green lines, under which the numbers were clear. "Each play is a dollar, so, that's easy. I can play 352 times. I'll win everything by then, and have 43 cents left over."

"You've had this the whole time?" he asked calmly, a smile creeping across Maisy's face.

"Of course. It's my 'just-in-case' money."

"But what about last night?"

"Darlene let me make food, and she paid me." She said this like it was nothing, feeding a five into the change machine.

"Right, but what if she didn't? You said you had twenty-two dollars."

"I did, but that was room money." Her voice was laced with an implicit word and that word was 'duh.' "This is 'just-in-case' money, and I'm going to win."

Like he'd disappeared in front of her, she plunked four quarters and then another into the machine before doing it twice more.

It was then that Maisy had had enough. She'd mouthed the words "she's obsessing" to the good doctor two times already. She wasn't waiting for the third time to be the charm.

"I'm so close." Iris muttered, leaning back and then forward, so her head struck the machine like a clapper on a bell. "So close. So close." She struck and hummed until Maisy held a hand between her face and the glass before the last set of quarters could go in. Her voice was as steely as before, not a hint of sugar but quietly calm, not the raspy frantic cat whisper she'd used with him.

"Iris, let it go."

"Huh?" The girl looked up from the machine, glassy-eyed.

"Let it go."

Chapter 34

I Feel Better

Receiving a few uneasy looks was common when out with Iris, especially in a place like Queequeg's. It was the fancy kind of place where young men with baby beards sat all day typing philosophical words into their laptops and handhelds, home of six-dollar coffee and the best baked goods aside from the ones the girl beside her whipped up every weekend. Iris had the menu memorized, just as she did most menus of the places she liked, but still she floundered. A few sidelong glances could be expected. The girls behind the counter here were downright staring. Even now as Iris touched every travel mug on the shelf, adjusting them so the price tags faced the same way, they gaped outright.

"Do you notice anything strange here, Doc?"

"Is it me or are these people staring?" Chris spoke from the side-of-his mouth, attempting to either whisper or start a new career in ventriloquism. It wasn't out of the ordinary for people to stare at a Queequeg's. This was the coffee she'd been craving all day that cost as much as a meal somewhere else, where she could be sure a young guy in a scarf would be typing away on his laptop in the corner. It was the fancy, ubiquitous coffee shop that had the type of clientele who would stare at any Joe off the street who called what was in his hands a large coffee, let alone the girl who was currently touching every travel mug on display one-by-one.

Maisy didn't think anything of it at first, but now that he mentioned it, this did strike her as a different kind of staring. Normally, there was an uncomfortable shuffle when she caught someone giving Iris a look. When she gave them the look right back that said, "What?" they shrank back as if embarrassed by what they'd done. The girls behind the counter were leaning over the counter to get a better look. They had no shame in it at all. Even the man-boys with the beards and scarves seemed to be looking away from their laptops and handhelds to get a look at the girl in the hat.

"Iris, are you ready to order?"

She knew this menu as well as she knew the one at the shop, and even so it could take 10 minutes for her to settle on what to have. Maisy was hoping this wouldn't be the case. The weird smiles from the counter girls were making her nervous.

I Feel Better

"Are we on hidden camera or something?" Her version of the sideways whisper was more comical than his. Together they looked like a pair of broken puppets. Iris scoured the menu. Maisy knew she'd end up with two cake pops and a chocolate milk but read along with her looking for suggestions. She couldn't help but think there was whispering behind her, not the gossipy judgmental whispering of spelling bees and dance recitals, but the kind of excited Christmas morning chatter of children trying not to get caught peeking at presents.

It was a pair of almost teen girls, bookends except for the braces. They stood close enough to sneeze on Iris if they wished, but far enough back to at least uphold the illusion of space between them. Maisy tried not to scowl at them. They weren't being jerks. They were doing that thing teeny bop girls did when they saw the pop star they liked, but why were they doing this to Iris? Christopher gave a shrug unsure what was happening around them.

The good doctor had noticed within seconds the clear change in what he'd begun to see as "normal folk" reactions to standard Iris behaviors. Maisy was right, this was off. Normally, there was an uncomfortable eye shift of the alleged looky-loo once they were caught, a quick glance away as if to deny the whispering or lingering glance had occurred. These girls behind the counter were not ashamed, and when they looked at Iris, they seemed not curious or accusing, as was custom, but engaged. They whispered loudly to each other, gesturing with eyes and mouths like excited kiddies about to get an unexpected treat. The girls were excited.

Even the two skinny young men seemed to look up from their tablets with curiosity that wasn't the variety she was used to. Their eyes widened as if they were seeing a tornado live in person.

"Do you think we should?" Maisy was about to suggest ducking out. There were dozens of stops between here and the next state, but Iris pushed by her in a determined rush.

"Do you have cake pops?"

The cake pops were on display right behind the girl at the register. Iris could see them, but this was the way she always ordered her cake pops at Queequeg's. It was polite to inquire and not demand. She'd been working on that.

The two girls behind Maisy had run into the coffee shop like they were being chased by a rolling boulder. They stopped short behind her with a little gasp and giggle. She shrugged at Christopher and he lifted an eyebrow much like his new friend.

The girl behind the counter smiled at the one at the coffee machine before answering. She talked in a forced, rehearsed way, like an infomercial lady selling a gadget no one needs.

"We have carrot cake, birthday cake, pistachio, and chocolate."

I Feel Better

Four choices. There were always three at home. The Queequeg's at home had three. They were strawberry, coffee caramel, and vanilla swirl. Iris' head started hurting.

Her skin felt like someone had poured steaming coffee onto her straight from the machine, and it hissed on her like a coiled snake about to take the death bite. This was not her place. This was a bad place and she shouldn't be here.

Maisy forgot the staring and the girls giggling behind her. She stepped up next to Iris and saw the girl's back had gone stiff. Her face had tightened into a look of pain and she drew her hands up into the wool cap like they were hiding for the winter. Her eyes drifted far away though they remained focused right in front of her. Maisy waved at Christopher to step up beside her and was about to speak calmly and casually.

Before she could open her mouth, the girl behind the counter said something strange.

"Know who I really like?" It was like she knew Iris wasn't going to answer because she paused looking at the girl at the coffee machine, who nodded at her to go on. "I like Dave."

Iris' eyes drifted sleepily back into focus and her answer was robotic. "What?"

"Dave Matthews. Do you like Dave?"

It was like a gunshot at the beginning of a horse race had sounded because Iris' face changed rapidly from tension to surprised confusion.

"I do," Iris said.

"You know he shot a movie down around here a few years back?" The girl at the coffee machine said with enthusiasm far too great for casual customer banter. The cashier girl added to the conversation none too casually. "He's got some great songs." She let it dangle in the air like bait.

Maisy could feel the girls behind her in line bouncing on their heels.

The cashier girl started tapping her fingernail on the register and the girl brewing the coffee went to grinding some beans. Maisy wasn't musical by any stretch of the imagination, but she could swear they were playing some kind of beat.

Iris looked at the cake pops. They were different. The rest of the menu was the same but they stuck out at her like chicken bones stuck in a throat. The air felt warm and the coffee smelled bitter. The beans, the girl's tapping reminded Maisy of something.

She was humming.

The girls behind her had started tapping their feet and clapping their hands to the coffee girls' beat. One of the baby-bearded boys was playing notes on his tablet. It was the song Iris was humming, a song she recognized but couldn't place.

In any other instance, Maisy would have pulled Iris out of the store. She would have taken a walk with her in the cool air, but she didn't. This time, she let her stay.

I Feel Better

Chris knew the song from long ago. It was a church song, an uplifting one they sang at picnics.

More people had funneled into the coffee shop. A tall, tough-looking truck driver with a hamburger in one hand hummed a bass note and a slender woman in a running hat clicked her lips together like a human drum machine. The makeshift tune had built in volume until there was a symphony of sound behind Iris' voice, which rose above it all like a cloud.

"I feel better, so much better, since I laid my burden down Glory, glory, hallelujah, since I laid my burden down."

The two girls behind Maisy had jumped ahead to the counter so they could beat on it like a drum. Two older women seated with cups of tea were singing along. By the time the song had surged into the sixth or seventh verse, more than half the people at the Truck and Rest Stop had found themselves singing together in the coffee shop. The cashier girl sang a long low note in harmony with Iris' tune and Maisy felt like she was witnessing something great.

One-by-one, truckers and tourists joined in adding their own versions of what they would do without their burdens in high smooth voices and rough growls until the one awkward moment of quiet when all eyes rested on Christopher.

"I'm sorry, what?"

Iris raised not one but both eyebrows as high as they could go.

"I don't sing." He tried to explain but the expressions were unrelenting. "I wouldn't even know what to say." He barely opened his mouth, so the words squeezed out like toothpaste from a clogged tube. The young men with tablets looked uneasy. The girls who were beating on the counter to give off the sound of drums shot him dirty looks. Like a camp counselor, Iris eased their worries, waving away their tension with a hand and a smile, talking simply to Christopher and to them. Her eyes didn't focus on any of them but on all of them. "Just think about what you would do if you could lay all your worries down. If you didn't have to feel burdened anymore." She nodded at the crowd who had turned from uneasy to helpful, their answers peppering the air with sounds like a spoken symphony getting in tune. Now she looked only at Christopher.

"How would you feel?"

His phone felt like a boulder in his pocket and his body still ached from the decision he'd made, his legs feeling like cinder blocks. Everything had been so hard this year, but the answer had been so simple that when he said it, the crowd surged in agreement, with the music picking up full swing. It was so loud Iris could barely hear him, but she knew just as well what he'd said.

Chapter 35

Cat out of the Bag

"D id you know about this?"

She hit the button and Eric picked up before the phone could ring a second time.

"Hey, M—," and just as quickly, Maisy spoke before he could get out another word.

"How long have you known?" There was accusation in her voice but it wasn't hard. It was softened by faint amusement. There was tension and excitement in her voice. Maisy didn't like not knowing anything, especially when it came to Iris. Being one step behind was as good as not walking at all. At the same time, the girl's joy was infectious. Through the window, she could see it. The coffee shop brimmed with smiling people who not moments before had trudged through the rest stop.

"Known what?" The last word was muffled. He was rubbing his beard like he did when he was tired. He was slow in the morning before his second cup of coffee. Maisy ducked out of the coffee shop into the silent hallway and crouched over her phone like a lioness over a gazelle. Eric had been waiting for this call.

She ducked into the hallway outside, which was silent now that most of the customers at the Truck and Sip were funneled into the Queequeg's getting a look at the newest VueClix star.

The crowd buzzed like a hive and Iris was the queen. She spoke animatedly with a young girl holding a doll from the crane machine. That single fact alone would have brought the girl to a standstill only moments ago, but here, with the sounds of the song still hanging in the air, it was something completely different. Her hands weren't tucked into her hat. She waved them for emphasis to whatever story she told, and a smile stretched across her face, her forehead free of worry. It was going to be okay. Christopher nodded at Iris just then, as if the two were thinking the same thing.

"Can I have your autograph?" A girl with a sparkly bow in her hair thrust a coffee cozy toward Iris, which she quickly scribbled on with a complimentary pen.

"What did you do when you hit a million views?" asked the hip guy with the beard as if he was too tired to speak, yet his eyes twinkled with excitement behind his pointy glasses.

Cat out of the Bag

"I." She looked at Christopher, who shrugged just as surprised as she was. "I didn't do anything considering I've only just found out."

The other dashing guy stepped forward, adjusting his hat not self-consciously but for affect. "Your donut video hit the million mark within a day of posting, and the one that you sang at the soda machine?" He poked and swiped at his tablet like he was conducting a symphony. "It's at 700,000 already." He held up the device and there was Iris as she stood at the Stuckey's making music with the soda machine. "This one with the plates is headed the same way. If you don't mind, I'd like to post this little concert. Do you mind?"

Iris felt a rush in her cheeks that wasn't itchy or hot like fire. It wasn't a panicked, sick feeling but a warm, tropical feeling like something good was going to happen. "I don't mind."

"Did you say plates?" Chris leaned in. He wasn't much for social media. It had taken the university nearly twisting off his arm to set up his academic page.

"Yes, that's right." The guy in the tight jeans lifted his laptop beside his friend's tablet. In the short film, she was building a fountain out of kitchen items back at Jack's kitchen. Whoever had taken the movie had framed her in such a way that the light glowed behind her as she sang. She looked like someone Christopher couldn't place until he remembered the boy with the tablet.

"An angel."

He saw Maisy's hands waving emphatically from the hallway. He had no idea who she was talking to but he could venture a guess.

"Iris is some kind of viral star?"

Eric made the noise he made when he forgot to restock the cooler at the store, the same noise he made when he let that old lady leave without paying, the one who muttered to herself about the husband she swears is going to meet her one day.

"Kind of. Well, yes. I saw it yesterday." She could hear the whisker scratch sound again. "I meant to tell you this morning. I didn't want to worry you."

"Worry *me*?"

In just one day, Iris had spread across the internet like ink in water. Her song at the donut shop was featured on TV Music and the BuzzBee website, an entertainment site with an audience of millions. One of the late-night hosts had already tried to emulate her beat boxing. In short, the girl had become a sort of cult celebrity in the course of a day.

In any other situation, Maisy would have paced, fretted, and pulled out her hair thinking of ways to break this kind of news to Iris, who panicked at the attention trick or treating would bring. In this case, she leaned against the partition between the coffee world and where she stood looking in on Iris as she talked energetically with the people around her, smiling like she did in the spinning teacup ride on the boardwalk. Her shoulders rested in line with her collarbone, her neck held tall and straight. She was a regal-looking girl when she wasn't crippled by anxiety. She rocked not forward and backward in fear, but happily from side-to-side like any other teenage girl talking about a band she liked.

Maisy expected to feel panicked, but she looked at Iris and felt happy.

"Hey kid, that was something else, wasn't it?" She nestled in between the little girl who wouldn't leave Iris' side and a trucker she didn't look at.

"Something other than what exactly?" There was no tone that would indicate this was a smart teenage response. She said it as serenely as a yogi chanting om and as Maisy responded she almost tripped over her words.

"Nothing. I. It was a strange saying. I just meant, wow."

The man turned as she was speaking and he looked like he walked right off the set of her favorite show.

"She's great, right?" He asked. His smile reminded her of one of the *Ghostbrothers*, at least that's what Iris called it. She followed the adventure of the sibling who watched out for his younger brother as they fought off creatures from the other world. He looked like the older brother, all tough swag on the outside, but the way he was smiling at Iris, was uncanny.

"Ahem. Yes, I know she's my—"

"We're related." Iris had been working so hard on not interrupting. Yet, she'd cut Iris off midsentence.

The young girl with Iris giggled, making her stuffed owl turn figure 8s in the air.

"I wanted one of those, but I couldn't get the crane to work." Iris said.

The room still buzzed, the patrons all riding high on the wave of song and laughter that had only just stopped. It took Christopher a minute to weave through all the people without spilling the contents of his overfilled latte.

"My dad can win you one, Iris. Iris, Iris, you're my favor-ite."

The girl struggled with the word like she was trying to lift a heavy object over a wall. Christopher handed a cup to Maisy and the *Ghostbrother* lifted his eyebrow with a shrug that looked more disappointed than happy.

"I'm sure she'd like her own dad to win her one." He shifted in his spot toward the girl who was still as attached to Iris as she was before. "Let's leave them to it, Lily."

"Leave us to what? That's not my dad. That's Dr. Christopher. He's my friend. Right, Christopher?" She snatched a hot chocolate from Christopher's hand and he nodded at the man and at Maisy, half-realizing the implication that had been tossed out.

"And I stink at those machines."

"Is it okay, Maisy? Can Mr. Eckles try?"

Cat out of the Bag

"Sean," he thrust his hand out more eagerly than intended. She took it just as quickly. It was a strong hand, the kind of hand that would hold strong if the bottom fell out from under her. It was warm suddenly, and Maisy felt like she needed to move.

Lily and Maisy talked like old friends as the machines buzzed and beeped around them.

"You know it's something else, running into Iris, here. Of all places. She's been watching VueClix the whole ride down. We're heading to Happy World. Little dad time, you know?"

Sean Eckles was talking and Maisy knew there were words coming out of his mouth and that they might have even been in English, but not one connected. She was watching more than listening, the curve of his lips, his straight white teeth. The resemblance was uncanny.

Maisy felt the blood rush to her cheeks. She'd been looking into his eyes unapologetically as if she were watching them on TV. They were bright green eyes with a yellow glow inside like there was a light shining inside, ethereal eyes, like a wolf's.

"I'm sorry, what?"

He smiled, that smile again. "You gotta get as much time as you can when you can, am I right?"

Even though Iris was the resident head scratcher, Maisy found herself pawing at her wavy hair as if she were trying to shake loose the cobwebs in her mind.

There was a guy who was a dead ringer for one of the 'idjits' she watched every day. Now he was plunking dollar after dollar into a crane machine to win a toy for her daughter while explaining how much he values spending time with his own child. She wondered if her coffee had been dosed with something.

"Got it!" He pulled the owl from the machine and from across the arcade Iris started flapping her hands like she was about to take flight. She and her new friend jumped up and down with delight, passing one owl into the hands of the other and then switching back.

"Daddy, Daddy, Ir-is is going, going to Happy World. Too-oo." The last sound extended further out from the sentence than it would have had anyone else spoken it. Iris didn't notice the difference. Maisy didn't let on. Sean appreciated the both of them more than his smile could ever show.

There was that glow in his eyes again, sparkling like a supernatural fire.

"That's great. Maybe we'll see you down there."

"Sure."

"Let me give you my number, if that's okay. At the risk of sounding too forward, maybe I can take you to dinner?"

"That would be nice." Maisy scanned her surroundings, as she did every few minutes for unforeseen sounds or surprises. Chris was in the hallway, clearly talking on his phone to someone.

She instinctively felt for her own.

Chapter 36

Georgia

The questions had started the second they pulled out of the truck stop, intermittent and gentle at first, like raindrops. Iris wanted to know how long it would be until they hit Florida, or how long it would take to get to the next state. Then it was an inquiry here or there about speed limits and car safety. This was how it went any time they drove, but this hadn't been any drive. By the time they hit South Carolina, the trickle of talk had become a deluge.

"Did you know South Carolina actually produces more peaches than Georgia?" She half muttered, poring over the tourist map she'd swiped at the last pee break. "That means Georgia is a liar. Why do they boil peanuts? Are there special peanuts in the south that are poison if they're not boiled? That must be it. It must be an issue with the shells so that would be why."

"Iris."

"They need to boil off the poison so the people don't die if they get the poison coating on the peanut that protects it from the heat."

"Iris."

Maisy's voice was calm but firm. She persisted but the girl didn't hear. She went on with theories about various peanut poisons as if her mother hadn't said a word. Frankly, Maisy wasn't fazed. On any car ride Iris grew anxious enough to prattle. Maisy was surprised it had taken this long.

"Iris. The peanuts aren't poison." The new presence of Christopher's voice snapped her from her monologue long enough to nod and shrug before moving on to the next pressing issue.

"It's illegal to sell electric eels in South Carolina, but it's the sweet tea capital of the world. Can we stop and get sweet tea? Do you think we will be late if we stop for sweet tea? Maisy, I let Christopher try my sweet tea icing and he liked it, but I'm not sure if that's what I'm gonna make at the Bake-Off because there are so many things.

Pineapplecoconutrumdrizzlebarbecue. Her words had become a continuous thread that sounded like music and she blinked her eyes and pressed her head to the seat behind her in a rhythm that rivaled any jazz drummer.

"Iris, take a breath!" Maisy tried not to shout and the girl looked at her as if questioning her volume, speaking again as if she were doing commentary on a chess match.

Georgia

"Pulled pork like the sandwich I ate? Do you think that would work? It could be delicious but the balance between sweet and savory is delicate. I wouldn't want it to taste like vomit."

Iris pulled her finger to her mouth and scanned the tourist map. It was filled with the kind of trivia that could keep her entertained for miles. Out of the side of his eye, Christopher looked at Maisy with a dip of his head. The calm had fooled him. Maisy knew better. She handed her phone over to the back seat even though relinquishing it meant no check-ins with home or the store. It was a sacrifice she was willing to make.

"Here, why don't you look up some flavor combos, or you can go to the Bake-Off site. See if they have a map of where we're going to be. Iris loves maps."

Within seconds, Iris had pulled up a 3D image of the contest site and a list of other competitors. With that, she cross-referenced other competitions and generated a list of recipes she would most likely see once they got there.

"You did all that with the phone?" Christopher asked with a smile of amazement that was in no way feigned for effect. He was still trying to set up his email.

Maisy was better but not by much. "Technology is pretty amazing."

For a good long while, no one spoke and the hum of the road had lulled Christopher into the peaceful road trance daydreams are made of. That's why when the scream came he almost drove off the road. The sound was so jarring the car veered hard to the right before he realized what it was. It was a high-pitched squeal that sounded half-rodent, half-robot. Iris sat upright while staring up at the ceiling, and her body was moving side-to-side. Before he could say a word, Maisy was turned to the back reaching for the girl's hand.

"Keep driving," she assured him. "Iris."

"Wheeee-uhhhhh. Heyccck." She rocked. "Mow, mow. Mow. We're still driving. Driving. Driving." Her eyes scanned the road like she hadn't noticed it before. "The trees are moving so fast, Maisy."

"Don't look at the trees, sweetie."

He hadn't heard this side of Maisy's voice. He'd heard the shrill panic voice and the fierce protective lion voice, but this was new.

"I don't feel so good." The girl looked scared and her lips moved so quickly the words didn't make sense. "Persimmons and snickety crickets walk wildly. Trees fasten margarine mugs in weasel fingers. Tantamount lemons. Lemons and wiener dogs." It was gibberish that ran in one long thread, a life rope falling overboard, but Maisy caught it.

She climbed into the back sitting so close to the girl they could be connected. She put her arms around her and squeezed, humming a familiar tune in her ear. It was a Dave song, but the words were for her little girl.

Georgia

"Sweet Iris, lay down, sing this song for me, forever and a while. Sweeeeeet Iris, lay down." Maisy's voice was sweet. All the nerves and edge had melted and she rocked with the girl whose eyes had grown heavy. Christopher, for all his training, felt like he knew nothing. He was a stranger in this car, looking onto something he'd truly never understand.

Iris rocked with Maisy as the song shrunk to a whisper only they could share and Iris had fallen asleep, stretched out with her pillow from her bed at home. Maisy climbed back into the front with the dexterity of a ninja, clicking her seatbelt back on, as if she'd just swatted a fly or changed the DVD, or some other menial car-bound task. Clearly, this was old hat for the both of them.

"It's really hard, being in a car, for her." Her voice was barely there. "I'm surprised it took this long." She mouthed the words and the doctor understood, wanting nothing more but to help.

For all his expertise, Christopher wasn't sure he could say anything as clearly as the woman next to him just had. He fought the impulse to be a psychologist and let quiet fill the car and his mind until the question burned its way to his lips.

"Is it ever hard for you?"

"Is what hard for me?"

"Doing all this?" He swallowed adding, "Alone?"

Maisy answered without a moment's thought. "I like being alone." She shrugged. "Some people don't want to be alone. I'm used to it just being me. I like it."

There was nothing to add, so instead he let the silence speak for him. In that beautiful stillness, the two drifted off to the places in their minds where time no longer mattered. He drove for miles and with the silence thick between them Christopher was left with his thoughts and his phone burning a hole right through him. Perhaps he squirmed in his seat or reached for it. Maybe he brushed a hand by it as teenagers do when waiting for that all important text. Whatever it was, he had to do something. It was like Maisy knew.

"You just cut and run, right? That's your story?" She was surprised there was no malice in her voice to hide. She wasn't picking a fight, just stating what they both knew.

"I didn't." Chris leaned in his seat thinking of all the words he wanted to say, while shifting from one side to the next. He tried to focus them, but none escaped. They all stayed where they were weighing him down like cannonballs. "You don't understand."

Everything Maisy said was a whisper that barely registered over Iris' deep snores. She felt like she was yelling all the same. She understood just fine.

"You couldn't stick it out, so you left. No warning. No nothing. Just adios. Rachel doesn't deserve that. For the rest of her life, she'll be wondering, thinking she wasn't good enough. Then she'll feel lonely, especially since she wanted you around. You'll see. She'll get used to it." The words came so quickly she was unsure if she was saying them out loud. "She'll never trust anyone, though. No matter how hard they work to show her they are worthy they won't be. She won't let them in." Her eyes hurt. The sun was too bright. "You might be gone but that doubt will stay with her."

She took a sip of leftover coffee not because she was thirsty but because she didn't want to say anymore. Not sure if it was an afterthought or an apology, she finally said, "She deserves better." They drove along in silence punctuated by Iris' deep snores until that weight in Christopher's head drifted down past his heart where it sat in his gut like sickness.

"I called her, you know."

There was an almost imperceptible jump in Maisy. Her mind was somewhere else.

"I miss my dog." He kept his eyes on the road though Maisy watched him. "I miss Rachel. I bet you didn't know that. I miss her. I miss us." He gripped the steering wheel like there was a downpour outside, but the road was clear ahead. A low sound came from him that wasn't quite sigh or moan. "She does deserve better, Maisy. That's why I left."

Before she could say what she was thinking, a word that meant excrement and male cows and at least two quarters in the swear jar, he spoke again.

"I know you think I just abandoned her, because every guy does that. Right? In your book, we all suck. I get that. No, don't explain. I get it." He rubbed his eyes like that could make the ache go away. It was too bright out here on this open road. "She was more alone with me around, Maisy. I'm not saying it's right, but I'm, I'm broken. She deserves better."

"You know why I quit my practice? One day, this kid is talking to me about something that happened to him. His grandpa." He swallowed. The air felt dry and sour suddenly. "Guy was a monster. There's this eight-year-old kid telling me this story. I got up while he was talking, walked out the door, and I didn't come back. I drove home. I put on my pajamas and I lay in bed for a week."

"When Rachel would try to talk to me I just stared." Out of the corner of his eye he could see Maisy watching him, not warily, but intently.

"I'm a doctor, Maisy. I knew what I had as long I could remember. I always had it under *control*." He finally looked at her. "Then I couldn't control it. The sadness. I couldn't take it, so Rachel took care of me like I was a baby." His voice felt raw, "And I let her. *That's* what she doesn't deserve."

Maisy's eyes were sympathetic but he cautioned her.

"Don't." His half-shrug wasn't scolding. "The pity is the worst part. That's the look Rachel gave me too. Like I was fragile. I'm supposed to be protecting her, giving her a life where she feels loved, not just needed." He rubbed his eyes. "You know, she's the most beautiful woman you could ever meet. Her eyes shine like the ocean when the sun catches it just right. Now she looks at me like I'm the sick puppy she's stuck taking care of."

"She's wants to be a mom." He smiled. "And travel, she goes hiking with Sasquatch every Saturday. For hours. Some days, I can't even get out of bed. Marriage shouldn't be a jail sentence." He took a gulp of his own cold bitter coffee, the leftovers were a welcome distraction from what was fresh in his mind.

"She does deserve better. She deserves to have the life that she wants."

"What if the life she wants is with you?"

The voice broke into the conversation from the back of the car and what was most unsettling wasn't that they'd woken Iris up, but that the voice wasn't hers.

Chapter 37

Resemblance

Maisy and Iris watched from inside the car, giving Christopher whatever privacy they could while he finished the call. They wouldn't be able to hear him with the windows closed and with him standing twenty feet from where the car was parked off the road. Yet he crouched in the tall grass, head jammed into his shoulder like he was whispering secrets.

"That was a dirty trick, Iris. What if he wasn't ready to talk to her? Did you ever think of that?" Maisy was building up steam as she normally did when she was about to outline a number of things that could have gone wrong. These speeches were as common as milk in the fridge and lists tacked onto the door.

"He was." Her words were flat like she was reading the ingredient list off the back of a cereal box. "He's been ready all morning. Didn't you see his eyes? They were sparkling. They were going to cry soon if he didn't."

They both sat with straight backs pressed firmly to the seat so they looked like odd bookends when he came back. It was the posture that feigned ease on the outside while inside he knew they were cringing. They were quiet like school kids telling secrets. He let them stew in it, not for cruelty's sake but because he too had some things inside he was trying to hide via some good old-fashioned posturing. He moved a hand casually over his face like his eyes were tired, wiping away the wetness that had bubbled up like a spring. A deep breath usually did the trick for most people. For him, it was a slow neck roll and a cough or two.

"Allergies." Maisy coughed too, not looking at him. She sat perfectly erect like the girl behind her, the two of them looking like mannequins that were put in the car for display. She cleared her throat and wiped the invisible offender away from her nose while he collected the last bit of himself he needed in the moment.

Iris looked out the window at everything and nothing, eyes focused somewhere only she could see.

"That was something." He turned to Maisy and looked back at Iris, who'd only noticed now he'd said a word. She tried to smile politely like she'd seen people do in movies but her lip caught on her tooth so she half snarled. "It's okay." It was as unconvincing as the little shrug that went with it, so he tried again, each word more thoughtful than the previous. "I think it went all right, as all right as it could. She evidently heard every word of what I said. Thanks for that, kid."

"It is amazing what those speakers can pick up. What?" Maisy's squinted, eyebrows lifted, and she gave Christopher a grin that pulled a note of mirth from him he hadn't heard in some time.

"It's okay, I think. She's upset. She doesn't understand that I'm actually helping her here. Being away from me is the best thing for her. She doesn't appreciate that yet." Whatever veneer of ease he'd put on had begun to wear down and he shifted gears. "I got to talk to Sasquatch. Have I shown you my dog?"

He pulled out his wallet like he was pulling a stickup and fanned out an accordion sleeve of pictures featuring not just the enormous dog but the tiny woman he was trying to put behind him. The irony of this was lost on Iris.

"She's very pretty, Christopher, like Spiderman's girlfriend in the comics. Is that her natural hair color or does she dye it?"

"It is natural. Here if you look at this one, it's a great pic of Sasquatch."

"He looks like a bear." Maisy prompted as Iris stroked the smooth plastic covering the image. It was cold under her fingers, like water in the morning while the shower heated up, such a cold feeling for a dog that looked like a teddy bear married a soft winter blanket.

"He's our big baby." He chuckled. "Not much of a bear. He's afraid of the dark if you can imagine. See here, in this one?" In the picture Christopher and Rachel lay on scant corners of a bed primarily covered by the dog sprawled on his back paws sticking straight up in the air.

"We sing him his little song. We rub his belly and in minutes he's snoring. Then I sneak off the bed and shut out the light. It's our whole bedtime routine."

"Was." Iris corrected and it caught him off guard.

"Sorry?"

"Was." She nodded surely. "You left."

He folded the pictures into a neat pile but didn't put them away. "Yes. Well, I suppose Rachel is still doing it."

Maisy shifted where she sat and crinkled her forehead at the girl who could look so much like her yet still surprise her at every opportunity.

"He sounds like a real teddy bear, Doc. I'm so glad you got to say hello."

"Speaking of which, aren't you due?"

"Due for what?"

"You haven't checked in with your pets in at least an hour or so."

"What's that sly look for?"

"It's just. I know you're very concerned. You can never be too careful when it comes to a betta fish."

"No you can't," Iris butted in, not concerned with the playful lilt in his voice or the raised eyebrow that meant he was probably talking about something else, "Call Eric."

All at once, Iris was the spitting image of the woman in front of her, the worry pushing her voice up and down like a balloon in the wind.

"You need to check on Sophie."

353

Chapter 38

Cowboys and Engines

Iris sat so far up in her seat that her face was almost between Christopher and Maisy. Maisy had taken the wheel at the last stop and she was happy she did. Though he tried to hide the fact, Christopher had been texting for the last twenty minutes. He'd punch in a message, wait a few seconds, and smile at his phone like it was talking to him. Eric hadn't picked up the phone on the first half ring as she expected but had replied with a clear text. *The pets are fine.* When she texted back there was no response, which meant he was busy at the store, which was also a good thing. Now, with Iris so close by, there was less to worry about. It was kind of nice to let go of the tension in her mind and let it drift out over the road like a balloon.

"That's fifteen, now. Fifteen billboards for the same place. Why are they putting up billboards every half-mile for the same place? Is it famous?"

Maisy took a breath to speak but Iris was curious, which made it hard to get a word in edgewise.

"We should go there. Are you hungry? Even if you're not, it says they have a komodo dragon and a reptile house. We have time. Check-in isn't until after 3. They're very specific about that in my prize package." She pawed through a frilly folder covered in pastel lace. "My park tickets aren't good until tomorrow."

The tension was coming back. It was a tightrope feeling, like Iris had one around her neck. The thought of another night in a room that wasn't her own squeezed her throat like a hand. She didn't want to think about it. Even more, what she didn't want to think about was that she was upset at herself for not being able to handle it. She thought she could. The night in the cottage had been torture. It was better with Maisy there, but she wanted her bed and her walls.

"That cowboy place at the border? Pecos something, right?" Christopher broke from the text conversation he was pretending not to have. "Home of the world's largest ten-gallon hat."

"We're staying at a cowboy hotel. See? We have to go. It'll help us prepare for the Old West Hotel." She pointed at glossy photos of gunslingers with thick moustaches serving milkshakes in the hotel saloon and rooms decorated with wagon wheels and tumbleweeds.

"Back when I was in college, we drove down to Florida and stopped there. It's not really much to sneeze at."

Cowboys and Engines

Iris instinctively felt her nose. It wasn't itchy at all. She pulled out a brochure from her contest folder package, the one with the reservations and tickets she touched periodically to reassure herself she still had them.

"It's a bit of a wreck from what I remember." Christopher added. "Cheesy plaster cactuses and lassos." Maisy gave a mirthless laugh of agreement. "I think there's a restaurant they call Tex Mex but it's really—"

"We need to prepare." The words burst from Iris like air through a pinhole in an overinflated balloon. Maisy had been laughing; her face went still and she spoke calmly.

"Okay."

It wasn't on the schedule and none of them had to go, but when the giant cowboy hat came into view, Christopher took the exit for PECOS PHIL'S.

It was a giant property that in its time had been impressive. Lines of kitschy shops and food stands lined a giant lot dotted with wooden cutouts of sheriff badges and cacti. The place was close to abandoned and by the looks of it had been forgotten by the hordes of tourists heading to the newer, shinier attractions further south. The garbage cans lay half open, overflowing not for the abundance of visitors but for the lack of being emptied. A sharp stench cut through the air that was both rancid food and spilled chemicals, as if old moldy cheese and nail polish remover were joined in one putrid stink. Whatever it was, the heat didn't help. It clung to the warm air like a ghost that wouldn't leave.

"Should we go in the hat?"

"I don't think we can, mouse." Maisy clicked her teeth and looked up at the tower that in its heyday looked like a hat, but for now looked more like what it really was: a rusted-out water tank leaning on its supports like a drunken old cowboy. Iris bounced on the balls of her feet anyway, just as excited about the broken ghost town as she was about the rest stop or about her trip to Happy World. The bright colors, though faded through years of neglect, exploded with possibilities. She could be a cartoon deputy or a runaway bank robber. It was all right there for her.

Food carts disguised as covered wagons and old train cars lined a path down a dirt road that led to the reptile house (closed) and the cowboy museum and ride (currently not running due to technical difficulties). Sure, the fabrics on the covered wagons were faded and for the most part looked like hot dog carts wearing hats. The attempt at the illusion was still very real and she appreciated it.

"Look guys, a car wash! Should we clean the car? Look, it's called Cowboys and Engines, get it?"

The theming was cheap and forced but it was there. Iris looked like a kid who'd never seen candy as she walked into Wonka's great chocolate factory. Maisy couldn't fault her for that. She'd seen the girl get excited for the cardboard box her desk chair came in. Once when Iris was really small, she'd asked for a dollhouse Maisy couldn't afford. When Christmas came, she showed as much excitement for a sweater and books, as she would have for the fancy dollhouse she wanted. Later when she'd tried on all her new clothes and colored every picture in the books, she disappeared into her bedroom where she crafted a full-size fashion dollhouse from a stack of books and some old gift boxes. Maisy couldn't fault her for playing pretend, for seeing the patch of asphalt and peeling paint for a real-life Wild West city. She couldn't fault the girl for lacking the cynicism she herself had in abundance.

"Here, here, here! Let's eat here!" There was a one wagon covered in electric green, boasting 101 types of guacamole, *ALL U CAN EAT.* Iris ripped through 37 samples before her face began to match the contents of the small bowl and she decided that was all.

It was a short break from the road and they were still well on schedule. Maisy didn't mind and Christopher lounged in the shade of a wooden cutout tree, where he seemed more than content to look at his phone.

It was like a ghost town here, which is why the gunshot came as such a surprise.

The sound cracked the space between Iris and safety in half and in an instant she felt as if the world had broken beneath her feet. She jumped before Maisy could move and ran full speed past the dilapidated gift shops and straight through the parking lot toward the highway.

The thing most people didn't know about Iris is, she's fast.

"Where is she going?" The man in the beaten-up excuse for a cowboy costume looked hurt. It wasn't often they got a chance to do the street show, the one with the showdown and the lassos. It was the whole reason he'd shut up the museum to change into costume.

"She, I'm sorry. It wasn't you. It was the…" Christopher tried at once to smooth over the cowboy's hurt feelings and watch Maisy rush across the lot after the girl who headed into a busy road. He'd seen Iris startle but not like this. Yet all the while, Maisy remained calm.

She walked Iris to the car where she buckled her into the seat like she would a small child. Iris took big, deep breaths, her eyes widening and narrowing as if they were a pair of back-up mouths sucking in air greedily like her life depended on it.

Maisy stayed in the back with her, murmuring a tune softly like hummingbird wings.

Moments later when the girl finally spoke, her words struck Christopher like sledgehammers.

"I hate that I ruin everything. Why can't I just be like everyone else?"

Christopher spoke without a measure of thought. "You are." Whether he knew he did it or not, he'd taken one hand from the wheel and rested it on the pocket that held his phone. "Everyone's got something, Iris."

Chapter 39

Doubt Mouse

So far, nothing had gone as Iris imagined. The Georgia boiled peanuts were not toasty nuggets of heaven. They tasted like bland rocks. Pecos Phil's was a faded billboard place that scared her half to death with its loud noises and no komodo dragon. Now she was afraid Happy World would be like any other cheesy park for young children with rides that looked like the wind-up toys in her room. Darlene's Tiki Cottage hadn't been disappointing. In that case, it had been Iris who was the letdown. Even though she thought she had been so prepared, Iris missed her room. In some way, every bit of this trip had fallen well beneath expectation. That was, of course, until Happy World had come into view.

"Oh my, I can't believe it." The hotel was built into a real mountain, or at least what was made to look like a mountain, right in the middle of Florida, and it wasn't a façade.

"The Riley Company trucked in tons of dirt and rocks from out west to build an authentic western adventure." Iris alternated reading from her folder and staring at the wonder in front of her.

"We check-in there in the middle of that big building that looks like the old-timey hotel. Look at the stained glass, Maisy. Do you see it?" The expansive property replicated the barren landscape of the wild American desert, rolling red sand dotted every once and again with flat stones. Maisy hoped these were the same animatronic creatures from the theme park rides she was seeing because large snakes lifted their heads from the ground on either side of the car as they drove by.

"It must've cost millions to build this." Maisy made the clicking sound she made only when she was impressed or thinking. Either way, it was warranted.

This was a whole world, a collection of buildings and a landscape that together made up an old western town. It wasn't the beat-up fading relic that was Pecos Phil's but a shiny Old West dream city in shiny, spare no expense Technicolor. Real horses walked the pathways that connected the sheriff's to the saloon and undertaker's. Like the mechanical snakes that looked all too real, there were tumbleweeds that really tumbled. There were no cutouts here, but actual cactuses that sprouted up in front of shops and hitching posts as if it were 1885. Real horses clip clopped between the newspaper shop and the stable, to the postman at a leisurely pace that made the guests heading in and out look frantic. At the center of all this movement was the showpiece, the main building modeled to look like a proper western hotel.

Chris pulled in through two tall wooden gates marked GUEST ONLY where he was met by an old prospector who asked if he could park the old covered wagon.

"We're packed fuller than a powder keg." He said with a tip of his hat, as at least a dozen people buzzed behind him like a swarm. "Let me see if I can find you a nice spot." He disappeared into a maze of metal that looked like every car in his town and at once the doctor felt a surge of panic. This wasn't a side-of-the-road motel where he could just crash for the night. This was the kind of place that took reservations months in advance.

"This place is pretty fancy. I don't think they're going to take too kindly to me sleeping in the car."

"You're staying with us, silly." Iris said without a thought and Maisy stopped on the spot with a look on her face that screamed without making a sound. Neither thing was noticed by Iris, who kept walking and speaking at the same rapid pace.

"I get a suite. It has its own kitchen, so I can practice my recipes, and a whole 'nother bedroom, so there's lots of room. We even have a pullout couch in case someone staying with me decides to snore all night."

Maisy was busy snapping pictures and sending them as fast as she could. It wasn't often they went away. She caught up in two long strides. "I don't snore."

"Yeah, you do. Don't worry. Look, check-in is here."

The lobby was cavernous, literally. One wall was made to look like a rock wall with a mine carved inside. A mine cart hung precariously out of the shaft twenty feet above on a piece of partially laid track. There were trees growing up through the floor that reached up to the ceiling, so far up it was hard to see. There were showgirls and cowboys walking among the tourists—bakers here for the contest sharing sugar secrets, crying babies, foreign accents, all over the ambient Old West noises that filled the large hall.

Of all this, two things drew Iris in so she didn't want to move. First was the smell. It hit her dead in the face as the doors slid open, evergreen leaf and freshly cut wood layered over the light perfume of popping popcorn and slow roasting meat. They tickled her nose in a good way and the more she breathed the more she picked up on the slightest hint of smoky campfire and dusty earth. Logic told her it was a smell that was piped in through a ventilation system. She had read everything there was to know about Mort Riley and the lengths his company would go to create an authentic experience for Happy World guests. Part of her wanted to believe that she was in the middle of Tombstone, Arizona, on her way to her fortune.

Apart from all the magic that was happening in her nose, there was a tingling on her skin like a gusty breeze that felt fresh, clean, and slightly wet. It was like cold air was rushing at her from the hole in the ground dead center of the lobby between two of the largest trees.

"That's the geyser, little lady." A man sat at a piano shined so glossy his face reflected back at him. "It goes off every hour on the hour. Quite a sight to see."

With that another scent played in her mind, of fresh water and snowdrifts, the freezing cold smell of first snow and slushee machines. She knew it was familiar.

An old-timey card dealer checked them in at a tall hardwood counter polished to shine just as bright as the piano. He talked in a lilting drawl that was almost musical, and though he kept in character it was hard for Iris to concentrate on his words.

"Yer about three floors up with all the other contest folks. And that'll do ya."

The prospector from out front had returned. He grabbed a bag and Iris jumped with a start. "What're ya gonna be baking tonight, little filly?"

"Tomorrow," she corrected, looking to the dealer who had rattled off her itinerary just a moment before.

"First round starts this evening at 7 sharp, at the Golden Horseshoe Review: Reception and Tasting. It's a little get together for all the contestants to get to know each other. You know, get a taste of the competition." The girl looked so stricken the dealer leaned toward Maisy trying his best to whisper so as to not get caught breaking character. "It's the ballroom down the hall." Iris started breathing very heavily and the prospector and dealer looked at each other uncomfortably.

"Judging doesn't start until tomorrow. It says so in the folder. I thought I had time. I need time to plan. I need time to get ready."

All of a sudden the slick, mustached dealer looked like what he really was, a college kid with an internship at the most joyful place on the planet who was having a difficult time making his guests happy.

"It's not for points or anything. It's just so people can mingle?"

"You got plenty of time, honey." The prospector assured Iris as she pawed through her folder.

The dealer repeated the speech he'd just given but without the accent and old-time flourish. "You get a tour of the park and welcome reception starts at 7 PM." It sounded like an apology when he said it this time.

"I thought it all started tomorrow." She muttered running her hand over the line that proved her wrong, over and over again. "I thought…"

Maisy, who hadn't said a word, hooked her arm through Iris' and nodded. "We got this."

Maisy had spent the majority of the past decade learning how to pick and choose her words, how to plan daily activities based on the least stress possible. It was a lot like walking on a balance beam, keeping her eye on every obstacle that could arise while keeping her head atop the strongest shoulders possible. She had to be unwavering. When she decided to forego the welcome reception and Iris' eyes welled up with tears she held steadfast, despite the cries and pleas, despite Iris' assurances it would be okay. It was already a crazy day, spent half on the road. There were cheesy cowboys and traffic and now a hotel.

They shuffled past groups of bakers and tourists through the ornate hallway that looked like it was torn from a history book. Christopher hooked toward the elevator before Maisy could stop him.

"No, Doc." She shook her head and wrinkled her nose and eyebrows as if the compartment behind the sliding doors contained a flesh-eating monster.

"Right," he motioned to the bags, suitcase, and sleeping bag dragging behind Iris. "Since we're on the fifth floor, why don't you let me take some of these things and meet you? Does that sound all right?"

Iris had her favorite bathrobe draped around her neck. She rarely found herself in the bath, spending years perfecting the art of the sponge bath and dry shampoo, and all methods possible to avoid water touching her in any way. The bathrobe, *Robey*, meant comfort and home.

"Just take good care of Robey. Don't drop her."

"I've got it, Iris."

"Her."

"I've got *her*, Iris."

He gathered bags and stuffed animals, pillows and the fluffy pink robe despite longing eyes.

She gave the parting advice to the good doctor as the doors slid shut, "Don't let anyone steal her."

Christopher disappeared behind the doors.

Iris felt unburdened with the heavy bag off her back. Yet her hand felt heavy, tracing the words on her itinerary like it were weighed there with a magnet holding it to the paper right where it said RECEPTION TONIGHT.

"It would be too much for anyone, Iris." Maisy's voice was softer than usual.

"Especially me," Iris' voice went dark the way it did when she doubted or panicked, but most of all when she felt like no one in the world understood her.

"Stop that."

"Stop what?"

"Stop the nonsense. We've come this far. Don't start in with the feeling sorry for yourself. You're better than that." She was short and to listening ears a bit tough on the girl, but she had to be. If she gave her room to spin her wheels, they would soon spin out of control.

"We'll settle in, get you nice and ready, and then." She let the words hang there like a half-built bridge.

"Then what?" Iris finished.

"Then you win this thing."

Chapter 40

Date with a Ghostbrother

It wasn't so bad getting up the stairs now that Christopher had taken the stuffed animals and cookbooks, the tape player, sleeping bag, and Robey. Their floor was noisy. It was a hallway wide enough so that small children could play catch from one side to the next. That made the sound carry that much more. People brushed past them on their way to the lobby or pool carrying all sorts of travel bags and big fluffy towels that scratched against the walls like cat claws. From inside the rooms, sound reverberated out, kids on school trips and little babies crying. It echoed against the flickering lights that buzzed in her ears. Maisy couldn't hear any of that, but she could see it on Iris' face. She was starting to get the look that troubled Maisy the most, the one where she was trying to look like nothing was bothering her. Her eyes went wide like she was putting forth a great effort to keep her brow from furrowing and the rest of her face looked almost plastic as she tried to keep it from moving. This was her "normal" face, and it sent a chill down Maisy's neck worse than any horror movie music in this great long hall.

"The map says, we turn here at the end and hook down this other hall. Iris? You with me, kid?"

"I really wanted to go the reception."

"Iris, it's for the best."

"It's part of the competition, and since I'm in the competition I should really go." The girl stopped to speak and hadn't moved. "It's not fair that I don't get to go. What if there's a secret competition before the competition and I lose because I wasn't even there."

"There isn't."

"What if there is?" Her eyes were strained and she stood so stiffly her body swayed just so.

"Iris, it's too much."

"*I want to go.*"

"We'll think about it."

They both knew this meant no, but it was enough to get the girl moving. She focused her eyes ahead of her and though singing a song low under her breath, she tried to keep her lips from moving. Her thin arms wrapped around her so tightly it was a wonder she could keep her balance sauntering through the hall in long labored strides. It was a quite a sight. Maisy was thankful that despite the hotel's packed capacity this hall was empty.

Date with a Ghostbrother

Until of course, they turned the last corner. At that point, Maisy would have been less surprised if they had run into a couple of ghosts.

"Well I'll be." His voice was the thing of long-drive daydreams, and his smile could still light up any TV. "Look what we have here."

"Iris!" The young girl shouted and ran with arms spread wide, and Iris didn't respond with her characteristic stiff arm, but in a real embrace.

"I knew you were coming to Happy World, but the same place? Wow."

The girls picked up their conversation where it had left off at the Truck and Rest Stop, as if there hadn't been hours and miles in between.

There was that smile again. Sean Eckles could be a *Ghostbrother.* The man was movie-star handsome. He was right here on her floor.

"When we checked-in, I saw the signs for Iris' contest and I thought, 'That's it. It's fate."

"It is pretty amazing."

"Looks like we're neighbors."

Was she blushing?

"Looks like it." She smiled and forgot for a moment how key cards worked. "I'm just gonna make sure this is the right place." She held it flat in front of her like she was going to hang it on the wall and a giggle came out of her she instantly regretted.

He leaned toward her and her stomach did an unfamiliar leap. As he flipped the card the right way, the door opened on its own.

"You've gotta see this place. Iris, you've got a gift basket. Oh, hello." Christopher caught himself mid-rave. The room was exquisite, a regular western saloon but this was even better. Maisy's face flushed crimson. He shot his hand forward. "Sean, right? Nice to see you." He leaned out the doorway, unable to hide the grin that bloomed wide across his face and wider when he saw two girls talking cheerily. "Lily." He tipped an invisible cowboy hat.

"Hey, we were going to catch an early dinner in a bit. Says there's a good old-fashioned steakhouse down by the saloon. We were going to take a little walk. Maybe take in the fireworks? If you're all interested?"

"We've got a lot of unpacking to do," Maisy squirmed.

"Done." Christopher smirked.

"All of it?"

"Pretty much. It's the least I could do." Now he grinned. "Not your clothes, of course. All of the animals, ingredients, and snacks. Laid out all to plan." He said the last bit loud enough for Iris to hear.

"Well, we've got that reception Iris wants to go to so badly. I'd hate for her to miss it." She lied. "It is part of the competition, so."

"No, it's not."

Date with a Ghostbrother

Iris looked up from her conversation with Lily without missing a beat and Maisy couldn't see it but she could feel her face go white as a sheet.

"We don't know that, Iris."

"Yes we do. It's no big deal."

It was Maisy now who was having a hard time not furrowing her brow. Iris looked more at ease than she had all day.

"We'd love to come to dinner."

The steakhouse looked like a rancher's cabin, all interlocking logs and lassos on the wall. Iris was just as taken with the decor as she was the pretzel breadsticks on the table she fed into her mouth like ammunition. Maisy supposed she should thank Chris for pushing her out the door. The girl looked content and even she was starting to feel a smile warm her cheeks. It wasn't often she got to spruce up and even less often that she dated. This counted as a date, didn't it? She was in the good polka dot dress and even dabbed her wrists with the vanilla perfume that had been sitting on her shelf since Iris had purchased it for her at her middle school Christmas bazaar. Even though there were two daughters coloring pictures with crayons and making up silly songs, it sure as heck felt like one. To be sitting next to a handsome man who hadn't taken his eyes off her since they'd sat down didn't just feel like a date, it felt like a darn good one.

The waiter had come by once to take orders and again to refill waters. He talked in a scratchy old-rancher voice though he couldn't have been more than 17, and there was a pop in his walk that was almost cartoonish. He was very attentive, even for a place like Happy World, a destination known for making its guests feel like royalty. After the second table check, a breadstick refill, and a set of new napkins they did not yet need, it was evident this was more than good service. He came back this time with the look of someone who couldn't get a sneeze to come out, that strange look that is suspended between relief and discomfort.

"I'm sorry folks, but I have to ask." His accent was gone and he looked over his shoulder as if he'd be swiped from the table any minute for breaking royal protocol.

"Are you her?" He smiled broadly toward Iris like no one else at the table was there. Iris stopped mid-chew, breadstick dangling from her bottom lip.

"Me?"

He nodded to her, ducking closer to the table like he needed to see her better or, more likely, so he wouldn't be heard by the manager who eyed his ranchers like a brutal overseer.

"From VueClix. You are her, aren't you?"

Iris' eyes darted around the table and her cheeks went red. She took a giant swallow of water and fiddled with her wooly but then took a deep breath and looked at the rancher who looked more like a boy.

"I am." She took another sip of water. "That's me."

Date with a Ghostbrother

The boy clapped his hands. "I knew it!" He lifted his hat with a smile and his accent returned. "I'll be right back with your food, folks."

He bustled off, stopping at the overseer no doubt to explain why he'd broken character.

"That's really great about Iris." Sean said. "What she's doing, I mean. She's really brought Lily out of her shell."

When the dinners came, Iris didn't ask for the food on her plate to be separated if it touched and Lily didn't complain once about anything tasting spicy or weird. The girls were too busy chatting and giggling. When Lily stammered, Iris waited, never finishing a word for her, never acknowledging there was a delay at all.

"She's been more at ease in the past two days then I've seen her in a year."

He spoke the words Maisy was thinking and it felt good not to be in this restaurant alone. Without thinking, she reached across the table and brushed his hand.

"You." She felt silly. "Had some. Glitter."

A few purple sparkles lay on the table where she brushed them. Sean smiled like he was about to say something witty, but the lights went dim and the rancher was shouting through the restaurant and heading to their table.

"Hey everybody, someone's hit the Mother Lode!" He had a giant golden bowl on a tray filled to the brim with sponge cakes and ice cream, dripping with caramel and butterscotch. Sparklers were placed at the top of the mountain of sweets and they lit up the restaurant as he headed to their table.

The lights went back up only after he'd deposited the giant sundae on the table, with a set of golden plates, spoons, and special bibs for just this occasion.

"Thirteen scoops of ice cream, six slices of our world famous French vanilla cake, four slices of our golden delicious apple pie, one and a half ladles of gooey topping, peanut butter chips, crème brûlée sugar crystals, and one whole can o' whipped cream. Enjoy."

Both Maisy and Sean looked on in bewilderment, knowing neither had ordered the enormous concoction.

"Compliments of the Old West Resort," he winked. "Dinner's on us."

The girls sunk into the pile of sugar and dairy and when they were too stuffed to say another word Iris asked if they could look at all the gadgets and gear that decorated the walls.

"It's okay by me." Sean laughed. "I don't think I can move."

He leaned back in his chair in a gesture of defeat, only remnants of the Mother Lode remaining.

"Is it okay by you?"

Maisy couldn't remember the last time she felt like this.

"Yeah, I think it is."

The girls disappeared through an archway that looked like it was carved into a redwood tree.

Date with a Ghostbrother

"About that glitter. I'm a little embarrassed. Lily and I." He seemed hesitant. "Craft." Maisy smiled. "We bring our supplies everywhere. Even restaurants. We made purple elephants at that last rest stop."

She watched him intently, the set of his jaw, the way his mouth moved when he spoke, and her mind went places it was not accustomed to going. Perhaps he picked up on the change in the air around them because his voice perked up and he sat up in his chair, leaning toward the table and her.

"You know, we're only a few hours from you. It's just a quick drive up I-95." He smiled. "We could maybe do this again sometime when we're not in Happy World."

"We're like four hours away from you."

He was devilish and heroic at the same time with a glimmer in his eye and a movie star smile. "I'm willing to take that drive. Are you?"

"I think I am." With Iris out of sight, she felt like there was something she was forgetting. She leaned closer to him so they were only a few inches apart. "You have a little." She brushed under his eye. "Glitter." Her voice sounded foreign, soft and removed.

If memory served her right, this is what it felt like just before a first kiss, though it had been years. The anticipation buzzed in her ears. In that dizzying moment she could make out his every eyelash, every deviation of green present in his eyes. She would have stayed there and floated in that moment for days if she could. It was warm and time-less like a favorite song that wasn't humming, but buzzing.

"What is that buzzing?" Snapped away from the warm cocoa place she looked down where her phone shook be-side her.

"Is that important?" He sat back from the table that was just moments ago set for romance. Now it reverberated with the insistent hum of repeated texting.

"I'll just check this. Sorry."

Now Eric decided he wanted to be long-winded. His texts had ranged from one- to three-word responses if there were any at all, and now he was asking questions like he was writing a book. *How crowded is the hotel? Is it packed to capacity? What floor are you on?*

"Give me a break." She muttered more to herself. "You know anytime I hear a noise I jump thinking something bad happened." She put her hands up. "Just the phone though. No biggie. Where were we?"

She tried her best to nonchalantly lean her elbows on the table but it was clumsier this time around. She was all of a sudden more aware of what she was doing and corre-spondingly self-conscious.

"I think here." He moved toward her in one motion that was fluid and solid at the same time. It was like he was some new element that exuded cool. She tried to hide the fact that she'd just gulped. He took her hands. She closed her eyes.

Date with a Ghostbrother

Then it was like the world exploded, not because he kissed her but because a shelf of old tools fell onto a tray full of guests' dinners, which all toppled over onto Iris' feet.

"Sorry," Iris spoke through the clamor as Lily went running to her father's lap and any hope for that first kiss came crashing down with the mess at Iris' feet.

Chapter 41

Next Day

"I'm really sorry."

"Iris, it's okay."

The girl had spent the hours she should be using to prep her recipes apologizing for the catastrophe in the restaurant. She woke up the next morning, if 4 AM could be called morning, with the same thing on her mind.

"I just wanted to see what was on the shelf."

"Iris, it's okay. It was an accident. No one is mad at you. These things happen."

Maisy flipped over her phone. There was one text from Sean making sure they were both okay. He signed it with a winking face that could have looked like it was blowing a kiss. She couldn't be sure.

There were none from Eric.

She'd sent him about a dozen messages after the date fiasco telling him exactly how he'd ruined her night.

"You know that's just like him. He blows up my phone with texts and then when I respond I get nothing, not even a phone call. He's completely thoughtless."

Iris, who had been working on consideration for the past ten years in therapy, was an expert by now, and her ears perked up. For once, she talked about something other than the restaurant.

"Not really, though."

"What?" Maisy was fired up already. Her voice said so. Christopher was still sleeping, as was probably everyone else on the earth. He was separated from the noise by a thick barn wood door. Even so, she tried to keep her voice low. Iris spoke at the same monotone volume she'd use for recipes or conversation or singing a song and she looked thoughtful.

"You said Eric is inconsiderate. He's really not, though. If anything, he's the opposite of inconsiderate, right? Or no. I mean, he's covering all the shifts right now, isn't he?"

"Yes, I guess. He's completely irresponsible. You know what he could be doing with all that football money? Instead he just hangs around at a bagel shop."

"You hang around at a bagel shop."

"Yes, but I work there."

"So does he."

"Yeah, but, he's like a teenage kid with that stupid motorcycle and that phone."

"It IS the Supernova 8." Iris paused with gravity. "He's using his motorcycle because we have his car. Without that phone, I think you would have gotten lost, according to your story." Maisy sat next to Iris and looked into her coffee cup like it was a crystal ball. The girl next to her had the answers. "It sounds like you want to be mad, so you're mad at Eric." She shrugged. "I have no idea why you picked him."

"For one, he broke up a very nice moment on my date with Sean."

"Ew, *that* was a date?"

"Well, sort of."

She shrugged again, "I'm sure you'll see him again. Lily said he likes you much more than the lady from Connecticut. She was boring. Lily said her daughter didn't like to share."

"Connecticut?"

"Yeah, they met her on the road wherever they stayed. Lily said her daughter was mean. Lily likes you the best, too. The lady at the pool let her son splash everybody."

"What lady at the pool?" Maisy looked confused. "Here?"

"Yeah, she's staying on the third floor. They met them this morning before we got here. Like I said, her son's mean. Lily likes you best, and so does Sean." Iris was scribbling in a notebook her top-secret plans. "So are you going to make like you don't like him now?

"What?"

"That's what you do, right? When you really like someone? You act like you don't like them? Murph says that's a thing. Pushing people away because we don't want to like them."

"I don't know, what I'm... When did you get so smart?"

Iris shrugged a three-beat noise that sounded like musical *I dunno.*

"I know I need more coffee. Just after I rest my eyes for five minutes." Maisy lay straight back like a board and stayed that way until the sun was well in the sky. When she opened her eyes she saw that Iris had cut her sketches out of the notebook and taped them up in the kitchenette.

"This is where my containers will go, and the spoons. Here's a cinnamon and my whisk." These words were meant for no one but Iris herself. Maisy just got to hear them because she happened to be in the room. This was part of preparation for anything and everything in Iris' world, the pictures and the words, the practicing and rehearsing. Maisy dare not interrupt.

On the nightstand, her phone blinked green but it wasn't a text. It wasn't from Sean.

It was from the man who spoke as if he'd been in the room just hours ago and had heard every word Iris had said.

Maisy, listen, I really didn't want to do this over the phone but...I got your texts. I get it. You had a bad night. I know I haven't been answering the phone. And yes, I'm not the best at texting. And I ruined your date. I get it. I drive you crazy. You went on a date, huh? Anyway, like I said I got your messages. You really bit my head off, but you know what, you can bite my head off, Maisy because I don't care. I'm not going anywhere. I'll be here when you're mad and I'll be here when you can't find your keys, and even when you're trying to push the world away. I'm here no matter what because you're not getting rid of me. You try so hard to do it all alone, and the thing is, I know you can. I don't want you to.

There was a pause like he'd hung up, but then he spoke again.

What I'm saying is—Maisy, I'm here.

Chapter 42

Day One of Contest

Energy buzzed out of Iris' fingertips. She touched her bags of ingredients. She ran her hands over the samples she'd made, taking note of smells and textures. She sifted through her entrant's folder for rules and schedules, maps and locations. She wondered what the day's challenge would hold and ran scenarios through her head like binary code rapidly deciphering what decisions she would make if she were asked to make a cookie or pie. What if she were challenged to make a dessert sauce? Could she do it?

Christopher had finally woken up and was sipping a tea that smelled like her cardamom brittle. She inhaled deeply the rich, sweet scent.

"I could add a vanilla clotted cream drizzle over the brittle and serve it in a tea cup and call it Chai Treat Latte."

"Kid, you're prepared for anything."

"What if they want me to cook without utensils? I saw that on a game show once. Do you think it would burn terribly if I used my hand to stir boiling sugar? If I wore a silicone oven mitt?"

"I don't think they're going to ask you not to use utensils, Iris. It's not that kind of competition."

"Anything can happen." Her eyes were wide and she bit her bottom lip hard.

There was no use in asking her to concentrate on other things. The breakfast buffet was made to look like a ranch. The theming of the AM Corral was lost on her, as she shoveled her breakfast down.

"Iris, look. That whole wall is a window into the lobby. You can see the big tree. Iris, the geyser is erupting." Christopher tried to distract her but it was no use. "Hey, the seats are shaped like cow prints." His every attempt at conversation was met by silence or a response that had nothing to do with his question and everything to do with baked goods. Maisy would have felt his pain but she was occupied by her own thoughts. Eric's message played in her head on a painful loop.

"You think I push people away?"

Chris had to work to not spit out his second Chai of the morning, putting it down to stifle the amused smile. It melted when he saw how serious she was.

"Maybe a little."

"Do you think people can be so wrapped up in their own stuff they go blind?" She clarified, the girl's head popping up as if she'd heard a gunshot. "Not literally, Iris, don't worry." She waited for her to settle back into the world of her treats and spoke in a quieter tone. "Like, blind to obvious things?"

Chris didn't answer, a habit he'd grown accustomed to in therapy. Instead, he nodded slightly, encouraging her to go on.

"It only makes sense then. I finally go on a date with someone. I just start to feel like I could do that. Of course, he's like." She rubbed her face embarrassed to say it. "A player. I should have seen it."

"Play what?" The nervous baker broke from reciting recipes.

"Not music, Iris. It's a dating saying," Maisy assured.

With that, she went back to listing all the possible uses of golden raisins after offering her final say in the matter. "Oh, ew."

"I'm sorry, Maisy." Chris said, trying his best to sound like a friend and not a therapist.

"Don't be, you know?" She stretched her arms out as if they'd fallen asleep. "The whole time we were eating I just had this weird feeling anyway. Like part of me knew it wasn't right." She took a big gulp of her coffee. "I kept feeling like I was forgetting something." She sipped again. "Or someone, which was weird, because Iris was right there."

He fought the urge to counsel now harder than ever because the answer was as clear to him as the cup in front of her face. Until, she got it too.

Baking for Dave

"It can't be Eric."

"Yes. It can."

"What do you mean? You can't even see him. Turn around."

Through the window, she could see a tall, strong-looking man, who could be Eric, but wasn't. This guy was clean shaven and had short, trimmed, if not styled hair. He was wearing brand new clothes that looked like they were from a magazine.

"Do you mind?"

"Not at all."

Maisy practically ran into the lobby to get a better look at the man in the smart shorts and striped shirt that stood at the check-in desk with his back to her. She hated doing this.

Excuse me?"

"Hey, stranger." He turned around with a broad smile.

Without thinking, Maisy crumpled into him like a tower of blocks wrapping her arms around him, burying her face in his chest.

He lifted her chin, "Hey. Hey, what's wrong?"

Maisy was shaking. "Everything. Nothing. I'm sorry."

His voice was warm and made the noise of the lobby around them disappear.

"I told you I was here."

With that, Maisy kissed Eric like she'd never kissed anyone before.

Chapter 43

The Grand Ballroom was set up like a giant maze, columns and rows of small kitchens set up in identical cubes. A long line of tables was set up at the front of the expansive room piled high with contestant numbers and official entrant aprons. Iris had her ticket ready and within seconds had the bright pink apron secured around her waist.

"Would you?"

Tying was hard, but she wasn't going to let it stress her. There was no room for stress today, just tastes and sounds if she could remember to breathe.

"There are so many people here." They passed wives and smart-looking young men, grandmother types and a lady square back who looked like she was ready for TV.

"We got this, Iris." Maisy gave her elbow a squeeze.

"We got this." Eric winked.

"We." Christopher seemed unsure if it was his place and Iris brightened. "We got this."

A clean white sign with startling pink lettering with Iris' name marked the kitchen she'd been assigned and any tension the girl had melted away the second she saw it.

"Number 41, Maisy. Can you believe it?"

"That's pretty cool."

Through the maze of people, she heard a voice she knew and saw a familiar face break through the crowd.

Lily came running. "Is it okay if I co-oo-ome cheer you on?"

"Of course it is," Iris beamed.

"Ca-an I help you?" The girl went to step into the kitchen and Iris stopped her.

"Can't. Sorry. Only I can enter the kitchen, or else I get disqualified. It's strict Sugarworth rules, says so right in my folder."

"You can stand here with us," Maisy said hoping to avoid the question she asked anyway out of fear of the inevitable awkwardness that was bound to follow. "Where's your dad?" Maisy asked too nervously for her own liking.

"He's ba-aa-ck there. With the coo-ooking lady."

Maisy muttered, "I guess I don't have to worry about it being awkward."

Iris entered her arena with a wave. There was a shiny, double oven that looked brand new, and a burner on the large counter where she could work. There was a sink in the corner and a smaller fridge and freezer, a trash can and a two tall white cabinets filled with ingredients and tools of all sorts. She didn't get to look through them all. She had just enough time to drop her bags on the ground next to the countertop in the center of her cube when the announcer started speaking.

"Welcome to the Sugarworth National Bake-Off. We here at Sugarworth pride ourselves on bringing the best products to the American kitchen because we love what we do. This competition is a tradition that is more than 100 years strong because of bakers like you. So from our hearts to your mouths, we wish you the best baking! Now before we blow that whistle, I'll tell you the first round is Hand-held Treats. Cookies, brownies, cakes, and candies are fair game." There was a buzz of excitement he let die down before he spoke again. "Your pantries are stocked and your ovens are ready. You have 90 minutes. Let the baking..." He paused clearly enjoying the noise that was building. "Begin!"

Iris had been expecting a whistle because of what the round man with the red face said. She was expecting the gym teacher sound, or even the long musical sound of a train coming down a track. What she didn't expect was an ear-shaking fog horn that shook the walls and silverware in the drawers. It carried through the ballroom like a shockwave that lasted ten Mississippi's and a half thousand. The worst thing that could have happened had. Iris had forgotten to breathe.

"Oh boy. Iris. Iris!" Maisy stood at the threshold where Iris stood frozen. From here, she looked like a plaything in a doll house frozen behind plastic. The only difference was that most dolls smiled. Iris stood with a look of terror on her face that gripped at Maisy's insides like ghouls. There was nothing she could do about it.

Eric put his arm up when she tried to run inside. "If you go in there, she's disqualified, and all of this is for nothing."

"Eric, look at her. Doc?" She pleaded with the doctor who watched from the side. The girl looked like she was in the grip of terror, her eyes in a far-off place filled with monsters and fiends no one else could see.

"Let's see how she does. We got this. Right?"

Maisy rolled her eyes in frustration, outnumbered and as helpless as the girl stuck in the kitchen.

Breathe. The voice inside screamed but try as she might she couldn't make it happen. Her eyes were pinched shut with glue. They felt that way and the weight of a million elephants sat on her chest. Deafening noise filled her head, a giant drum that beat faster and faster. It took over her ears and her mind so she could feel it in her skin and at her temples. It was her heartbeat, wasn't it? Her heart raced when she was afraid. She'd worked on this with Murph. She could hear her easing her through the panic as if she were right there in the office.

"Iris. Breathe. Calm down, and count to five. One. Two. Three. Four. Five." Breathe. "And again." It was like

Murph was there with her. It was so real, she had to open her eyes to see, half-expecting her therapist to be right there with her. It was real.

Murph was standing right there between Christopher and Maisy, her long curly hair pulled in the tight ponytail she loved so much, her smile just as bright as every Tuesday when she saw her.

"Hey, Iris!"

"Um. Hi, Murph!"

"Thought I'd come to cheer you on."

"Me too." From behind Murph, Iris heard the voice she'd heard speak only once before. It was strained like it hurt him to make the sound, but he did it anyway. Ryan leaned over from behind Murph and smiled just long enough for Iris to see before retreating back to the tablet in his hand.

"And me, honey!"

"And me!" Darlene and Jack framed Ryan like they were posing for a picture.

Iris was so busy smiling she didn't realize her breathing had started to calm. The beat in her head had quieted.

"Don't forget me!" Walter, the waiter from the ranch restaurant, waved wide and Iris looked his way.

"Hi, everyone." She waved, half-dazed. From the corner of her eye she could see Lily smiling a wide smile just like Murph's. Maisy was standing so close to Eric that if she would actually look at him, she could see that their fingers were almost touching. She wouldn't look at him. She hadn't since her outburst in the lobby and didn't plan to anytime soon. She focused on the girl in front of her, hands held out in front like she was smoothing out dough. *Settle down.*

Ryan had been tapping away on his tablet. He looked up at her with a quick shake of his head and a point of his finger, holding the device up high so it faced her.

She heard her own voice just then, singing. She hummed along. She could do this. She started unpacking her bag to the rhythm of the music, clanking down the ingredients she was allowed to bring from home. The crowd was a choir in the background, some singing and chattering, and she was no longer afraid. She drifted to the cabinet. It was a marimba turned on its side and she tapped, tapped, tapped as she found what she needed and brought it to the counter. She sniffed ingredients in the fridge for smells that floated in the air like her song, the kind of scents that could bring her to another time or place. The heavy ones that dragged like rot and grease were tossed aside making room for the ones that soared. This was how her recipes were born.

In the drawers, shiny forks were drumsticks and spoons were castanets and they made a sweet tune as she set up her kitchen to be a playground just for her. She filled bowls and cups with water, running her finger along the tops so she could line them up according to size. This was how she measured, by the sound they made when tapped and played. She needed to be precise. None of the people were there anymore. It was just her and her tools, her ingredients and what she would make with the song in her heart.

When she was ready, the kitchen was set for a masterpiece and she knew precisely what she would make of the day.

The day looked like it was over.

"Where is everyone?"

The ballroom had all but emptied. Lily and Ryan were still there, Eric of course and Christopher, but the other contestants were gone. Maisy had the look on her face she got when she knew Christmas was going to be light.

"The time limit is up, Iris." She shrugged like there wouldn't be a robot under the tree but didn't enter the kitchen. "You can still bake for us."

She looked around at the empty kitchens to the far end of the ballroom where judges stood from the long tables and headed her way.

"No." Iris said almost to herself. Maisy made a move to come in the kitchen and help her gather her things.

"No!" She said louder and her mother froze where she stood.

"Do. Not. Come in here. I'm baking."

"Iris!"

By now, the round man with the red face stood next to Maisy shaking his head so his cheeks looked like a railway sign.

"Don't you take another step in this kitchen." She cautioned the man before he tried again to enter her cooking area. Iris' speech became more rapid as she reached into the bag she'd spent the last 25 minutes of her cook time emptying. She fanned the folder open like a great poker hand and pulled from the center the piece of paper she searched.

"It says right here." She read methodically. "Cooking areas will be prepared for entrants to bake, at which point contestants have 90 minutes to bake. See?" They looked at her, puzzled.

"My kitchen wasn't ready. Now it is." Plates balanced on the scale she fashioned with a plank board on a stack of books. "This is how I measure." She pointed to the half-filled bowls and rows of foods arranged by color. "This is how I make sure I have everything I need."

The red-faced man sighed painfully and looked at his oversized phone as if reading what she'd just said. He rubbed his cheeks and looked at his watch.

"Finals aren't until tonight. You have 90 minutes, and not a minute more." His voice was stern but his eyes were smiling. Iris could see a grin in the way they twinkled. He proved it with the tiniest wink before adding in a principal voice. "Starting. Now!"

She didn't need the 90 minutes. Iris had moved like a robot in fast forward, efficiently measuring and scraping out fruits, reducing a bowl of pineapple juice down to a fine, rich syrup. She sang one side of Virginia Beach '92, and her creation was complete.

She looked out of her kitchen as if noticing for the first time that her friends were all still there.

"Is there a bell or something I should ring?"

"It's fine." The Sugarworth man had been waiting out of sight and ducked past Eric to see what she'd done. He gave the rotund man a nod that was both greeting and warning.

"Can you tell me a little about your dish, Iris?"

The plate of cupcakes looked like it came out of a children's book. Three perfectly white cakes topped with icing that was both implausibly fluffy and impossibly green sat on the plate.

By the look on his face, he was doubtful.

"I call these 'Road to Sugarworth' cupcakes. They're coconut angel cakes, soaked with a spicy rum pineapple caramel." She hesitated as he inspected the bright green frosting up close. "It's an avocado buttercream." She added like she was sweetening the deal, "With lime."

For a big man, Mr. Sugarworth took a dainty bite, knowing from his years of experience he should always be prepared for the worst. In this case, he was happy to be wrong.

Chapter 44

Believe

There were a few hours before the final, time needed to set up the giant stage where the three finalists would compete. Iris didn't think about that stage at all. It was harder for her to order a sandwich at a store than it was for her to stand in front of hundreds of people. Maisy had a lump in her throat just thinking about it, yet Iris strolled through the hotel like she was already walking through the theme park.

"I can't believe you did it!" Eric looked like the man in the moon with the sleepy grin on his face.

"You can't? You look weird without your beard." Iris meant no malice. It was hard to recognize people when they changed. Had it not been for his big frame and that crooked grin, she might have mistaken him for some other ex-football player staying in the hotel.

"Uh. Thanks? What about you, Maisy? You like it or hate it?" He winked and she found herself suddenly interested in her own shoes.

They looked like a small herd moving through the lobby, Iris leading the pack like a shepherd. Murph chatted with Darlene and Jack, smiling as Ryan tapped away on one of his games. Christopher walked with his hand in his pocket, no doubt waiting for a message he'd not yet received. Maisy tried hard not to look at the man she'd so recently thrown herself upon. Iris froze in front of the geyser, watching the water push toward the sky. "Should we celebrate? Says here there's a Sugarworth parade in the park? What do you think, kid? You want to hit a few rides before the final?"

Maisy chose that moment to break the vow and gave Eric a pained look.

"No. No. No." Iris shot the words out like bullets and repeated them like a mantra. "No rides. No park. I'll go tomorrow. After the competition. Maybe then I'll try the bumper cars, but for today. Cakes. Much to do." In a shock to all of them, she headed straight for the elevator and pushed the button for the fourth floor. "It'll save time."

The four of them bid a short farewell to the friends who opted to take in Eric's parade and all the sights Happy World had to offer. It was roomy in the compartment, but Maisy felt like she was in Eric's lap. She tried to banish that thought away as soon as it surfaced.

Believe

"Why's your face all red, Maisy? Are you having a reaction?"

She was, but not one she'd like to share with Iris. "No, Iris. I'm fine. I'm." She stammered. "Warm."

"It's cold in here. They keep the Riley resorts at a cool 64 degrees. It makes for perfect baking. You might have a fever. Or maybe, you're going through early onset menopause."

"Iris!"

"What?" Iris' attempts at whispering were rarely successful but that never stopped her. She leaned into Maisy so she was almost pushing her over. "Are you embarrassed because you know you love Eric now?"

Now any semblance of pink that had dissipated from Maisy's face returned with a burning red vengeance both Christopher and Eric tried to ignore.

"Look at that. We're here." Christopher ushered Iris out of the elevator as soon as the doors cracked open, leaving Maisy, red and speechless, in the compartment with the one person she was trying to avoid. He went to speak and she lunged out after them.

In the room, there was forced conversation. Maisy found reasons to be in the other part of the suite as Eric filled them in on last-minute flying with frequent flyer miles and the perks of being an ex-NY Bomber.

"That's how I'm here. Guess it pays off that they knew who I was. Turns out there's always an open room somewhere if somebody knows you."

Eric was used to Iris' quiet days and even more used to her mind going somewhere else, especially when she was planning. Maisy's nervous milling around was as common as a sunrise. He felt bad leaving the good doc with no conversation at all. Talking to Chris took his mind off that thing in the elevator he wasn't supposed to hear.

"I spent all yesterday getting coverage for the shop." He spoke loud enough so even those trying to avoid the conversation could hear it. "I made sure to reschedule deliveries."

He said slightly self-consciously, "I got my hair cut. You know, I am a business owner after all. I should probably look the part. I don't want to just sit back anymore. I want to be part of something." He was more aware of himself suddenly. "I shaved?" He touched his chin thoughtful. "And, oh! I almost forgot." He'd shot up out of his seat. "I gotta get something from my room."

"Now?" Christopher was perplexed.

"Yes. Right now. It can't wait."

Iris, who'd been alternating among scribbling, reciting, and singing in the room where Maisy folded shirts for no reason, broke from her trance telling her directly. "You should go with him."

Maisy attempted to shrug off the suggestion and before she could speak Iris held up her finger the way Maisy did when her daughter was about to make an excuse.

"Go with him."

Believe

"What about?" She looked for a reason to stay and Iris said out loud what she'd been trying to say all along.

"I'll be fine."

Chapter 45

Fine

"You didn't have to do all that."

Maisy spoke after the world's quietest elevator ride brought them upstairs to the floor only accessible by key card.

"Do what? It's not costing me anything. Isn't that crazy? Just because I am who I am. Was. Whatever that means."

He slid his card and the doors opened with a whoosh. In any other instance, Maisy would be silenced by the opulence around her, the gilded wainscoting and velvet tapestries around the windows, the quiet concierge in the tuxedo who acknowledged them with a tip of his hat. All of that would have rendered her speechless. None of it even registered as she looked at him.

"The whole—this." She motioned to him. "The look. You didn't have to do that. You were." She corrected. "You are. Fine. You said you wanted to be part of something. You always have been." She reached for his hands, hers looking like a child's in his. "I just didn't see it." This time he kissed her and it wasn't in a rush of panic and when they pulled apart she didn't look away. They'd stopped in front of an ornate double-door. "Is this, you?"

"It is. You too, if you like." He opened the door with a flourish. "Would you care to join me? There's something I'd really like to show you."

"How long are they going to be gone?"

"Not sure." Christopher turned his phone over. Maybe the battery was on the fritz or his connection was bad.

"No Rachel?"

"I thought maybe she'd have messaged. That would be silly, right? I mean, I left. So, I can't really expect to be her favorite person or something. I just, we were having a good talk. And."

Iris didn't understand much about relationships but what she did know was this. "It's hard."

Christopher's eyes looked like he was trying not to be sad, but unsuccessfully. "I just want her to be happy."

Before Iris could tell him that was something she knew a lot about, there was a knock at their door.

"Maisy has a key. Who would knock?"

His heart leapt with near impossible hope though he felt foolish to admit it even to himself. "I'll get it."

"Maybe it's Lily, or Ryan. Or Murph. Or maybe it's another gift basket from the judges. I already finished the one we got at check-in." Iris followed behind him rattling

Fine

off hypotheses, none of which proved to be true when she looked through the peephole.

It was Eric and Maisy, leaning against each other like bookends in the doorway, bookends that smiled like grade school children. Eric wasn't holding up homework or a ball so she could see.

He was holding up Sophie the fish.

Iris was bouncing into the door unable to get it open quickly enough and when she did was already talking to the tiny purple fish in the bowl Eric cupped in his hand. She was so busy cooing and asking the pet how she'd been that she didn't see what Maisy was holding in her hand. She set down the clunky box unhinging the door so Oscar the cat could walk freely.

"How did you get them to let him in?"

"It helps when you're a NY Bomber. Ex, that is." He corrected. "Who knew?" Maisy knew how much he hated using his celebrity. She'd watched him hide it behind the counter of a bagel store for longer than she could remember.

Iris disappeared into the happy familiar world her pets provided, the warm soft place where hours didn't exist.

"Iris."

"Yes."

"It's time."

Chapter 46

Let Her Bake

The cooking area was in the center of the Grand Ballroom. It wasn't what she thought it would be. For one, it wasn't on a tall stage at all. This wasn't necessarily bad. She'd imagined cooking on a rock star stage from which she feared she might trip or fall. This wasn't like that at all. Three kitchens sat side-by-side, at least three times the size of the cube in which she cooked today, separated by a thin white curtain. People funneled in from all directions to get the best seats in the house. Iris made her way through the rows trying not to take note of them. She'd have to count them if she did. She didn't have time. She would not let herself run out of time again, not now. So, instead of touching the soft silk cushions on each seat, she stared at the floor shuffling up the center aisle like it was a thick plank on a pirate ship.

She didn't hear a sound but the ocean that threatened to swallow her whole if she wandered from the aisle. It wasn't until she saw the glinting steel appliances and long counter laid with ingredients that she noticed several people were calling her name. Darlene and Jack were there with Ryan, who wore a Dusty Dog cap with floppy ears, no doubt acquired in the park along with the glittering yo-yo that had replaced the tablet normally in his hand. Murph had come back and she snapped pictures with one hand while waving with the other.

The judges spoke intently with the woman who looked like a TV cook show lady, who was more confusing to Iris than she'd been before. She was smiling and making gentle motions with her hands like a hula dancer, no more like the game show ladies showing a prize, maybe a bracelet or a watch. Her eyes were so angry. They were spitting dragon fire. She was speaking so closely to the red-faced man, Iris smiled. If he wasn't careful, he would be cooked alive.

"Iris!" Lily called from the front row with an outstretched hand. There was a little girl seated next to her in a knit cap not so unlike the one Iris wore, who smiled like she knew her and turned to Lily with giddy excitement when Iris waved hello.

"You made it!" Lily repeated it so many times it became a song.

"I did." She confirmed, still watching the judges and the lady, less amused.

Let Her Bake

It was loud in here all of a sudden. She could hear people shifting papers and moving seats. Sweet baking scents that didn't go with the fancy clothes smells of perfume and cologne made her head hurt. At just that moment, the red-faced man came huffing toward her like a bull and she wanted to find a dark place to lie down.

"Iris." She felt Maisy's hand on her back and jumped, stiffening like a scared animal about to play dead. "Iris, we've got this."

"Miss Heller." The judge said, his cherry cheeks flattening with his serious tone. "Although we cannot help but commend you on your flavorful and inventive cupcake creation this morning, I regret to inform you that you will not be able to proceed into the final round."

He looked reluctant to say what he said, his eyes scanning the crowd hovering on the two little girls who leaned forward in their seats to hear what was happening.

"The rules."

He looked to the girls and to the cook show lady who cocked one eyebrow so high she looked like Captain Hook. All she needed was the moustache. The judge looked just as much like Mr. Smee, uncomfortable and shrugging. He sounded rehearsed, reciting.

"Although the rules *did* allow you to continue and finish your round, you still exceeded the time limit allotted for advancement into the next round, as has been pointed out to us by a fellow contestant."

"But."

"It's the way Sugarworth has run for more than 70 years."

A flash of folder gleamed bright in her head like a beacon. She could see the words and recited better than Mr. Smee himself could have.

"The use of compensatory time will be permitted in the event of extenuating circumstances i.e., power outage, health emergency, tornado, flood, act of God or man, and will be left to the discretion of Sugarworth Inc., a subsidiary of Sugarworth International, representative or living relative of the Sugarworth family."

Mr. Smee straightened up at this with a smile to the front row as if he'd found something he'd lost. "Well, this is true, isn't it? I'd forgotten about that."

He headed back to the table of judges and the other finalists, including the manicured lady with the dragon eyes, armed with his new information.

One other judge nodded. Another looked like he was smelling pickles. One other contestant gave a happy shrug and dragon lady made a huffy growling noise. The noise wasn't just there. As they conferred, a murmur came over the audience, first with the front row, then trickling down the aisle like a wave until it grew so large it flooded her head. Her eyes filled with water about to burst and if she started crying she would not be able to stop. It would hurt her stomach and burn her throat and all of this would be for nothing. Iris didn't think she would be able to take another second of the sounds until she heard a familiar voice break to the surface.

"Let her bake." Christopher shouted with all his might. "Let her bake." Maisy echoed the doctor, then Eric sounded-off with a lion's roar voice. Afterwards, Murph with her squeaky voice, Darlene, and Jack followed. The little girls said it in unison. An old lady Iris didn't recognize shouted it with a salute to Christopher, who clapped his hands with a hoot in reply, repeating her words like they were an order. The shouts became a chant that lifted up over the crowd like a fist beating the judges over the head.

"Let. Her. Bake. Let. Her. Bake. Let Her. Bake."

The red-faced judge brushed his hands together like he was wiping away crumbs and the other contestants split from the table, scurrying like ants to their places. He didn't come to Iris. He walked to the cooking area, speaking directly into the microphone.

"Welcome to the final round of the Sugarworth National Bakeoff. If our finalists can take their places in their respective kitchens please: Yvonne DeYoung." He held out a hand and the dragon lady took her place in the first kitchen. "Jonas Marples." The college-age man who shrugged at the table took his place in the second kitchen, adjusting his baseball hat with an apologetic tug.

The crowd began to murmur. The Sugarworth man cleared his throat for attention.

"Let's not forget Iris Heller."

Chapter 47

And the Winner Is ...

Sometimes everything moved slowly so Iris could hear every single movement of her own muscles against the air around her. Sometimes when things got intense, she could measure each second as if they were years that passed inside her mind, taking in every last detail. The moments leading up to the final were not like that. The round-faced man called her name and the world seemed to get so noisy at once that it was quiet, all the colors around her so blank they went blank. The next thing she knew, she was cooking in her kitchen, filling bowls as quickly as she could like she was an airplane on autopilot. Spoons clicked and clanged, making music and her hands floated in front of her like a conductor.

Voices surfaced from all directions, not just the rows in front of her but from the sides and behind. People were up from their seats circling the cooking area like sharks.

"Iris." She heard her name once and then again.

"That's the girl from VueClix."

"Go Iris!" Unfamiliar people called her and even stranger, sang songs she knew she'd made up just yesterday and the day before. Young and old voices, girls and ladies, and boys and men were all singing and cheering like they knew her. She let the song fill her like water and measured out ingredients in a rhythm that made no mistake of time.

If Chris wasn't seeing it, he wouldn't have believed it. Iris was so comfortable, so in charge of her own movements, she bore almost no resemblance to the scared girl he had seen at the ferry terminal. She was focused, laying out ingredients and tasting batters with wooden sticks she promptly threw into the wastepaper basket. She saved not one wrapper and moved deftly from her stove to her oven. She poured batters and whipped frosting, boiling together sugars into a golden syrup. All the while, she checked off the steps she'd written out on a list one-by-one and when the sounds of her spoons got the best of her, she leaned back on the table, took a deep breath, and started again. Even with the chanting voices that called her name, Iris was in command.

The VueClix fans had found her and it was strange to the crowd that fanned out around her kitchen, blooming out of the ballroom and into the hotel lobby. Familiar faces Chris swore he'd seen before drifted in and out of view. Was that the girl with blue hair from the donut shop? Even those hipster boys from the road? He was almost sure of it. Maddie had arrived with a flourish, Ronnie and Bud at her side.

"What else were we going to do this weekend?" His new friend gave that old dry laugh he'd become fond of even in that short time they shared coffee. There were some other tourists from the sing-a-long this morning who'd made signs, and the ladies from the donut shop up north. If he wasn't seeing it, he wouldn't have believed it. All these people, this outpouring for one girl. It was heartwarming, and body warming? He felt like someone had a hairdryer against the small of his back, set to low. And wet.

He turned to see not the throng of singing Iris fans but a small black bear with a dopey grin, who'd left his back right leg soaking wet.

"Squatch!"

He dropped to his knees, throwing his arms around the dog attempting to fight back the tears, ones that reemerged seconds later when he lifted his face and she was there.

From this angle, she looked like an angel with lights and sounds behind her with nothing but love in her eyes. She held out her hand to him and he stood to meet her, wondering if he'd finally lost his mind for good.

"You came."

"I came."

The dog had an air of pride, or more likely he caught the scent of bacon sizzling from a nearby kitchen. He perked up and so did Chris.

"Are you sure about this?"

Rachel pulled a crumpled paper that looked like it had been taped in several places from her purse; he immediately recognized it as his note.

"I couldn't let you do this alone."

"I'm not even baking." He smirked, not intending to, yet, he did.

"Not this." She motioned with her hands in a big circle. If they were in water it would have sent his ill-timed joke the other way. "Any of this. I'm not letting you go."

"Well, okay then." He smiled, not because he was making light of the situation, but because he had to. The warmth he felt inside was real and had nothing to do with Sasquatch's breath.

"How did you?" He looked down as Sasquatch shook his jowls clean, showering those in a two-foot radius with his own special brand of slime.

Rachel buried her hands in the dog's fur, digging for the new red collar he'd earned every Saturday for the last three weeks.

"Say hello to your new therapy dog." She patted Sasquatch, whispering a word and the dog went to Christopher leaning into him like a warm, yet giant security blanket. "We would've gotten here earlier but we had graduation this morning."

It was a lot to take. That was a saying that had nothing to do with stealing but meant there was a lot going on, and there was. There were people singing and strangers she didn't recognize chanting her name, and strangers she did clapping the rhythms she knew so well they made her feel like she was at home. This kitchen was nothing like home. It was big and open to the watching eyes. It let in sounds that filled her head like a balloon. There was no way she was going to let it happen. Her masterpiece was almost done.

When the red-faced man blew the whistle, she heard it this time. This time she had her plate ready and her kitchen clean. She marched right up to the tasters' table with her head held high. The sound of the crowd was a roar.

"Iris, you rule!" A young man shouted above the crowd and she believed it. She was a queen now and this plate was her legacy.

"That's a dark chocolate cake made with chipotle peppers and cherry compote." The icing is fudge. With whiskey. Like cowboys drink." Her words were terse but there was intensity behind them. "On the side is an ice milk smoothie with fresh mint."

She made her way back to the staging area where Maisy and Eric ran to her, the latter grabbing her tightly into a hug that lifted her three feet from the ground. She was swarmed by her people, hands touching hers and patting her back. Christopher broke through the throng with a smile that made her feel like there was a candle inside her heart. His eyes were as happy as his face.

"Iris, I want you to meet someone."

Before she could see who, the small pixie woman had her in a hug that made her think of her happiest thoughts. She was like a magic being, this wonderful lady with cherry red hair whose eyes sparkled like blue gems.

"You're Rachel, aren't you?"

"I am."

Iris, now getting a fair amount of licking from the beast who accompanied the red-haired fairy, spoke as plainly to Christopher as she did the first time she met him.

"Don't ever leave her again."

Christopher gave Iris a salute of sorts with a wave and a smile, disappearing into the crowd with an arm around his wife and one hand on his dog. Just as soon as he disappeared into the colorful cloud of people, the rainbow of limbs and shirt styles broke like clouds and two little bodies emerged heading straight for her. It was Lily, as happy as ever, holding hands with another small girl, the one with the wooly just like Iris'.

"Hi, Iris!" She beamed. Her friend smiled shyly, one hand behind her back.

"Well, go-ooo ahead, silly. Aa-ask her."

The smaller girl pulled a wooden spoon from behind her back that was comically large compared to her tiny body. Her free hand was wedged firmly between her top and bottom lip, from between which she spoke.

"Can you sign thif for me?"

And the Winner Is …

"Um. Yes." Iris said reaching at her sides for a pen that did not exist.

Lily quickly turned, ran to her father, ripping a pen from his hand as he spoke lazily with a lady who had familiar yellow hair and a giggle Iris recognized. She tried not to let it gnaw at her head.

"Here you go." She said trying to add a fancy flourish to the 's' and the girl chirped with delight like a baby bird as she too ran back into the crowd. It had its own pulse, this crowd. It moved like a jellyfish in the ocean until again, there was a tiny ripple.

The blue-haired girl from the donut place was taping her again. The red light shone like an eyeball. Iris looked directly at the camera with a wave.

"Um, thank you all for coming and for watching and seeing me." She scratched under her wooly and stopped herself. "I mean it."

A young man with a beard noticed the girl, taking a place beside her with a camera of his own.

Iris looked at both of them.

"Hi. I don't really know what else to say. Just waiting to see how I did."

Two girls screamed just then. "Iris, you did great!" It was followed by the resounding hoot sound people make when they're excited.

Maisy and Eric stood together smiling at her and they looked at each other as if they finally realized what everyone else knew all along. This was good. Right then, Maisy looked different, like she did all those years ago when Iris was young and they danced together in the living room to the tapes in the shoebox. Maisy looked happy.

Iris knew those people were right.

In a while the crowd hushed, though it still hummed with excitement like a live wire. The round-faced man wove his way through the crowd that mingled and moved around Iris. He bobbed past the sandwich maker men still in white and smiled as men do at attractive women like Suzie, until finally he stood before Iris where he cleared his throat, like he needed to get her attention. He didn't. She'd been watching him the whole time.

"Ms. Heller."

"Yes."

"I want to tell you that your cupcakes received an incredible score from our judges. They were moist and delicious and in the history of Sugarworth, we've never seen such creative use of ingredients or a kitchen for that matter." He gave a little laugh but it was a sad laugh.

"I didn't win, did I?"

For the first time, the red-faced man did not seem rehearsed or polished. He looked like a sad old horse at the end of a long ride.

"Unfortunately, no."

He looked at his feet like he was sad because he actually was. His eyes said there was real pain there, not the

And the Winner Is …

polite fake pain of bad news. "You see, I was rooting for you, Iris. I have to be unbiased. My granddaughter Agnes, well she's quite taken with you."

From behind the judge, Iris saw the wooly girl flying her spoon in the air like an airplane.

Iris looked at the people around her. She could hear her song swelling out from the crowd, and laughter from little girls, people talking about nothing and everything at once like they all mattered. She saw Ryan smiling with his tablet and Murph and Christopher and Rachel arm in arm, Sasquatch licking at his massive jowls. She looked at Maisy watching Eric when she didn't think anyone was looking, and how she smiled like the world wasn't there.

"I'm terribly sorry, Iris. I really wish you could have won."

"Mr. Sugarworth, I did."

Chapter 48

A Letter from Your Friend Iris

Hi, everyone. A lot of people ask me lots of questions about my big adventure. I have addressed a few below:

1. What happened after the big contest? I can say that after the crowd cleared out, there was one person who came into my kitchen who didn't want to taste a treat or get an autograph. He wanted to know if we could sing a song. I'm not going to say who he was, but I will say he was as big a fan of me as I was of him. Wink wink.

2. Did Maisy ever kill me for taking the car? You know that's just a saying, right? A terrible one, really, because she'd be in prison

right now if it were true and my mom would never make it in prison. No, she didn't kill me, though it will be quite a while before I get my learner's permit. (Truth be told, I don't really want it.)

3. What are you up to now? I have my own VueClix channel and it has several million views, which means I'm famous, I suppose. It doesn't really change much except I did get to go up on stage with Dave one time at his show in New York City. That was really cool, except for the big, tall buildings, because they were terrifying.

Also, I'm working on a collection of recipes for kids who want to cook with homemade measuring instruments.

4. Last, to answer the question I get asked most and it's probably the most important one. Yes, I finally went into Happy World. I spent a day with all my new friends going on all the rides...including the bumper cars!

About the Author

Melissa Palmer is a writer, nerd, baker, part-time kitchen dancer, wife, and full-time mom. She pulls from her experiences with her own daughters—the two superheroes who shape and guide her life—to create the world and characters seen in *Baking for Dave*. When she's not writing, she's biking or running (either on the road or after one of the many animals in her menagerie).

Her short story "Mrs. MacMillan's Garden" was nominated in 2013 for the Pushcart Prize. Melissa was a finalist for the Eric Hoffer Award in short fiction, which was featured in the book *Best New Writing 2014*; she won the Atlantic Cape Community College Teacher Pioneer Award in 2016.